JINX, You're It

HIS LUCK IS ABOUT TO CHANGE.

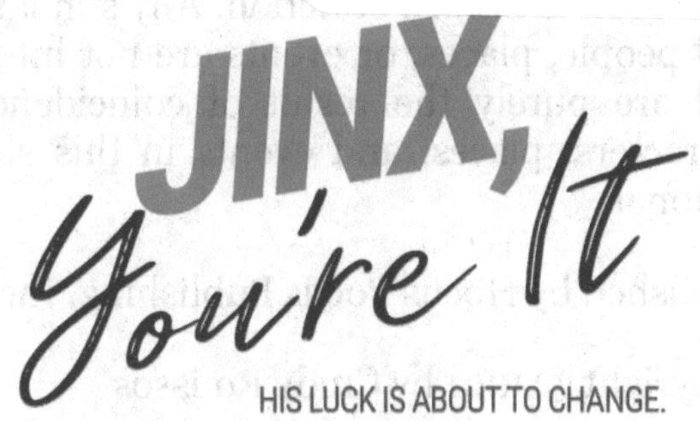

New York Times & *USA Today* Bestselling Author

CYNTHIA EDEN

PROLOGUE

"This is a mistake," Ali whispered right before her mouth surged up and pressed greedily against his.

"Oh, absolutely," Jinx assured her in that low, deep, sexy rumble that pretty much just made her panties want to fall off. "Probably the worst mistake ever." He kissed her again. A long, drugging kiss that had her rising onto her tiptoes so that she could get closer to him. "That's why it is so much fun."

Her hands curled around his broad shoulders. Her fingers bit into his skin. There were a million reasons why she should walk away from Jinx.

And one very big reason to stay.

I want him.

The case was over. She'd be disappearing come the morning. This night was going nowhere. It was just about hot sex. Incredible pleasure. About the insane attraction that she'd felt for Jinx from day one.

He was not her type. Okay, fine, Jinx was probably everyone's *type*. He had a body that was sculpted to pure perfection. The man possessed the bluest eyes that she'd ever seen in her entire life...and his smile. *Wow.* He possessed the kind of slow, wicked smile that had her body tensing and quivering every single time she saw his lips curl.

Physically, the man was pure temptation.

But...He's too reckless for me. Jinx didn't take anything seriously, not even the danger that they had recently faced on a mission she'd been sure would fail. He mocked and he joked, and he didn't seem to care about death. Or, well, anything else.

She liked reliable men. Steady men. Men who didn't laugh when bullets went flying.

She *liked* those men, but in this particular instance, as desire flooded through her body...she *wanted,* no, *craved* Jinx. Jinx and his particular brand of madness.

The mission was over. They'd survived. Gotten the job done. Managed to *not* even get shot. Wins all around.

His tongue dipped in her mouth. His hands locked around her hips as he lifted her up and pinned her between his rock-hard body and the wall.

They were in some no-tell motel. They'd flown back in the country and paused in this little town for the night. Not like she'd ever be visiting this place again. She never came back after a mission was done. Her job was to fade away. To vanish. She was good at that job.

"God, you taste delicious," Jinx growled as he pulled his mouth from hers. She stared up at him, aware that her heartbeat was pounding out of control. If possible, his eyes were even bluer as they burned down at her with the force of his fierce lust.

Jinx hadn't hidden the fact that he'd wanted her. He'd been upfront about it from the beginning. And she'd told him it would never happen...

Never say never.

"I swear," he added roughly, "I could eat you right up."

Oh, the visual that popped into her head at that moment. *Do it, yes, please. Go right ahead.* Instead of saying those wild, desperate words, Ali squeaked, "Only once."

He squinted those bright blues at her. "Once? Baby, it is gonna be a long night. I don't see why on earth you'd limit a guy like me to just making you scream with pleasure only once. You are hurting yourself."

She swallowed. "I meant...only one night."

His lips curled.

Her body tensed. Quivered.

"Ah..." A sensual sigh. "So I *can* make you scream over and over?"

He was such a confident jerk. And, yes, she was pretty sure he'd be able to back up that confidence. God, she hoped he could back it up. Ali couldn't remember the last time she'd had screaming-good sex.

Okay, wait, she could...it had been never. Sex had *never* been so good that she'd screamed, but she was more than ready to give it a shot.

"Maybe I'll make you scream," she said as her hands grabbed his shirt and shoved it up.

He tossed the shirt to the floor. "Full disclosure, I'm more of a roaring type. Or gutturally growling. You know, hardcore, sexy stuff."

He couldn't even be serious...*now?* Her hand went to the snap of his jeans. Yanked the snap open. Tugged down the zipper.

His fingers curled around hers. "I'll give you one night, but what if you want more?"

Her mouth was dry. She licked her lips. "That confident you're so good?"

His lips hitched into a half-smile that stole her breath. Not that she'd ever let him know the impact that *any* of his many smiles had on her. Jinx wasn't serious. Not about missions. Certainly not about her. This was sex. Only sex. Physical.

"What if you go falling in love with me?" He still held her hands. "What if you just can't get enough of me, and you can't imagine your life without me in it?"

Ali sucked in a sharp breath. "Then we'd better make a rule. Good sex doesn't equal love. So *no* falling in love."

A nod. "Any other rules? I've noticed you tend to be very...rule follower-like."

Guilty. She liked order. What was wrong with that? Just because Jinx had apparently lived his life rule free didn't mean that everyone did. But if he was asking for rules... "We keep this secret."

His thick, dark eyelashes lowered. "You want me to be your dirty little secret?" A rough edge entered his voice. An edge she'd never heard him use before. "Don't want anyone else to know you jumped into bed with me?"

Yes, actually, she would prefer the others not know about this situation—thus the rule. "We may have to work on other missions in the future. If that's the case, I don't want the others on the team to know we got naked together. I'm not the kissing-and-telling type."

His head bent. His mouth feathered over hers. His tongue teasingly swept inside. He took his time kissing her before murmuring, "Shocker, but...neither am I." Another kiss.

So they had two rules. Rule one, no falling in love. Rule two, what they did had to remain a secret. She was good with those guidelines. Very good.

His mouth...

His lips lifted from hers. "I have rules, too."

What? "Since when?" she blurted. Her hands were still caged by his. Caged and right above the straining erection that surged toward her. Jinx was built along *very* big and strong lines, everywhere.

"Since...you." His mouth pressed to her throat. Kissed her skin.

Her whole body shuddered. "What are the rules? And could you hurry and say them quickly?"

A soft rumble of laughter. "What's the rush?"

The rush was that she wanted to strip away the rest of their clothes and pounce on him. "Jinx!"

"You tell me everything you like. You tell me instantly if I do anything you *don't* like. You come harder for me than you ever have for anyone else."

Another kiss to her neck. "I think that about covers it for me."

Her knees were jelly. She was going to fall in a puddle right there, and she couldn't even blame her weak knees on the two tequila shots she'd had before coming into the motel room with him. "I can handle that."

"Good. Then time for you to handle *me*." He let go of her hands.

She reached for his cock. Curled her fingers around him and pretty much ignored everything else. The real world could wait. She was going to forget everything else for a while and just enjoy herself. She stroked his cock. Caressed him. Loved the warm strength of him, and she wondered how he would taste. Ali began to slide down—

"Oh, no. Remember my rule? You have to come harder for me than anyone else. That means you don't make me break my control until *after* I've driven you completely insane." He scooped her into his arms. Headed for the bed. He lowered her onto the sagging mattress and proceeded to completely strip as she stared up at him.

His body...

Shoulders that were huge. Abs of steel. Corded strength in those powerful thighs. And his cock—

He quirked a brow at her. "You know this goes easier and faster if your clothes are off, too, right?"

Heat flushed her cheeks. She kicked off her shoes. Shimmied out of her jeans and tossed her shirt away. She kept her panties and bra on because tossing them aside seemed...she didn't know what it seemed. Ali just left them on.

He didn't move. Just stood statue still at the side of the bed.

What was he waiting for? "Um, I thought this would go faster when I stripped?" Her voice held a slightly nervous edge. Ali hoped he didn't notice. She was trying to act like she did this sort of thing all the time.

She didn't. This was, in fact, her first ever one-night stand.

Not her first time for sex, but usually, she dated a guy for a while before becoming intimate. Got into a relationship. Took it all slow and steady with her *reliable* boyfriends.

"I was admiring the view." Jinx put one knee on the bed. His hand rose, and his knuckles slid along the curve of her hip. Then skated over to the crotch of her panties. She'd spread her legs for him, trying to be all helpful. "You're wet."

And he was hard. That should make things way easy for them. "Could we do this?" The words broke from her. So much for being cool. *Fail.* "I want this. I want you." This intensity wouldn't last. No way could it last.

His fingers crept under the edge of her panties. "What's the rush?"

He dipped a finger into her.

Her breath caught as he pressed that finger of his knuckle deep into her.

"You're tight. You will feel fucking fantastic."

The lights were on. It would be so much easier if they were off. Why hadn't she turned off the lamp? She'd just forgot about the damn thing.

He slid his finger out of her.

Ali's breath huffed out, too. Okay, he was giving her a minute to—

He yanked the panties off her. Jumped onto the bed. Parted her thighs and stared down at her like he'd just found some kind of amazing prize.

Yes, fine, whatever, he could—

He put his mouth on her. Put his mouth right on her without any other preliminaries. And with the first lick of his tongue against her clit, Ali knew that Jinx was about to make good on his boastful words...

You come harder for me than you have for anyone else.

Her hands grabbed the sheets. Fisted them. Her whole body arched as he stroked her with his fingers and licked her with his tongue. There was no fumbling. No awkwardness. Just him lapping her up like she was the best treat he'd ever had, and Ali could feel her whole body tighten as an orgasm just swept right through her and—

Detonated.

She choked out his name. Maybe gave a muffled scream. She didn't know. She didn't care. She just felt *awesome.*

"Now, you're ready." He grabbed for a condom. He'd had one in his wallet. Of course, he had. This was Jinx. He probably did this all the time and—

"Hey." His voice was low. Demanding. "Look at me."

Her lashes lifted.

"Where did you just go?"

He was lodged at the entrance to her body. How could she possibly have gone anywhere? "I'm right here."

His gaze wasn't mocking or teasing. There was a new intensity there that she hadn't seen before. He caught her hands. Pinned them on either side of her head, and then he was surging into her. Not fast and hard. Slow. Steady. As if he was testing to make sure he wasn't hurting her. She was arching her hips against him because she wanted more. Wanted *everything,* but Jinx was taking his precious time and driving her absolutely crazy. "Jinx!"

"There it is." A fast kiss. "Scream for me, baby."

Seriously? He was—

He sank all the way inside. Then pulled out. Drove deep.

Now he was hard and fast. Now he was driving into her like a man obsessed, and she was moaning and arching and twisting against him because the ravenous need was back. Pleasure was surging again, and she wanted more and more and more.

He gave her more. He gave her everything. He pumped into her with fast and furious strokes until her whole body broke apart, and her orgasm sent wave after wave of pleasure surging through her. Did she scream? Maybe. Ali had no clue. She didn't care. She was only feeling, and she felt *incredible.*

He was with her. His body hard and powerful. His face had locked into intense, almost possessive lines as he stared down at her. There was a greedy hunger in his gaze. Something she understood because in that moment, she wanted more, too. Wanted everything that she could get from him.

He came inside of her. A long, hard jerking of his body, and she tightened her inner muscles around him even more because she wanted to feel every single moment with him. Every single thing that he had to give. She wanted it. She wanted Jinx.

Over and over and—

Wow. Dangerous. Stop the thought.

Her breath heaved in and out. Her heart thundered. He was still in her, already getting hard again, and their hands were still intwined.

He stared at her. The lights were on. Everything was so bright. He'd seen her, every moment. She'd squeezed her eyes shut when the pleasure hit so she hadn't been watching him. But she realized he'd never taken his gaze from her.

Ali felt vulnerable, far too exposed.

He's still in me.

And he wasn't smiling. Wasn't flashing his killer grin. Instead, if possible, his face tightened even more.

"Jinx?" She started to wonder if she'd done something wrong. The sex had been helluva good for her. But maybe it hadn't been that way for him?

He didn't speak. Her hands flexed in his hold.

"You're not getting away," he rasped.

What?

Then he smiled at her. His easy, carefree smile. "It's going to be a long night."

Oh. "Then...you weren't disappointed?"

Again, his expression changed. But the change was so fleeting that she thought she'd imagined it. "Hell, no."

She risked a smile of her own.

He stared at her mouth. "Why the fuck would you even ask that?"

"Because you looked so serious. So intent. Like something was wrong."

"Everything is right. *You're* right." But he pulled out of her.

She gave a quick gasp because a little aftershock had hit her.

"Be right back," he promised. "We'll need another condom." A pause. "Maybe a whole damn box. There's a gas station across the street. I'll go there and get some."

He was planning to use a whole box of condoms with her? That was impressive.

Exciting.

He ditched the used condom in the bathroom. Dressed quickly. Then leaned over the bed. She'd shimmied under the covers while he took care of the condom-ditching business, and she held a sheet up to her chest.

He stared into her eyes. "Don't move. I'll be back in five minutes." A quick kiss. Only...

This kiss felt different.

Possessive?

Jinx didn't get possessive. She'd worked on several missions with him before. She'd technically known him for at least two years. He didn't get possessive about anyone or anything.

The door closed softly behind him. Ali raked a hand through her hair. That had been—wow.

Jinx.

And he planned for more. A whole night more. Then they were going to put all of this amazing sexing behind them and work together as a team on future cases and—

And I will always be picturing him naked. I will always be remembering what it was like to have him inside of me.

No way would she ever be able to erase those memories.

Oh, she had majorly screwed up.

Her phone rang. A loud, jarring peal of sound that had her jerking and then reaching toward the nightstand. She'd put the phone on the worn nightstand earlier...before she'd given in to that reckless urge to kiss Jinx.

There was no picture on the screen to identify the caller, but she knew that number, and unease slithered through her. Ali lifted the phone to her ear. "Hello."

"The car is waiting in front of your motel."

Her heart slammed into her chest. "I just finished a mission."

"And you're starting another. You're needed now. Deep cover."

Ali didn't move. She stayed in the bed—the bed that smelled of her and Jinx—and realized that she didn't want to go anywhere. She wanted to be right there when Jinx came back. She wanted to spend the night with him. She wanted to get lost in him.

She didn't want another case. Didn't want to have to become someone else. She was tired of pretending. "Find someone else." Words that she had never, ever expected to say. Not in a million years. The job was her life.

"There is no one else. A car is waiting, and it's time to move." Her handler's voice was implacable. "You need to be gone before he gets back."

Goosebumps rose onto her skin. "Were you...watching us?"

"Not us, you. I was watching you because I am here to take you to the next case. A case that can't wait. So get your gear and move." A direct order.

Because he was her boss.

Except...

"This is the last one." She'd been feeling adrift for a while, and she hadn't expected to say those words. They just kind of came out. But she wanted *more*. More than shadows. More than bullets raining down on her every time she turned around. "I do this, and I'm out."

"There is no out."

"There is for me." She rose from the bed. Jerked on her clothes even as she kept talking to him. "Consider this my two weeks' notice."

"The case will last longer than two weeks. It's deep cover. I told you—"

"And I just told you, I'm done. This is it. I want to be normal." She'd never realized how much she longed for it until it was gone. Until it had been ripped away by the choices she'd made. But she'd paid her debt. *More* than paid it. "Put in the paperwork, do whatever you need to do, but erase me. I'm out of your files, and, after I finish this case, my number will disappear from your phone."

Silence.

She looked around. She had to leave a note for Jinx. She couldn't just vanish.

How much time had passed?

"Fine," he gritted, his voice rumbling in her ear. "But get your ass outside, now, before the boyfriend comes back."

"He's not my—" She stopped. She didn't need to explain Jinx to him. He *knew* Jinx. They'd all worked together. "I'm on my way." She hung up the phone. Found a motel room pen near an absolutely ancient-looking notepad. Ali bit her lip as she stared at the pad. According to mission protocol, once you received an assignment, you had to go dark. No texts. No calls. Nothing.

But she wasn't just going to leave Jinx. And there was no rule about scribbling out a quick message the old-fashioned way. As long as that message didn't give away any mission secrets...

What was she supposed to write?

Thanks for the best sex ever.

That would go straight to his already inflated ego.

Thanks for a night I'll never forget.

But...it hadn't been a night. More like an hour?

A horn sounded outside. Jeez. Impatient, much?

The pen flew over the notepad.

Then she was out the door. And five minutes hadn't passed because Jinx wasn't back.

***

Silence.

Jinx knew something was off as soon as he opened the motel room door. He gripped the brown paper bag in one hand as his gaze swept the small area. "Ali?"

The covers were rumpled. Her discarded clothing gone from the floor.

He took a few fast steps inside. "Ali?" Sharper, harder.

No response. It took only seconds to realize she wasn't in the bathroom. She was gone. She'd left him.

Holy hell, she'd *left* him. After what he thought was pretty fucking great sex, she'd left him. No woman had ever done that before.

He whirled toward the door. She couldn't have gotten far. He surged forward, then stopped when he caught sight of the notepad. His jaw locked as he stalked closer to it, then read...

I got a call. You know the kinds of calls we get. There was no choice.

His nostrils flared.

If there'd been a choice, I would have stayed.

Well, fucking hell. Ali had always been incredibly honest.

Thank you for showing me the kind of incredible time that a woman will never forget.

His breath shuddered out. He'd intended to show her that incredible time over and over again. Like, not just for the night. But for the next week. Because while Ali might be honest, he was a world class liar. Always had been. He'd never intended to only have one night with her. Hell, no, he'd been playing a long game with Ali for a while.

His gaze lingered over the last line she'd written...

And I was wrong. It wasn't a mistake.

Jinx swallowed. He hissed out a breath and dropped the paper bag on the old desk. Then he yanked out his phone. He sent a quick text to Ali.

I will see you again.

No response.

But then, he hadn't expected one. When an operative went out on a mission, the order was to immediately go radio silent. *That* was why she hadn't texted him before she'd left the motel room.

At least she'd left him a note.

He grabbed the note.

Fuck, he could still smell her on him. Her sweet, strawberry scent.

The mission wouldn't last forever. He *would* see her again. He *would* have her again.

He tucked the note into his pocket.

He could wait. He could be patient. Patience was a virtue, after all. Granted, it had never been one of *his* virtues, but he could try. Unfortunately, he'd always found virtues to be rather boring. Jinx much preferred vices to virtues. And as soon as he had the chance, he couldn't wait to lead Ali down the road into wicked temptation with him.

I will be seeing you again, my Ali. Count on it.

CHAPTER ONE

"Sex on the beach is incredible."

At those low, rumbling words, Alison Carter whipped up in her beach chair. "Listen, buddy, I am not in the mood for—"

"The drink, of course. I am talking about the drink." The tall, muscular, freaking Greek-god-looking guy beamed at her. His smile was absolutely killer as it revealed his perfectly even, white teeth, and the aviator glasses he wore hid what she knew to be almost astoundingly blue eyes.

Jinx. He's here. Right in front of me. This could not be happening.

"It's sinful. Designed to help you cast your inhibitions aside and just soak up the pure sensual pleasure that waits in the world."

He didn't have on a shirt. Just dark swim trunks. Trunks that stretched across his muscular thighs. If possible, he seemed even more muscular than he'd been the last time they'd been together. She wasn't staring at a six pack. Had to be an eight pack. Maybe a ten? Was that a thing?

Stop staring. Her gaze snapped up to his face. Luckily, she was wearing sunglasses, too, so Ali didn't think that he'd noticed her gaping at him.

Hopefully. "What are you doing here?" she demanded.

He lowered his long body into the beach chair beside hers. Two women nearly fell as they peered back at him. They *had* been jogging down the beach until they caught sight of him. But when Jinx came into view, they did a quick about-face. It looked as if they might even come over for a chat.

Uh, obviously, he's busy.

Ali shooed the women away with a flick of her hand.

"Why am I here? On the beach, you mean? I'm enjoying the sun. The waves. The beauty of the day." A shrug of his powerful shoulders. "Same as you."

No. This could not be happening. Of all the beaches in the world—and there were *lots* of beaches—what were the odds that her personal kryptonite just happened to be on the same one that she was? "Odin," she gritted out.

"Hmmm...What about him?" Jinx shifted a bit on the chair, making himself more comfortable.

"Odin said this was a free vacation for me." Odin Shaw. A guy she'd considered a friend. He'd told her that this trip was his way of paying her back for all of the favors that she'd done for him and War—Warren Channing. War owned Trouble for Hire Private Investigations, a fairly new venture. New and surprisingly successful. The PI biz was growing leaps and bounds for War and Odin. Former special ops guys, they had turned their talents to solving local crimes. And, so far, they'd had their names splashed plenty in the news because they'd helped nab two big killers.

Their names had been splashed in the news. She'd quietly helped on those cases, and because War and Odin knew how much she valued her privacy, they'd kept her in the background. As a thank you for her services, she'd been given an all-expense paid trip to the Emerald Coast of Florida.

At the time, the trip had sounded too good to be true. But she'd needed to get away, so she'd jumped at the opportunity to put her toes in the sand.

No one had mentioned to her that she'd be sharing her beach with Jinx. *Jinx!*

This could not be happening.

"Did you just growl?" Jinx wanted to know. Then, before she could sputter off a reply, he added, "Sexy."

"Stop it." She glared at him as her toes curled into the sand. Only they weren't curling in some happy way. They were more *digging* into the sugary white sand of the beach. "I'm supposed to be relaxing. Not having to deal with you."

He sucked in a pain-filled breath. "That hurts." His hand went dramatically to his heart. "And here I thought we were friends."

She shot to her feet. Grabbed her cover up and hauled it over her body. The last thing she felt like doing was parading around in front of him just wearing her bikini.

"The ocean is fucking *that* way," Jinx suddenly snapped as he glared at a guy sitting nearby. Some guy in a red shirt with a ball cap pulled over his brows. "Stop looking at my girl's ass."

Not happening. She tugged the cover up down to her thighs and immediately moved to scoop up her oversized beach bag. She would go back to the condo. Lock herself inside. And forget about Jinx.

Not like it was the first time she'd had to work this routine.

But before she could race away from the scene, Jinx stood in front of her. "What's the hurry? Why not sit down and catch up with an old friend on this beautiful day?"

Her lips thinned. With one hand, Ali made a quick, nervous adjustment to her sunglasses. "We are not friends. We worked on a few cases. That's it. Not like we exchange Christmas cards or anything."

"Right. I did notice that I've never gotten a Christmas card. Wondered about that omission. Thought it had gotten lost in the mail." Her reflection stared back at her in his glasses. His arms crossed over his chest. "I can buy that we weren't friends. Fine. But we were lovers."

"*Shhh!*" Immediately, she glanced around. It had sounded as if Jinx had just *shouted* that last bit of info.

He shrugged. "We were. The kind of dirty, hot lovers that like to rip each other's clothes off and fuck in cheap motel rooms."

"No." A hard shake of her head. "I refuse to do this with you. Not now. Not here." Not on a public beach, for goodness' sake. Ali sidestepped him and began stomping—or attempting to stomp because walking in the sand was always a major effort—her way past him.

But Jinx followed. "Where would you like to chat?" His voice trailed her just as he did. "Are you inviting me back to your place? Suggesting we take this somewhere nice and private?"

Ali spun toward him. Sand flew in her wake. "Why are you here?"

"Oh, don't you know?" A wide, too gorgeous smile spread over his lips.

Her body tensed. Quivered. *Dammit.*

"I live here now," Jinx casually revealed. Just dropped that bombshell. *Boom.* "And imagine my surprise when I walked onto my favorite beach in the area and saw...*you.*"

She sucked in a deep breath.

"The lovely lady who left me high and dry," Jinx continued, "and holding a giant box of condoms."

A very loud gasp came from the right. Ali did not even glance that way. Her cheeks burned, a burn that did not come from the sun because she had SPF'd the heck out of her skin. "I left you a *note.*"

He stepped closer. So close their bodies nearly touched. "And then you never called me when the mission was over."

He actually sounded angry. And surely, *surely* that had not been a hint of hurt in his voice. No way, no day. "Not like you were mooning over me. You just found some big-breasted, fake red-haired, tight-jean wearing singer to hook up with and you didn't look back. So spare me the weird scene, would you? We had a night. Not even a night. More like an hour. It was great. It's also over. And we have both moved on." Her chin lifted. "Now, excuse me, but I have to go wash sand out of my bathing suit." Ali did another fast turn and resumed her sand-stomping routine.

She didn't get far. Suddenly, Jinx was looming in her path.

She frowned at him. Her frowning reflection glared back at her from his mirrored glasses.

"That was awfully specific." He'd turned musing.

"What was specific?"

"The big-breasted, fake red-haired, tight-jean wearing singer story."

Uh, oh. "Was it?" Her voice rose a little too much.

"Um, yes, it was. As in...you saw me with someone like that." He rocked forward onto the balls of his feet. "You came looking for me after the mission."

Dang it. She had.

"Oh, Ali. Don't hold back on me now. One of the things I always enjoyed about you most was your honesty."

He'd enjoyed it? He wanted more? Her grip tightened on her beach bag. "I might have come back to catch up with you. Not like I had anything else big on my agenda. And, yes, I did happen to see you with the redhead. Not that it mattered. We weren't involved. You were free. I was free. End of story."

"Sonofabitch." A low, vicious curse. The lethal edge in his voice caught her off guard. "All this time...and *that* was why you hid from me?"

Hid. That one word set off alarm bells. Yes, she was hiding, but not from Jinx. "I need to go." Once more, she moved to step around him.

He stepped with her in the same instant, as if he'd anticipated her movement. "It was one dance. *She* danced with me, if you want to know the full story. And, yes, she offered to take me back to her place when the dance was done."

"It doesn't matter." This whole insane conversation didn't matter.

"Didn't realize you'd seen that. How the hell did you even know where I was that night?"

She stared at a random point to the left of his face. "You know I'm good at finding people." One of her gifts.

"Yeah, I do. That's why I was sure you'd come back to me, only you never showed up, so I thought you were ditching me."

The sun beat down on them. The waves slammed into the shore.

"If you were there, you should have seen me send her away."

She hadn't. She'd left after seeing them together because...it was Jinx. Jinx didn't get involved with anyone seriously. Jinx didn't take *anything* seriously. It was just who he was. Not like he was magically gonna change. Not for her or anyone else. She'd realized that as she stood in the doorway of that club.

Realized that I didn't know what in the world I was doing. Realized that I didn't want him to tell me—to my face—that we were one and done.

"Judging by your expression, I guess you missed the magic moment when I sent her on her merry way."

Her gaze darted to his. "We...weren't involved. You could—*can*—date or—or fuck—whoever you want." Okay, she'd seriously stumbled over what should have been a casual, breezy, sophisticated, I-don't-care statement.

"That really how you feel?"

No, at the time, she'd felt like clawing the redhead's eyes out. And as for how she felt *now*...

"Because it's not how I feel," Jinx stunned her by saying.

Had she heard him correctly? The surf's roar was awfully loud, and she was so tempted to ask him to repeat himself.

"It's been months," Jinx continued grimly, "but the idea of you fucking anybody else..." He lowered his mouth near her ear. "It makes me want to damn well destroy someone."

What? No. No way. Jinx had not just said those words to her. She'd misunderstood.

He put his mouth to your ear so that you could hear perfectly. You know you didn't misunderstand.

"Just so you know where I stand." His breath teased the outer shell of her ear.

A shiver traveled through her body.

Jinx's dark head lifted. "I'd like more."

"More?" she repeated.

He just stared at her. If his glasses weren't in the way, maybe she'd be able to read the emotions in his eyes. Then again, maybe not. She'd never been able to read him. As far as she knew, no one had.

"More of you." He reached for her left hand—the hand *not* gripping her oversized bag. As soon as he touched her skin, a bolt of pure energy zipped up her arm. She gave a quick, little jerk, one that he had to notice.

It had always been that way for her. She'd had an instant attraction to Jinx. The man was walking sex appeal, so how could she not want him? And he was just too perfect. Perfectly symmetrical features. Perfectly sexy bit of stubble on his perfect, square jaw. Thick, dark hair that had just the lightest bit of curl. A voice that sounded like warm sin.

Jinx had always been able to attract anyone he wanted, and she'd certainly been no exception. There was a line to get in his bed.

But...

She didn't intend to stand in line any longer.

"No reason we can't pick up where we left off," Jinx continued in that warm-sex voice of his. "You're here. I'm here. I'm sure there is a bed close by that you and I could wreck."

She swallowed. When that didn't help to clear the lump in her throat, Ali swallowed again. What he was offering was ever so tempting but... "No."

"Excuse me?"

"I get that most women probably don't say this word to you, but I'm saying it...No. Or, rather, no, thank you." Because she'd been taught to be polite.

His jaw seemed to drop.

"Now, I'm afraid that I have to run. I've got an important meeting tonight that I can't miss."

"You have a date?" Guttural. Not warm-sex any longer.

Ali pondered his question. A date? Not that she'd call it that, nope. "I have a meeting." That was all she'd tell him.

His hand flew up and—

Snagged her sunglasses. Oh, no.

"Much better." He stared into her eyes. His eyes were still shielded by the aviators, dammit. "Always liked staring into those pretty brown eyes of yours."

She narrowed said eyes at him.

His head cocked. "You're hiding something from me."

"I want my sunglasses. The sun is bright."

He took a step back. "Are you scared of me, Ali?"

She snatched back her glasses. Screw waiting for him to give them to her. "You don't scare me." With somewhat shaking fingers, she plopped the glasses back on her nose. "And believe me, it is most definitely in your best interest to stay the hell away from me."

With that, she surged past him. She didn't look back.

Her heart pounded, nearly bursting from her chest, as she left him in the sand.

*It really is better this way. So much safer...*Because Jinx had no idea just how dangerous her life had become.

***

"I thought I told you to stay the hell away from me," the low, snarling words came from the man who sat at the end of the bar.

Ramsey.

Big, tough, and supposedly the baddest bastard in the bar.

Jinx lifted his shot glass and saluted the fellow. It was, after all, Ramsey's place, and if he didn't at least *act* vaguely polite, he'd probably get thrown out the door. "Just wanted to check in on my favorite criminal."

Ramsey slammed one tattooed fist onto the scarred bar top. Then he heaved to his feet and stalked toward Jinx. "I am not in the mood for your shit tonight."

Jinx dropped his empty glass back onto the bar. As he did, the nearby saltshaker spilled over.

Oh, hell. Bad sign. As if he needed more of those. Jinx snagged some of the salt and tossed it over his left shoulder even as he whirled toward Ramsey. The guy was in full-on charge mode. *You aren't in the mood for me?* "Oh, right, like I am in the mood to deal with your sorry—" He stopped. Put his hands on Ramsey's shoulders.

"*What in the hell are you doing?*" Ramsey demanded in the tone that said *don't fuck with me.*

But Jinx just tightened his hold and craned around the guy. "Oh, hell, no." Horror hit him. *I knew that salt was gonna lead to trouble.*

"I want you out of this bar." Ramsey's words were low and cold. Icily furious. "I want you out of my sight. If you come near me again, I will kick your ass."

"You and what army?" Jinx replied automatically.

Ramsey waved one hand vaguely in the air. Immediately, half a dozen chairs were shoved back in response to the small signal. The legs of the chairs groaned and creaked as men and women shot to their feet.

"Right." Jinx nodded. "That army. Almost forgot they were here." Total lie. He hadn't forgotten. He just hadn't cared. What he *did* care about...she was standing near the doorway. *She should not be here.* "I'll leave, but I'm taking her with me."

"Her?" What could have been vague curiosity filled Ramsey's rough voice.

"Um, yes, the angel who just strolled in obviously looking for a bit of hell. She's mine." A total declaration of intent. "How about you let your little army know so that no one gets the dumb idea to so much as put a finger on her? Because if that happens, I'd have to stop being so nice." He let go of Ramsey. Started for his angel.

Only Ramsey was now turning and staring at her, too. Shit. The *last* thing Jinx wanted was for Ramsey's attention to wander to her. Not today, not freaking ever, thanks.

The angel was still in the doorway. Deep, thick brown hair spilled over her shoulders—brown hair shot with the faintest of blond highlights. Were the highlights natural? He didn't know. Didn't care. They were gorgeous. So was she...with her full lips, cute little nose, those high cheekbones, and the deep, dark eyes that could sometimes make him forget his own name.

Well, his *real* name, anyway.

She stood in the doorway, and her gaze darted around the shady bar as if she was looking for someone.

Lucky for her, she'd just *found* someone.

Him.

Jinx made his way right to her. Her head had been turned away as he approached, but as he closed in, her focus changed. Her head angled toward him, and her eyes locked on his. Stunned awareness flooded into her gaze. "*You.*"

"Me." He smiled.

She didn't.

She *did* look worried.

The same way she'd looked worried on the beach. The faintest hint of fear slid into her eyes before she masked it. Damn odd. Once upon a time, he would have sworn that Alison Carter didn't fear anything or anyone.

Apparently, he'd been wrong.

Not exactly the first time that situation had occurred.

"What are you doing here?" she said. Her breath caught. "Did you *follow* me?"

"Ah, yeah, sweets, I was here first." He jerked a thumb over his shoulder. "I was at the bar, enjoying shots...oh, wait, you enjoy them, too, from what I recall of our acquaintance." Yes, he'd just gone there. "Want to have one with me, you know, for old time's sake?"

Her adorable chin whipped up. "I am not here to drink."

"Really. Huh. You're in a bar, and you're not here to drink." He paused. "Now just call me curious but I am dying to know...why *are* you here? It's definitely not the atmosphere. Don't tell the owner..." Who was glowering at them. "But the place is a shithole."

She didn't immediately answer him. He waited. Jinx had a suspicion about why she was in the bar, and it wasn't a good one. Ramsey's wasn't exactly the type of place to attract tourists. Quite the opposite. It attracted a much rougher, shadier element.

The people in Ramsey's were usually either criminals or people looking to hire criminals. Since he didn't know of any law that Ali had broken, that made him think she belonged in category number two...

People looking to hire criminals.

"Is this the meeting you couldn't miss?" he asked.

Her gaze swept around the bar. "What I'm doing here is none of your business. Now, if you will excuse me..."

"No."

"What?"

"No, I will not excuse you. See, it's bad form to leave a *friend* in a dangerous situation. What kind of man do you think I am?"

"We covered this," she hissed. "I am not a friend, and I can handle myself. I can—"

"Why the hell are you still here?"

Jinx didn't stiffen at the thundering voice. He did sigh, though. Leave it to Ramsey to interrupt at a delicate moment. "I'm still here," he tossed back without looking away from Ali, "because I happen to be talking to my *friend.*" He used that word deliberately.

And Jinx saw the mutinous set of Ali's jaw.

"I told you," she began, "I'm not—"

"Any friend of Jinx's..." Ramsey's voice boomed out. "Is *not* welcome here."

Oh, how excellent. Ramsey had responded just as Jinx had hoped. He winked at Ali because he was feeling so pleased.

She gaped back at him. "What is going on?"

It was Ramsey who replied. He snapped. "You're getting your ass tossed out. You and your boyfriend." He put his hand on Jinx's shoulder. Tightened his grip. *Hard.* Then he leaned in and whispered to Jinx, "*I don't want to be fucking saved. I won't tell you again. Stay away.*"

"Well, you don't have to be rude about it," Jinx huffed.

"Yes, with you, I do." Ramsey let go of Jinx. Glared at a confused Ali. "Don't know why he brought you here, but you won't be getting through those doors again. I will make sure the bouncers know to never let you in."

"But, but—" she sputtered.

"But nothing." Jinx reached for her hand. "You heard the man, love. We'd better be going." Then he let his own gaze sweep the crowd. He was conscious of all the eyes on him. "Don't look like the friendly sort. Bet the bartender doesn't ever offer Sex on the Beach to anyone."

Ramsey pointed to the door. "Get the fuck out."

Jinx tugged Ali with him. "Going."

"But I was supposed to meet someone!" Ali was digging in her heels. "I had a meeting with Ram—"

Jinx lifted her up and tossed her over his shoulder. He was sure she'd be pissed as hell, but desperate times did call for desperate measures.

Catcalls and whistles burst into the air. Oh, yes, sure, *now* the crowd there responded to him. What the hell ever. He carried a squirming Ali past gawking bouncers and out into the night. He didn't stop walking, didn't ease up his grip on her, not until they were away from the bar and beside his motorcycle. Only then did he lower her to the ground.

She came up swinging. Luckily, he was fast at ducking. She missed him. When she swung again, he caught her fist. "Baby, your skills are with computers, not hand to hand." Actually, he knew she had passable hand-to-hand skills.

He was just *better* at fighting than she was. Mostly because he loved to fight dirty.

Even as he had that thought, Ali kicked his shin. Hard enough to have him wincing.

"Fine," Jinx growled. "I deserved that one. But I was actually being the hero tonight."

"Heroes don't toss women over their shoulders and carry them out of bars!"

"Sure, they do. If the bar in question happens to be a criminal cesspool and the woman is in serious danger—a true hero would totally help her get out of that situation." He braced his legs, ignored the throbbing in his shin, and stared at her. "What the hell were you doing in a place like that?"

"Oh, come on. I'm hardly some innocent. You and I both know that." She sniffed. "I've been in more hotspots in this world than most people can ever—"

"You've always been behind a well-trained team that watched your sexy ass." He wasn't playing. Not teasing. This shit was serious. "I didn't see a team in there with you. I just saw you, walking straight into more trouble than you could possibly realize."

"I knew exactly what I was walking into!"

"Really?" He could practically feel steam burning from his skin. "You knew you were walking into a bar filled with some of the roughest criminals in the area? Guys who would as soon stab you as look at you?"

Her mouth parted. Closed. "I—"

He edged even closer. It was all he could do to keep his hands off her. His fingers flexed and clenched. "What the hell was your plan? People go to a place like that if they want to hire someone for a job. For a theft, a smash and grab, or even a murder. Now you and I both know you can steal anything you want without someone else's help." *That* was part of her talent. A talent that he also possessed, and that was why they'd been teamed together before. "Smash and grabs have never been your game. That leaves our third choice." A dark choice. "It makes me damn curious, baby, and I just have to know...who do you want killed?"

CHAPTER TWO

The night surrounded her. Insects were chirping in the thick woods around the rundown bar. The parking lot was filled with an assortment of vehicles—from high-end rides to cars that had duct tape keeping taillights in place. Music blared from inside of Ramsey's, not that she could see the bar any longer. She had a giant, angry wall in front of her that blocked her view of everything else.

The wall was Jinx. A Jinx she'd never seen before. One that made her nervous. She forced a light laugh. "I'm hardly looking to have someone killed."

He didn't smile. None of the fierce tension left his body. They were in the shadows as they stood next to the motorcycle, so she couldn't read his expression clearly. Ali thought that might be a good thing.

"Who were you meeting in there?"

She needed to get out of that place. And get *away* from Jinx. "Look, none of this is really your business."

"I happen to think *you're* my business."

"I'm not. We had a one-night stand, and that's it. What we did—one time—does not give you any say regarding what I do with my life." The words trembled a little, but she thought they came out pretty cold. Ali was grateful for that win. She wanted Jinx away from her, stat.

For his own safety. He wouldn't get that, though. Because she wasn't sharing that bit of information.

Anyone close to her? *In danger.* She didn't want danger touching Jinx. Not danger that came because of her.

"You'll want to think the fuck again on that." Anger vibrated in his voice. "When it comes to you, I'm very damn involved in what happens."

Where was the normal laughing, teasing Jinx? "Who are you?" she whispered.

"I'm the guy who wants to know what the hell is going on." A pause. "Were you there for Ramsey?"

Yes, she *may* have been. Because word in the dark corners of the world was that for the right price, Ramsey could make problems disappear. She had a problem that needed to vanish. One that she hadn't been able to handle on her own, despite her attempts.

"Shit." He'd obviously taken her silence as an affirmation. Which, sure, it was. Jinx backed up a step and raked a hand through his hair. "Not happening."

"Well, yes, unfortunately, it's *not* happening. Because of you." He'd ruined her fine plans.

He froze with his fingers in his hair. His head turned toward her.

"You got us kicked out. The man shouting obviously hates you, and since he thought we were

together, he didn't want me in there, either."
What a mess. "So now I'll have an even harder
time meeting Ramsey—"

"You already met him," he snapped. "He's the
bastard who said you could never come back. That
means any business you wanted to conduct with
him? You can forget about it."

Her stomach knotted. "Why does he hate
you?"

"He doesn't. He freaking loves me. Just has a
twisted way of showing it some days."

Her hands flew up in frustration. "Now you're
back to your jokes? Seriously?"

"Not joking about a damn thing."

Uh, yes, obviously, he was. "The man threw
you out of his bar. He threw us *both* out. Not
exactly showing the love." Since she'd been with
Jinx, she was painted as guilty by association.
There would be no help coming from Ramsey or
his associates. Dang it. She'd have to switch to
Plan B. A plan she didn't like because it meant
dragging people she cared about into her mess.

But not Jinx. He won't know. She squared her
shoulders. "It's been, uh, not fun, Jinx, so you will
understand why I'm leaving." She took two steps
to the left.

He dropped his hand. Moved immediately
into her path. "We aren't done."

"We are." She swallowed and fought to keep
her voice steady. "In fact, we've been done for
several months." *Break the tie. It's safer this way.
Better for him.* "You stay out of my way, and I'll
stay out of yours."

He looked down, glancing at their bodies.

"Uh, you're in my way right now," Ali pointed out softly.

His head lifted. "You think I don't know?"

There was a lot she thought he didn't know...about her. Because she was working hard to keep her secrets. Instead of answering, she remained silent.

"I can all but feel your fear, baby."

That knot in her stomach grew tighter. "What could I possibly have to fear?"

"I don't know...why don't you tell me?"

A truck's engine revved to life. A loud, bursting growl of sound that told Ali someone had been playing a whole lot beneath the hood of that particular vehicle. The growl had made her jerk in startled reaction, and Ali heaved out a long breath. She didn't intend to tell Jinx about her problems.

As it was, the longer he spent with her, the greater the potential for a target to get painted on his back. *If one isn't already there.*

Had she been watched at the beach? Seen with Jinx? Was she being watched right now? She'd tried to be careful when she came to Ramsey's. Ali knew how to check for tails, and she *thought* that she'd done a good job.

But the guy after her always seemed to be several steps ahead.

You don't know he followed you down here. You were careful. The vacation gift from Odin had seemed like a godsend. She'd thought she could vanish down in the coastal area. Maybe she had. Maybe she was jumping at shadows when she was actually safe and just needed to calm down.

Her hand lifted and patted against Jinx's chest. His ever-so-hard and muscled chest. "Thanks for the concern, but I'm good." Another pat. She would *not* let her fingers linger, even though they wanted to. Even though they were itching to caress him. *Nope. Not doing it.* "I was just out tonight. Seeing the town. Doing the tourist thing." It was fairly easy to lie. She'd had to lie before, of course, when she was undercover. But she tended to *not* lie at any other time.

She'd never actually lied to Jinx before. Would he be able to tell she wasn't being honest? She doubted it. None of her other marks ever had. "I knew this club had a bit of a reputation, but you see, I've got a wild side, too. I was told that Ramsey offered one hell of a fun time to the people in his bar." She started to pull her hand back.

Too late.

Jinx's hand had lifted, and his fingers curled around her wrist. He kept her palm trapped against his chest, over his heart. "That is adorable."

Uh, oh. "What's adorable?"

"The way you think you can lie to me—right to my face—and I'll believe you." He leaned toward her. So close that she thought he might kiss her.

Super bad plan. "Jinx..."

"This place isn't for tourists. You came here for a deliberate reason, and it wasn't so that you could party it up on the dangerous side of town. You were looking for a very specific brand of trouble. Lucky for you, you didn't find it."

Trouble. Unfortunately, yes, that was what she needed.

He was still holding her wrist. Still leaning in as if he was going to kiss her.

She remembered what it felt like to have his mouth on hers. Remembered how she'd gone from a simple kiss to wanting to rip away his clothes in about fifteen seconds.

You're too close to him. Move back. Don't risk Jinx.

Because while he might have been an overbearing asshole so far that night, Jinx tended to be one of the good guys. He'd always fought for the weak. Always followed orders like a champ. Never left a teammate behind. Never hesitated to do the right thing even as the world went to hell around him.

Because of what he'd been to her...he was in danger. So while Ali might want to push onto her tiptoes and put her mouth against his, she couldn't. Going down that road with Jinx again wasn't an option.

"You don't know me," she managed to say, voice husky. "You might think you do, but you don't."

"Sure about that? Here I thought I knew you biblically."

Her cheeks burned, but the darkness hid her flush. "Good night, Jinx." She tugged her hand from his hold. "How about we try to stay out of each other's way for the rest of the time that I'm in town?" *You need to stay away. Far away.*

He took a step back. Motioned for her to pass him. "You don't want me, you won't have me."

Oh, he didn't get it. She most definitely *wanted* him. She'd stayed awake plenty of nights thinking about him. But being with Jinx wasn't an option for her. Ali gave a curt nod and headed past him. With every step, some of the tension slid from her. It had been hard, it *was* hard walking away, but it was for the best. Ali risked one final glance back at him. "Wanting you has never been the problem."

"Ali?"

"Goodbye, Jinx." Final. Flat.

***

She fish-tailed it out of the parking lot. Jinx watched her go with narrowed eyes. He knew fear when he saw it, and Ali was definitely running scared.

A low whistle came from his right. Like he hadn't known the sonofabitch was there.

"I think that's the first time I've ever seen you get shot down by a woman." A considering pause. "Usually that smile of yours works wonders. Guess she's immune."

Jinx put his hands on his hips. "Not even close." His gaze darted around the lot. No one else was there. No wonder he'd been given this precious chat time.

Ramsey didn't like for them to be seen together too much. Jinx glanced toward him. A big shadow in the dark. "You will stay the hell away from her."

"I assure you, I have no interest in your friend."

"My worry is that she has interest in you." He scraped a hand over his jaw. "I think she was here to hire you for a job."

No response.

"Did you recognize her?" Jinx pushed because he felt as if he was missing something big.

"No."

"Did she call you? Because she told me that she had a meeting—"

"I *was* told by someone that a new client might be showing up tonight."

Jinx closed in on him. "You won't take her on. Whatever she wants—refuse."

"Doubt that she'll be back. I think she heard me when I said you both needed to get your asses out of my place."

He stared at Ramsey's shadowy figure. "You're on the edge." He could see it. "I can't predict what the hell you will do next." All he knew was that Ramsey wasn't letting him help. *And* Jinx had a pretty strong suspicion that Ramsey was taking secret visits related to a certain obsession of his. "Have you talked to her?"

"I just told you, I don't know your friend, and I have no interest in—"

"Not talking about *my* friend. I'm talking about yours. About the lady everyone thought was dead, but who just turned up very much in the land of the living. The woman who doesn't remember you, but who you can't seem to forget. *Her.* Have you talked to Whitney or are you just hiding in shadows and watching—"

Ramsey lunged at him.

Jinx had expected the move. He'd taunted the other man into taking it. So he didn't flinch. Didn't back up. Just waited.

Ramsey's fist was inches from his face. The guy's self-control had improved over the years. Back when they'd been kids, that fist would have slammed into Jinx's jaw. Jinx would have pummeled him back, and then five minutes later, they would have been best friends again.

Best friends. Best enemies. The way only brothers could be.

"Don't mention her again," Ramsey ordered.

"No? Well, thought you'd be interested to know she's back to staying at her house. Back to her job at the college. Your Whitney seems to be back to resuming—"

"She's not mine." A growl.

"My mistake. For a bit there, you had me confused."

"Stop messing around in things you don't understand, Jinx."

He understood plenty. Like the fact that his brother was hurting. Like the fact that Ramsey had locked himself off from everyone and everything. That *he'd* let this happen to Ramsey because he'd been too freaking busy saving the world. Jinx hadn't realized the person who might need saving most was the one person closest to him.

"She doesn't know me." Ramsey spoke without emotion, the way he so often did. "Doesn't remember a damn thing about me. And that's for the best."

Was it? Jinx doubted it. "You know, she might not remember. But you do. And some memories can haunt you. They can slip into your head late at night. Make you long for things." *Make you remember how a woman felt when she was wrapped around you...when she was screaming your name...when she was...*

"Trouble, Jinx..." Ramsey was saying.

"Sorry," Jinx muttered. "Got lost in my own memories." Not like it was the first time that happened. "Could you say everything to me again? All the bits that came after me telling you that memories can make you long for things."

Ramsey gave a long sigh. "I said...your *friend* is in trouble. You want to help someone, you want to play hero? Go play with her and leave me the hell alone." Then he turned his back and walked away.

Jinx climbed onto his motorcycle. Curled his hands over the handlebars. Ramsey didn't quite understand him. That was okay. Most people didn't. Not even those blood related to him.

But the thing was...when it came to Ali, he wasn't playing.

He drove away from the bar. The road was pitch black, only his headlight cutting through the night. Wind blew against him, and the motorcycle roared as he sped forward. He didn't need Ramsey to tell him that Ali was in trouble. Jinx knew that for himself. He also knew that she had to be damn scared if she'd come to Ramsey for help.

He hugged the curve. Heard the distant crash of the waves into the shore. He zipped forward again and—

Lights flashed on behind him as a powerful engine snarled. The lights were bright—too bright, blinding—but Jinx didn't waver with his hold on the motorcycle. Some prick wanted to pop out of the dark and give chase?

Fucking fine with him.

He shot the bike forward, racing faster.

The engine behind him rumbled louder and gave chase. Seriously? Jinx had to deal with some wanna be *Fast and—*

The truck hit the back of his bike. Tipped it and had Jinx surging forward. For just a moment, the motorcycle started to careen out of control. The blinding lights behind him kept burning, and the truck's engine was snarling for all it was worth.

A swift glance back showed Jinx that the guy was coming at him again. This prick was looking to do damage.

But he'd picked the wrong prey.

Jinx took his motorcycle off-road. Revved it and cleared the shoulder, then he spun back toward the road, kicking up dirt and rocks as he whirled to catch sight of the truck that had blasted past him. Jinx could see the rear taillights. *No license plate.*

The truck screeched to a stop. Then it began to reverse. The driver had seen Jinx go off the road, and he was coming back for him.

Come on, asshole. Come at me. Jinx didn't know who the hell this creep was but figured he was probably an enemy of Ramsey's who'd seen them talking in the lot. Jinx had been sure that lot was empty. Apparently, he'd been wrong. If this piece of shit thought he'd hurt Ramsey by coming at Jinx, then he needed to think again.

Jinx saw the flash of more headlights in the distance. Other cars were edging around the curve and would be on them soon. The driver of the truck must have spotted those lights, too, because it stopped reversing. Instead, it leapt forward and burned rubber as it screeched its way from the scene.

Jinx considered giving chase until he saw that one of the cars rounding the curve? It was a cop car. So Jinx just kept sitting his ass right there and pulled out his phone. If he zoomed up and gave chase, he'd wind up having a long chat with the cops. Not something he needed right now. Not when the situation involved Ramsey.

He dialed his brother.

"Are you fucking kidding—" Ramsey began.

"Someone in a big-ass, souped-up truck just tried to run me off the road." Flat. "Consider this a warning that one of your enemies may know who I am to you."

Silence. Then... "You hurt?"

"Takes more than a sloppy bit of driving to hurt me, but I'm touched by your concern. Deeply, deeply touched."

"Fuck off."

"I assume that means you'll find out who the jerk is? Because he wasn't sporting tags which tells me he thought he was being clever." The cop car had passed him.

"I'll take care of him."

"Good to know. Because I take someone hitting my bike very personally." He had killed the engine, and now he walked around to inspect his precious wheels. "Jackass left a dent. He'll pay for that."

"Told you...*I'll take care of him.*" Then Ramsey hung up.

"Well, good freaking night to you, too," Jinx muttered. Talk about some shitty luck.

***

She wasn't a quitter, so Ali didn't stop drinking her milkshake until she'd drained every single drop of chocolate goodness from that baby. She'd lucked up and found a small, twenty-four-hour diner on her way back to the condo, and to her utter delight, the place had served the best shake she'd had in ages. She'd hunched in her booth and drank away her sorrows and tried not to think about just how great—and tempting— Jinx had looked when she'd first spotted him inside of Ramsey's.

Now isn't the time to get involved again. You have enough to deal with as it is. Stuff she knew, sure, but...

This was Jinx. And she'd always had a bit of a weak spot for Jinx.

And that's why he's off-limits.

Ali left some cash on the table near her empty shake and made her way to the door. As she stepped outside, some joker in a souped-up truck turned on his brights. They blinded her and whoever else in the restaurant had the unfortunate luck of glancing that way. Automatically, she lifted her hand to shield her eyes—and then she heard the vehicle lurching away.

Jerk. Shaking her head—and lowering her arm—she hurried to her rental car. It waited for her under a flickering light in the parking lot and—

The light flickered. Came on. Went off. Came on...

Something was wrong with the driver's side door of her sensible ride.

Ali's steps slowed.

The parking lot light flashed on. Hummed. Went off again.

She inched closer to the vehicle.

Then she was swearing and pulling out her phone. She turned on the flashlight and shone the light at the door as she crouched forward.

Slut.

Someone had keyed her car and left a very distinct message. Instantly, she shot upright and swung around.

The truck...the truck with the bright lights.

Lights that had only turned on when she'd exited the diner. As if...as if the driver had been waiting for her.

Sonofabitch.

He *was* in the area. He'd found her. And if his message was anything to go by, he was about to start his same sick games again.

Jinx had been right. She had been in Ramsey's bar because she was looking for a very specific brand of trouble. The kind of trouble she could hire for a dangerous job.

But Jinx had shut down that option for her.

She looked back at the ugly taunt that had been carved into her vehicle.

Looked like it was definitely plan B time.

And plan B meant turning to some old friends for help. Considering that those friends owed her, they had darn well better take the job...*and* promise not to mention a word about it to a certain too handsome, too wild, good luck addict named Jinx...

CHAPTER THREE

At 8 a.m. sharp, Ali lifted her hand and rapped against the office door for Trouble for Hire. She'd texted War, the owner of the PI office, earlier that morning and told him that she needed to meet. She'd left out the part about it being a life-or-death situation. She figured they'd get around to that bit in person.

War had assured her that his office would be open and waiting. She wasn't sure how he was going to respond to her case. But she was ready to remind him of just how much he owed her. And you couldn't turn away a person when you owed a major debt, could you?

"Come in." A gruff voice called.

She twisted the knob and went inside, only to find herself in some kind of lobby. An empty lobby. Biting her lip, Ali hesitated for just a moment, then she hurried forward on her quest. She found another door, one partially open, that had TROUBLE FOR HIRE PRIVATE INVESTIGATIONS etched on the glass. Ali squared her shoulders and pushed that door open. "Thanks for meeting me."

The chair was turned away from her, but she saw the back of War's dark head. He was staring out the window. He must have been watching her approach. The PI office was on the second floor of the historic building. The first floor was for Armageddon, War's bar. The bar was completely deserted right now, another reason why she'd been so eager for their early morning appointment. She wanted to keep this visit as quiet as possible.

"I sure didn't think I'd ever be one of your clients." She shoved her hands into the back pockets of her jeans and rocked forward nervously. "But desperate times have called for, you know, desperate measures and all that."

He hadn't spoken.

"I'm out of options, and I could really use a friend." There. Truth. "I'll pay whatever you need, but I am in some trouble—"

The chair swiveled toward her, slowly, and her words froze. Her throat seemed to close up as she stared at the man sitting in that lush chair. A man who was very much *not* War.

Oh, no. A thousand times, no.

But, yes, it was Jinx who gazed back at her. Jinx who had the same dark, thick hair that War possessed. Jinx who had broad shoulders and a build just like War.

Jinx...who was very much *not* War.

He didn't flash his killer grin. His bright blue eyes didn't twinkle. Instead, he stared at her with an icy gaze and with an expression that was both savage and angry.

She backed up a step.

He rose. Put his hands on the desk. "Who..." Jinx began in a voice so cold and chilling that she was surprised icicles didn't immediately cover the desk. "Who the fuck wrote the word 'Slut' on your car?"

That was the first question he had?

She shook her head.

"*Who,* Ali? Because the fucker is gonna pay."

This was...She released the breath that she'd been holding. "Where is War?"

"Getting coffee and the damn donuts that he likes for breakfast." His hands remained on the desk. "I told him I would take care of you."

She looked over her shoulder. "I'll just...wait for War."

"You're getting *me.*"

Her head whipped back toward him. "Uh, listen up, bossy. I came for War. I have a private matter to discuss with War. So I'll just be doing that, thanks."

He shoved away from the desk. Stalked around it. Headed for her. She retreated, a quick, fast retreat that had her ducking out of the doorway, slipping back into the hall, and darting to the lobby. When Ali realized that she was practically running from Jinx, she stopped. "This is ridiculous."

"I don't find it funny at all." He'd followed her.

She waved toward him. "You're not a PI. I'm here to hire a PI. So I'll just wait in the um...lobby."

He shook his head. "Wrong, sweets."

"Excuse me?"

"I am a PI. A new hire of War's. Odin and War brought me onto the team. Turns out that if your PI office stops two crazed killers, you are suddenly in ever so high demand. War had so much work he needed more staff."

She stared pointedly at the empty lobby, then looked back at Jinx.

He shrugged. "The clients aren't all here now. But trust me, we have plenty. So many that it turns out War and Odin are both already committed to other cases. If you want help, then you will be getting me."

This could not be happening.

He waved toward the office. "So why don't you come back inside, have a seat, and tell me what's going on?"

She hesitated.

"What's the hold up? Are you afraid that I'll bite?"

He had before. Sensual bites in an experience that she couldn't forget. "It's a bad idea for you to get involved."

A muscle flexed along his jaw. Then he closed in on her. "Why?" Jinx bit off. "Why can't you trust me to help you when you are obviously scared to death? You'll go to some criminal in a rundown bar before you turn to me?"

It...wasn't like that.

The lobby door opened.

"So we fucked," Jinx announced loudly.

Oh, hell. War had just walked in. Juggling coffees and a box of doughnuts. At Jinx's pronouncement, he jerked to a halt.

"We fucked and we both came so hard that we wrecked the bed," Jinx continued roughly.

War snapped his mouth closed. Ali squirmed.

"Then you ran away," Jinx accused.

Her spine snapped straight. "I didn't run away. I had a case—"

"Now you've got something happening that scares the hell out of you. You need help. You need *me*. And baby, that's exactly what you're going to get even if you can't stand me any longer—"

Can't stand him? Why would he think that? She dreamed about the guy nearly every night!

"You made it loud and clear you want no part of me, but you don't have an option. You're in danger. So much danger that you come slinking in here—"

"I did *not* slink!" She'd never done that a day in her life.

"You want to send me far away, but that shit is not happening. You want a PI? Then you have—"

"You're in danger!" Ali exploded, driven to the absolute edge. Jinx always did this to her. Ripped away her careful control. Pushed her too far and too fast. "I'm trying to protect you, you jackass! The same way I've been protecting you for months!"

He blinked at her. "Say that again?"

Oh, no. She almost slapped her hand over her mouth. But it was too late. The words were out. Her secret was out. Ali could tell by the gleam in Jinx's bright blue eyes that there would be no going back.

Ali cleared her throat. "I, um..." Her gaze darted to a watchful War. "I'd like some coffee, please." She snatched a cup from him. Mostly to give herself something to do and some time to think.

"Ali." War offered her a faint smile. "How about you go in the office and wait for us a moment? I need to update Jinx on a client situation."

Sure, yes, anything to get away from Jinx for a moment. She nearly flew back into the office—the one she'd fled from moments before—and Ali kept her death grip on the coffee.

***

The door slammed behind Ali. Jinx stared straight ahead even as her angry words rang through his head. *"You're in danger! I'm trying to protect you, you jackass! The same way I've been protecting you for months!"*

"I hired you because I thought you were a people person."

War's smooth voice pulled Jinx back to reality.

War tilted his head to the left. "You are generally a pretty charming guy. Much more so than Odin."

"That's because Odin can't work charm for shit." Everyone knew that.

"Um." Neither agreement nor denial. "I had to give Odin a list of rules for handling clients. Things to say. Things not to say. Because, as you noted, sometimes charm can be an issue for him."

Jinx turned and took a step toward the closed office door.

"But, obviously, I should have covered some ground rules with you, too. Like, rule one, if you've had a previous sexual relationship with a client, don't shout it to the heavens."

Jinx's head jerked toward him. "I wasn't shouting." He didn't *think* he had been.

War quirked an eyebrow. "No?"

"I was stating a fact." He and Ali had fucked and come so hard they'd wrecked the bed. True story. One he'd like to experience over and over again. And in his dreams, he did.

"Yeah, so...on to rule two—"

"Never been big on rules." Jinx marched away and threw open the door. "What the hell is going on?" He crossed toward Ali—she was sitting on the couch in the office—and stood glowering down at her. "Spill it. Every detail."

"Rule two," War sighed as he trailed him inside. "Don't try to intimidate the clients. Be nice."

Jinx pasted a big smile on his face. "Ali..." He drew her name out like the caress it was. "What the hell is going on?"

"Jeez. Just because you smile, it doesn't make the shit you say nice." War sounded disgusted. "Why don't you go chug some coffee? Maybe it will help calm your ass down."

Coffee never calmed him down. It just primed him up. Didn't it do that for everyone? And, come to think of it, Jinx doubted there was anything that could calm him down in this particular situation. Ali was in danger. Some jerk had defaced her car. Jinx had been staring out the window and he'd had a clear view of the handiwork on the car door.

No one calls Ali a slut. No one.

"Jinx, I didn't want you involved," Ali said.

"Obviously. Since you have gone to every single other person in the world for help but me." A point that grated.

"I haven't gone to every person," she muttered. "Just a few others. Except when I go to them, I keep running into you first."

Hell, yes, she did. He folded his arms over his chest. "As I told you before, I'm the only PI available here so—"

"Uh, Jinx—" War began. "You know that's not entirely—"

He fired a hard glare over his shoulder. "I am the only PI currently available here," he repeated. "You have that big case you're working on, and Odin's time is full." He held War's stare. "So it's *lucky* that I'm available." He focused back on Ali. "But I need to know what I'm dealing with here. I can't help, I can't give the prick a world of pain that he will never, ever forget, not unless you give me more details." So, again, he returned to...*spill it, sweets.*

She sipped on the coffee. Darted a glance toward War. "No one else is available?"

"Well—" War hesitated.

"I am highly qualified," Jinx assured her. "You should know that. You've seen me in action. You know I can kick ass all day long without breaking a sweat." Now he shook his head. "And that's why I'm confused. Why the hell would you think you were protecting *me*? I am more than capable of protecting myself." It was just insulting.

"I'm protecting you because we slept together." The words were soft. Her lashes had lowered to conceal her warm chocolate gaze from him. Her hold tightened on the coffee cup. "Did you see what I did there?" she asked, her voice still low. "How I quietly said that because it's personal and private? How I didn't yell it?"

"Didn't know War was going to walk in when I made my little announcement." And why did everyone keep saying he'd yelled? He had a strong voice. He just naturally projected. "Besides, not like I mind other people knowing about what we— oh, hell. Right." Now he did recall that point she'd made before...the point where she hadn't wanted others on their team to know that they'd been together. That had been a rule, hadn't it? Maybe rule two? Why were so many damn people big on rules? Ali and War...plus Odin. The guy freaking *loved* rules.

But as for Jinx, he'd always enjoyed breaking rules. Or, at the very least, bending them as much as he could.

Since he, War, and Odin weren't active duty any longer, he hadn't thought keeping the relationship secret still mattered. War was out of the SEALs, Odin was no longer Delta, and as for Jinx and Ali...he'd stopped doing his special services for Uncle Sam, and word on the street had been that Ali turned in her notice, too.

Her lashes lifted. "It was supposed to stay just between us."

War strode closer. "Don't worry. I'm not going to broadcast it to anyone."

Broadcasting was more of War's wife's thing—Rose was a local reporter who'd worked with War to crack a case involving a serial killer. Unfortunately, Jinx had arrived in town after their wedding. A real crying shame in his book, especially since Odin had told him there had been a phenomenal open bar at the reception.

"Unlike some people I could name," War shot a pointed glance at Jinx, "I do know how to keep my mouth shut."

What the hell? Seriously? Not like Jinx had told anyone about him and Ali before this particular morning. And he hadn't known War was going to walk inside right at that exact moment. Was he supposed to be psychic? "Let's stay on topic, shall we?" And the topic that interested him... "Your case." He nodded toward Ali. "Consider this your lucky day, because, as of this moment, I am officially in your employ."

"But...how much am I supposed to pay you? I—"

"You already have been doing favors for the office," War said. "We owe you. No payment, so don't even try to play it that way."

Ali exhaled. "Thank you."

War waved away her thanks. "You've answered phone calls from us in the middle of the night and immediately got to work helping our clients. I'm the one who should be thanking you."

Because Jinx was watching Ali so closely, he saw the slight sag of her shoulders. It was as if she'd been carrying a big burden, and she'd finally let some of it go. *About time, baby. You should have come to me immediately.*

"Who keyed your car?" Jinx wanted to know. That would be a starting point. He'd work back and get every detail after that.

"I-I don't know. Not exactly." She was still holding her coffee. Cradling the cup like it was the most precious thing in the world. "I was at a diner last night, after I—after you and I parted ways."

"After you ran from me, check."

He felt War's stare, but didn't look his way. Jinx wasn't going to take his eyes off Ali. Mostly because her dark gaze was on his, and he couldn't look away.

"I stayed at the diner a bit. Had a milkshake..."

He nodded. "Because chocolate soothes your soul, I know. Carry on."

A furrow appeared between her eyebrows.

"Keep going," he urged.

"When I finished up, I went outside, and this creep in a souped-up truck nearly blinded me with his brights." Ali shook her head. "I was muttering about him and not paying enough attention to my surroundings—an amateur mistake, one I am well aware I committed. Then I got to my car and found the message that had been left for me. When I looked around, the lot was empty."

Jinx stiffened. "How long after you left Ramsey's did you see that truck?"

"About an hour."

"And this truck...was it dark, maybe gray or black, with no license plate, and a big-ass grille on the front?"

"I—" Her eyes narrowed. "Definitely a grille. And I think it was black. I didn't get a chance to look for plates." A pause. "How do you know all this?"

Jinx shrugged. "The usual way."

She stared at him, expectant.

Another roll of his shoulders. "The prick tried to run me down right before he paid you a visit at the diner."

She leapt to her feet. *"What?"*

"He came up behind me after I left Ramsey's. Tapped my bike. Thought he'd make me crash." He could see the fear and fury in her eyes. "No worries, I'm a whole lot tougher than most folks expect. In fact, I was about to show him the error of his ways, but then more cars arrived, including a patrol vehicle. When he saw the lights from the other vehicles, he flew out of there." And, the SOB had gone after her. But that raised an interesting—and worrisome—point. "How the hell did he know where you'd gone?" Because the perp had hung back and followed Jinx. No way he could have kept a visual on Ali at the same time.

War cursed. "He tagged her. We need to search her ride."

Ali's plump lips parted. "You think he's got a tracker on my rental?"

"It's what I'd do if I wanted to keep tabs on a target." Actually, it was precisely what Jinx *had* done on serval occasions. He'd be sure to personally check Ali's car because he knew the best places to hide a device like that one. He'd also be sure and get her door repaired. Screw it—he'd get her a whole new ride. He knew it was a rental, anyway. They'd repair it and send the vehicle back. Get her something new in its place. *Or maybe I'll just be her chauffeur for a while.*

Ali's left hand brushed against his arm. "He tried to run you down last night?"

He looked at her hand. The delicate fingers. The smooth skin. His gaze rose to her face.

"This is why I wanted to stay away," she said. "Because of our past, I knew you'd be a target."

He suddenly had an idea where this was going, and Jinx damn well didn't like it. But for the guy to write *Slut* on her ride, for him to target Jinx... "Stalker? Is that what we're dealing with here? Someone who couldn't let go after the relationship ended?" Someone who'd taken his obsession with Ali too far.

But she shook her head. "There was no relationship. I'm very, very careful about my involvements. I choose *safe* men. Good men."

A rough bark of laughter came from War. "Yeah, unless you run background checks on them, you can't be sure about just how safe they truly are..."

She kept staring straight at Jinx.

And he knew she'd done just that. Used her sneaky skills to peek into the backgrounds of the men she'd dated. "Fuck." He felt his eyes widen. "Did you do the same on me?" There were many, many layers to the mystery that was Alison Carter. She'd always been guarded like a crown jewel on missions. Her tech skills were top-notch, way better than his, and he was damn good. She could also slip in and out of any building like a ghost. She was a dead-eye shooter with her gun, and he'd never seen her back down from a confrontation.

For this guy to have rattled her...*what am I missing?*

"Yes, I ran the same check on you." Now her gaze darted to War. "And you."

Wait. Sonofabitch, was she saying that she and War—

Even as a growl built in Jinx's throat, her hold on him tightened. "It was basic research because I needed to trust the people on my team. When I'm in the field, I have to have total faith in the individuals around me." She let him go. He realized she'd put down her coffee cup. Their bodies were close, almost touching. "This guy—he started contacting me on my last mission. The mission that...took me away from you."

The faintest of stumbles there. Probably because she hadn't wanted to say...*the mission that had me slipping out of your bed.* Though it technically hadn't been his bed. Just a cheap bed in a shady motel that had never been good enough for Ali. She needed wining and dining, not a savage fuck in a rundown hole in the wall. But, unfortunately, that was what he'd given her.

"I was supposed to be working undercover. Get in, get access to the intel, get out. It didn't happen that way, though. The mission was a complete failure." A small hesitation. "Because of him."

Now they were getting somewhere.

Ali slipped away from Jinx. Headed to the window. Stared out at the street below. "I knew the target." Her voice was careful, her body tense. "That's why I was picked for the mission because our paths had crossed before. Because it should have been easy for me to get close—I already had his confidence. When I arrived in the area, I made contact. Resumed our acquaintance. Everything was going according to plan, then I received the first phone call." Her spine was perfectly straight. "The caller told me that the waiting game was over. He'd been patient, he'd learned my moves, and that he was ready to win." She shook her head and darted a confused look back at both War and Jinx. "I had no idea what he was talking about. I alerted my handler, but he assured me the mission wasn't compromised. We were good to go." Ali raked a hand through her hair. "I was supposed to go to dinner with my target. We did. Dinner. Drinks. Everything was normal. The next night, he had a party at his business. I was invited, just as the plan had stipulated. I got access to his security system. I got what I needed. I walked away, and...the next morning, I learned that my target had been shot to death in his Paris apartment."

Damn.

"I learned about his murder when I got another phone call. Same mystery guy. His voice was raspy, disguised, and he told me that he wasn't going to share me with the world. Told me that what had happened to Jacques had been unfortunate, but necessary."

Fucking hell.

"It was a professional hit. He'd disabled all the cameras in the area, all of the security footage went down before he killed Jacques. The calls I received couldn't be traced. *He* couldn't be traced, and trust me, I tried. I used all of the resources at my disposal to find him. I couldn't. *I couldn't,*" she repeated, and there was anger and confusion in her voice. "I can usually find anyone. Anything. But this creep? He does know my moves. He knew everything I was doing to track him. He kept reaching out to me, no matter where I went or what I did...he was there. He'd call or leave some kind of taunt for me. Something to let me know he was watching."

"Like what he did to your car," War muttered.

"Yes, like the car. But I already knew he was here, or at least, I feared he was." Her fingers wiggled in the air. "It's like a tingle on the back of your neck. An awareness that just comes when you know you're being hunted. He's hunting me. I knew it. I hoped I was wrong. I *wanted* to be wrong, but..." She stopped. Seemed to refocus. "I knew he was watching me when I came back to the country after Jacques's death. When I..." Now her stare flickered toward Jinx. "When I came back to see you."

She'd been *hunted* back then and hadn't told him?

"It was right after Paris," she whispered. "Just days later. I didn't realize he was going to be able to track me so well. I thought I could escape. I was using an alias in France, and I'd always been so careful to cover my identity. I had told you I'd come back, so I-I did..." Her words trailed away.

He finished, "And you saw me with the freaking singer. Like I said, that was *nothing—*"

"He saw me...going to you. I had barely stepped foot out of the club before my phone was ringing." Her voice thickened. "When I answered, he asked me...how many men would have to die before I understood how serious he was?"

That was why she'd stayed away?

"And now you say that he came after you last night." Guilt was clear to see as she added, "You have a target on you because of me, and I am sorry, Jinx."

Oh, hell, no. "War, I need the room a minute."

"Uh...you sure about that?"

He dead-eye stared his friend. "War, I need the room a minute," Jinx repeated flatly. His words were code for...*Get the fuck out because I need to make sure Ali understands some shit about me.*

War nodded. "Right. So...I'll just get started checking her ride. Take the room. Have a minute. Have ten." He sauntered toward the door. "Not like it's *my* office or anything. Not like I'm the one who came up with Trouble for Hire. No, no, go ahead. Act like it's your place."

Jinx followed him to the door. "Thanks, I will." Once War had cleared the threshold, Jinx slammed the door shut and locked it before whirling to confront Ali. He stared at her, taking her in, every beautiful, glorious inch of her. And he could only shake his head. "Have you *met* me before?" He took a surging step toward her.

"Ah, yes...?"

"You've seen me in action? Seen me in fantastic battle mode as I cut through my enemies with no hesitation?" Another step.

"I've seen you fight and shoot, yes."

"And I'm spectacular. The best you've ever had, am I right?" Another step. Two more.

Her brows rose. "Are you talking about your fighting skills or something else?"

"Both." Another step.

"I—"

"I can kick ass and fuck all night long." The words were mocking but he felt *anything* but teasing. His back teeth had clenched, and he gritted out, "So why the hell would you face this jackass alone? Why in the fucking world would you ever think that I needed to be protected?" Why would she have wasted even a moment being afraid when she could have come to him at any time, and he would have dropped everything for her? Didn't she get that? Didn't she know that he would be there for her in an instant, that he would—

A faint tremble of her lower lip. Then she bit that delectable lip. Took a moment and quietly admitted, "I didn't come to you because the man who is doing this to me? He's someone on the inside. Someone who works for the same group that we did."

His gaze sharpened on her.

"I was able to find out that much, at least. He's *part* of the black ops group that used us before. He has access to all of our private information. He *knows* us, inside and out, and because of that, he knows our weaknesses. Our friends. Our families. He knows how to wreck us. I wanted to protect you from that. I *tried.* I was going off book last night, going to *criminals* for help because I thought they were people he wouldn't be able to control."

"You think he can control me?" No one could.

"I think that I didn't want to imagine what he could do to you. I have a stalker, all right. Someone with access to every single bit of intel Uncle Sam has on me. On you. Someone who knows how we operate. How to anticipate our moves and wreck us." She shook her head. "I was trying to protect you. I wanted to protect all of my friends. Coming in today at Trouble for Hire was my last option. I want to turn the tables on this bastard. I want to stop letting him hunt me, and I want to hunt *him*. I realized last night, I can't do it alone. He just won't stop. He'll keep coming and coming, no matter where I go. To end this, I need backup."

"Done." Easy. Should have happened months ago, but at least it was happening now.

"What?"

He tucked a lock of hair behind her ear. His hand lingered against her cheek. "Sweets, you're staring straight at your backup." He winked at her. "Your backup, your white knight, your loaded gun, the attack dog you let rip and destroy..." A roll of his shoulders. "Whatever the hell you want me to be, just consider it...done."

CHAPTER FOUR

"Just like that?"

His hand was still against her cheek. Slightly rough, callused fingertips that she was far too aware of as they pressed to her skin. Ali swallowed.

"Just like that," Jinx told her.

He was so close that if she just leaned up onto her toes, she'd be kissing him. Not that she intended to do that. Bad plan. But… "You realize there's lots of danger here? We're obviously dealing with someone who has one hell of a lot of power and who is also super unstable."

Not a flicker of concern showed on Jinx's handsome face. "Yes, but I already have a killer plan."

Was he serious? For the life of her, she could not tell. Typical Jinx. "Do not jerk me around on this," she whispered. "You don't know what it's been like for me. He is always there. Always ahead of me. Why do you think I was so eager to run down here? I wanted breathing space. Room to think and plan."

"Told you, I already have a plan, and it's genius." His gaze slid to her mouth. "But it will have to look convincing, so do keep that in mind. Practice will make perfect."

"What are you talking about?" And *why* was she starting to push up onto her tiptoes as if she wanted to kiss him?

A hard rap shook the door. "Are you done with *my* office?" War demanded, obviously disgruntled.

"Not quite finished working out the details," Jinx called back cheerfully. "Why don't you go make another donut run?"

"Screw you, man!"

Jinx's mouth hitched into a half-smile.

"Can nothing rattle you?" Ali had to shake her head. "I mean, this jerk came for you last night. I just told you that he killed my last target. You're in his sights now, and you act like this is all a joke."

He blinked. "It's no joke."

Okay...

"Nothing about your safety is ever funny to me. Don't forget that."

"Nothing about your safety is every funny to me, either," she muttered. He'd better not forget *that*.

"You should have come to me sooner," he said. Now he sounded almost as disgruntled as War. "But you're here now, and my plan will work. You don't want to be hunted, and I don't plan for you to be prey."

She didn't plan for that either so...

"He seems to have a whole sexual issue going on with you. One of those asshole types who thinks he can control a woman completely. Weak-ass bastard."

Her brows climbed.

"If I can't have you, no one will...that kind of bullshit. Time he learned his lesson. *Past* time."

Her heart thudded hard in her chest even as War pounded on the door again. "I'm coming in *my* office!" he declared.

"Good for you," Jinx tossed back. He didn't move away from Ali. "You stayed away from men because of his threats, didn't you? Because you were afraid if you took a new lover, if you showed interest in anyone, he'd hurt them."

"He said he would. And he killed Jacques. *Not* that I was involved with him. I wasn't. I wasn't involved with anyone but—" She stopped. *You.* Though they'd hardly been involved.

One night.

No, one hour. One super-hot, singed-into-her-memory hour of her life.

Jinx waited as if expecting her to say more. When she just kept her lips clamped together, he sighed and said, "Me. You slept with me, and I was the first guy you'd let close in a long time."

Her chin jerked, but she didn't respond.

"That's cool. Better than cool. Fucking perfect, actually. And you're not asking, but I'm telling you..."

The office door swung open. War must've had the key to the lock on him.

"I'm telling you," Jinx continued as his voice roughened, "that I haven't fucked anyone since you."

"*Seriously!*" War's voice rang out. "What is it with you and your sex life, Jinx? Can you please stop oversharing with me?"

"So...since there hasn't been anyone else for me..." Jinx acted as if War hadn't just had that mini explosion. "Then it will make sense to the freak after you that I haven't looked at anyone else because I'm completely hooked on you. After all, he's a man who understands obsession."

"I do not like where this is going," she warned him.

"Don't worry. You'll love it before I'm done."

Doubtful. "No. I don't think I will." Because the hard twist in her gut told Ali what Jinx was going to say even as his lips parted...

"He doesn't want you with a lover. Too bad. When he sees you with me, when he thinks that we've hooked up again, it will drive the bastard crazy. He'll make a move, he'll come from the shadows, and we'll end him. Simple. Perfect. Beautiful."

Beautiful?

"Like I said," Jinx added proudly, "genius."

No, not genius. "He will come for *you*."

"Right. You've got it. Knew you'd be on board."

"It's barely eight thirty," War muttered. "And the man is making me want to drink. Why, *why* did I think bringing you into the agency was a good idea?"

"Because I'm a superstar."

"I don't think that was why," War mumbled.

Seeming to ignore that comment, Jinx asked, "Did you find the tracker?"

"Yeah, it was on the inside portion of her hubcap, on the left rear tire. There could be others, so I want to do a more thorough check."

"Not necessary. She'll be ditching that car. I'll be getting it repaired before we send it back to the rental company. Then she'll be driving around with *me*."

He was trying to steam roll over her. "Jinx, I haven't agreed to this insane plan!"

"How many times do I have to say that it's a genius—"

"You getting hurt or killed isn't genius!" It was dangerous. Deadly.

He laughed. *Laughed.* "Baby, I dodge bullets for fun. I want him to come at me."

She didn't want that. She'd been trying to avoid that whole situation—thus her avoiding Jinx. "This isn't some wannabe thug. I told you, I think he's high up in ranks. We could be looking at someone who is former military, who went special ops, just like you did. Someone who went off book and who plays rough and dirty."

"Rough and dirty. The only way I know how to play, too."

Helpless, she peered at War. Surely, he'd be the voice of sanity. "I came here for the team. Because I thought we could combine forces and track this man. I didn't come here so that Jinx could put a giant target on himself as he parades around town and yells, 'Come and get me!'" She sucked in a breath. "You're the boss here, War. Would you tell your PI that it's a horrible idea?"

War's shoulders rolled back. "Actually, I think Jinx is on to something."

Sweet heaven above. She closed her eyes. "I forgot that the two of you often feed off each other's crazy." Where was Odin when she needed him? He was usually the calm and rational one.

"It's not crazy if it will work," War mused.

Her eyes cracked open. "You want us to pretend to be involved?"

"From the sound of things, your stalker already thinks you *are* involved with him. Probably believes you came down here so you could be with Jinx." War rubbed his chin. "Have the two of you been together publicly since you arrived in the area?"

"Jinx found me at the beach yesterday," she admitted. "Then somehow, we wound up at the same bar last night."

"Because you were looking to hire some seriously shady criminals. Bad move, when you should have just come to *me*," Jinx chimed in to declare.

Why was he missing this point? "Sometimes, you need shady people to handle the monster in the dark." Something he shouldn't have to be told. But when she cut him a fuming glance...

His eyes were on her. All bright and focused hard. "I am the monster in the dark." No smile. No humor in his voice. "Something you should have learned by now, it's always easy for a monster to hide behind a smile."

Okay, that was creepy. And intense. And so not her Jinx.

Wait. He is not mine. Never has been. Never will be.

"What were you going to do with Ramsey?" Jinx's voice had lowered to little more than a sensual whisper. She didn't think War could hear his words. "Get him to kill for you?"

She sucked in a sharp breath.

"Ramsey won't kill for you," Jinx continued in that same barely-there whisper, one that had goosebumps sliding over her body. "But I will. In a minute, I'd do that for you."

Ali felt as if she were staring into the eyes of a stranger. His blue gaze had never looked colder. "Jinx?"

He blinked. And his eyes were gleaming again. Filled with the mocking humor that she realized he wore like armor. "It's settled. We'll pretend to be the best fuck buddies in the world, we'll drive your asshole stalker crazy, and the case will be closed in record time." He backed away from her. "And we'll have yet another satisfied client at Trouble for Hire." His gaze flickered toward War. "My first big case for you," he said with a dramatic sigh. "I swear, I will do you proud."

War shook his head. Then lasered his attention on Ali. "What do *you* want to do?"

She wanted to go back to having a normal life. Wasn't that why she'd told her handler she was out even before that last mission had begun? Unlike War and Jinx, she wasn't former military. Jinx had been right when he said she'd always had a wall around her on their missions. Her job hadn't been the fighting and the explosions and everything else that could still give her nightmares. She'd been about retrieval. Infiltration.

And the way she'd gotten that job? A long and twisted road. A road that had begun when she'd broken the law and been given two options.

Option one...jail.

Option two...work for the government.

Either way, she'd been told that she had to do her time in order to make the crime go away. *I didn't have my own life for too long. I want it now. I want to be like everyone else.*

"He's already coming after me." Jinx grabbed for one of the donuts. Started munching as if he didn't have a care in the world. "And this morning, seeing as how he was tracking your ride, I'm sure he knows you came here. To me."

But she hadn't been going to *him*. She'd been going to Trouble for Hire. She'd been hoping War and Odin would keep this whole matter off Jinx's radar.

And that didn't happen.

Jinx watched her carefully. "You can walk away and try to keep handling things solo, but the guy has me in his sights, and based on what you've said, I doubt he's just going to let me tra-la-la on my merry way. He'll come for me again, whether you're involved in the plan I have or not."

Her twisting gut told her that he was right.

"If we work together, at least you can watch my sexy ass." Jinx finished the donut. Licked a little glaze off his finger.

And she had a quick flash of what he could do with that talented tongue of his.

Not now.

But her cheeks were flushing. Jinx, of course, noticed. "You'll move into my place. No sense staying at a condo that probably has BS security. I'll keep you close. We'll put on a show the stalker will never forget, and when he comes in from the dark, we'll have him."

The plan sounded simple enough, but she knew it *wasn't* simple. There were about a million things that could go wrong.

"Do you have another option?" Jinx wanted to know.

If she'd had another option, she wouldn't be standing there.

Jinx's expression said he knew as much.

So...

"Looks like we're going to be lovers again," he told her. He seemed absolutely gleeful.

***

Jinx ducked out of the office because he had to make a fast phone call. War was going over some details with Ali, and Jinx wanted to get his ass back in there ASAP, but first...

"What the hell is it now?" Ramsey demanded when he answered the call.

"The attack last night wasn't about you. I don't think our connection is known."

"What?"

"He was coming for me, and he's been trying to hurt something that's mine." Jinx wasn't going to say more. Ramsey didn't need to know more about Ali. "I'll be taking care of him. Consider the problem eliminated."

"Jinx—"

He hung up. Mostly because he'd just caught sight of War. The guy had shoved his head out of the office door.

Most days, he liked War. Got along great with him. Considered him family. But War didn't know all of Jinx's secrets, and the man could be like a dog with a bone...

"Everything good?" War asked as he slipped fully out of the office and pulled the door shut behind him.

Jinx considered how to play the scene. Decided to go with straight honesty. "No." He shoved the phone into his back pocket. "Ali's been on her own handling this for too long. She should have come to me sooner." *I will be pissed about this for a while.*

War tilted his head. "She should have come to you...because you had a one-night stand with her?"

Jinx smiled at his friend. Strolled toward him. Slapped a hand on War's shoulder. "Who said I had a one-night stand?"

"Uh, you did. Loudly. Not even thirty minutes ago—"

"I had a beginning with her. That's what I had. Now I get to have the rest."

War's eyes widened. Then narrowed. "It's a show, isn't it? An act..."

"Sure, the whole world's a friggin' stage. I'm sure someone famous said that once."

"It was Shakespeare."

"See? Someone famous." He let go of War. "Now, if you don't mind, I need to get back to my girlfriend."

"Your *pretend* girlfriend."

He sidled around War.

"Is there something else I need to know about?" War asked.

His question stopped Jinx just as he was reaching for the doorknob.

"Because I swear, lately with you, I feel like I'm missing pieces of a puzzle. You've always been secretive, but this is a whole other level."

Jinx didn't open the door. Not yet. "You are one of the closest friends that I have in this world. You and Odin got me through some dark times, and I would kill for you two any day of the week." He looked back. "I'd also kill for the woman in that room. You, Odin, and Ali have my loyalty, and I hope you all know it. Any secrets that I carry would never hurt you. I wouldn't let them hurt the three of you."

War nodded. "I believe you, but you don't have to carry things alone. That's what we're here for, remember?"

"Tell that shit to Ali. She's the one that's been stalked while we didn't know a damn thing about it." A situation that had now changed. He yanked open the door.

***

"It's pretend, you get that, don't you?" Ali asked softly as they parked beside Armageddon later that night.

Why did people keep telling him stuff was for pretend? Jinx just shook his head.

As typical for a Friday night, War's bar was packed. There was a line of people waiting to get in—War did have the best whiskey in town, after all—but Jinx knew he wouldn't be standing in that line. There were perks that came from being buddies with the owner of the place. Immediate entrance? Perk number one.

She climbed off the motorcycle. Clung to Jinx's shoulders for just a moment before she stepped back. During the ride over, she'd been plastered ever-so-wonderfully against him. Her arms had wrapped around his waist, and she'd held him as if she'd never let go.

For the cover, of course. Just like everything else that was about to happen would be for the cover, too.

"I'm not looking to...ah...pick up where we left off." She handed him her helmet. He secured it. Then took his time getting off the bike. He'd already removed his own helmet.

"Why not?" he asked, truly curious. "I'm pretty sure you told me the sex was phenomenal."

"I—" Her nose scrunched in thought. "Did I say that?"

He was sure she'd meant to say that. "Phenomenal...incredible...same thing, am I right?"

She swallowed. "It *was* incredible."

"On that we agree." It was one of the reasons he hadn't hooked up with anyone else since having her. When you had something that good, why settle for anything less?

He wasn't the type to settle. He reached for her hand. Curled his fingers around hers. For the cover and what not.

She searched his eyes. "I can't tell if you're teasing me."

Now that was interesting. "Are you sure?"

"Jinx, I've known you for a long time. You practically have a revolving door with women."

He put his free hand over his heart. "Hurtful. Maybe I was just looking for the right woman. You ever consider that?"

She glanced away from him and peered at the long line.

He lifted their joined hands. Brought *her* hand to his lips. Pressed a kiss to her knuckles.

Her breath hissed out and her attention swung right back to him. He felt her tighten up and knew she was going to try and pull away.

"The cover, remember?" he chided before pressing another kiss to her hand. "You have to get used to me touching you. Kissing you. Otherwise, you might tip off our creepy stalker."

She licked her lower lip. "Just—just so we agree it's only pretend."

Ah, back to that, were they? He sidled closer. "What's so wrong with making it real? We both agreed the sex was incredible."

"Jinx..."

He let her hand go. "We don't know what eyes are already on us. You might want to look a wee bit more like you just can't live without me, know what I mean? Go for a whole soulful, he's-mine-and-I'd-die-for-him vibe, if you could." He straightened his t-shirt. Not that it needed straightening. He was wearing an old-as-hell shirt, battered and torn jeans, and what he thought were truly styling kicks. He'd always been a sucker for a stupid expensive pair of shoes.

His gaze swept over her. "You look hot as hell, by the way."

"Because you insisted I dress like a stripper."

"Strippers wear a whole lot less clothes. I don't know which strip clubs you've been to, my love, but if they dress like you, they are not going to be getting enough tips."

She was wearing skin-tight jeans. Jeans that hugged her ass in a truly world class way. A top that dipped low and revealed the upper swell of what he knew were perfect breasts.

She'd insisted on wearing canvas shoes, saying there was no way she'd ride his motorcycle in high heels. A pity, because he'd picked out truly sexy, fuck-me heels for her.

His eyes returned to her face. She'd gone with smoky eye shadow. Slick red lipstick. And her hair had been curled to tumble around her face in a carefully tousled look.

Hot. "You know, I take it back. If you were at a strip club, I bet you'd score a ton of cash. I'd personally make it rain hundreds on you."

"Jinx!"

He caught her arm and led her across the street. Right past the line. And right past the new security guy that War had hired to keep said line in check. The fellow recognized Jinx—as he should—and waved him inside.

I do love perks.

"What exactly was the point in us stopping here? Do you need to check in with War?" Ali asked as her gaze swept around the bar.

"The point is that I have a schedule of events for the night. Don't worry, you'll love everything." He began leading her through the crowd and toward the bar. "You did before," he added.

"What? What did you say?" Ali asked.

They were at the bar. He tapped the gleaming wood. "Two glasses of the most expensive whiskey that War has in stock." He inclined his head to the bartender. "And, Imari, be sure you put that on War's tab, will you?"

Perk two. War didn't know about that perk, not yet, but he'd figure it out soon enough.

Jinx turned back to Ali, wrapped his hands around her waist and easily lifted her onto the stool. He let his hands linger on her. "You look fucking beautiful."

Her eyes widened. Then she gave a quick nod, as if to say...

The cover.

Whatever she needed to tell herself.

He leaned toward her. He wanted her mouth. It had been entirely too long since he'd tasted Ali.

"Here you go. Twenty-three-year-old Pappy's. I do hope you enjoy it," Imari told him.

His head turned toward her. Her dark gaze wasn't on him. It was on Ali, and for a moment, her stare appeared assessing.

Imari's dark hair had been cut to frame her heart-shaped face. She was dressed all in black, like most of the staff at Armageddon. She moved with an easy grace as she slid away to take care of other customers, but her gaze returned to Ali a few times.

A few times too many. He was pretty sure he'd just seen recognition in her eyes. *How the hell would she know Ali?*

He reached for the whiskey. Gave one glass to Ali.

"So..." Ali smiled at him. A smile that seemed to say he was the only person in the room. She lifted her glass to toast him, and as Jinx moved in ever closer, she asked him, "Why does War's bartender have cop eyes?"

Because that was exactly what Imari had. Eyes that picked up every detail. Eyes that were way, way too sharp.

He tapped his glass to Ali's. "Because I think she may be an undercover cop."

"Does War know that?"

He didn't think so and that situation certainly made things interesting. Imari had been hired two weeks ago. War had told him that she came with great references.

Let's revisit those references, shall we?

"Bottoms up, baby," Jinx told Ali.

They drained their glasses.

The burn on the way down was oh, so good.

"Imari," he called. "We'll have two more..."

"You realize, of course, that those are one hundred and ninety dollars each," she told him as she pressed her hands flat on the bar.

"Um, I'm sure War knows." He turned his head toward her. Assessed. *Yep. She was screaming cop.* It was something in the shoulders, in the posture, a readiness that told him she was on edge. "He'll appreciate us taste-testing for him. War likes it when we check things out for him. Sometimes, he can miss a mark or two. It's good that he has friends who can watch his back. Look out for trouble, you know?"

Imari swallowed. Grabbed the empty glasses. "I'll be right back."

While she was gone, he turned back to Ali. She was still on the stool. He just happened to be standing between her legs.

"What now?" Ali whispered.

The next part of the plan. "This," he told her. Then he leaned forward and took her mouth.

CHAPTER FIVE

She could taste the whiskey. Could taste the rich, decadent flavor that was pure Jinx. His mouth was open, his tongue was thrusting against hers, and for a moment, Ali froze.

Then...

She grabbed him. Locked her hands around his powerful shoulders and held on tight. He was obviously trying to put on a show, and she'd go all in for that.

Just pretend. Just pretend. Except, it didn't feel pretend.

He had crowded in close between her spread legs. His hands were back around her hips. He was pulling her ever closer to him, and his mouth took hers as if he'd been starving for her.

Or, wait, maybe *she* was kissing him like someone starving and desperate. Because she *was* moving against him desperately. Arching. Trying to get closer. Opening her mouth wider. Sliding her tongue against his and that throaty, breathy moan? It had totally just come from her.

"Here you go." Glasses clinked on the bar top. "Enjoy."

The bartender was back. The too expensive whiskey was back. And Jinx was ever so slowly lifting his mouth from hers.

He didn't immediately move to take the shots. Instead, he stared down at Ali. She tried to calm her frantic heartbeat. A task that was not easy. Especially since she was still gripping his shoulders and wanting—with all her soul—to yank him back down toward her.

Pretend.

She forced her gaze off him. Her stare jumped to the right to find Imari's dark eyes on her.

The woman's face was carefully expressionless, but there was something there. Something...familiar. "I'm sorry," Ali said, not sorry at all, "but have we met?" The woman was undeniably beautiful, with a face that should have been unforgettable, but Ali couldn't quite place her.

I just know she's giving me serious cop vibes. It's in the watchful eyes. The way I saw her survey the whole crowd before she realized I was watching her. When the woman *had* realized that fact, her attention had sure sharpened on Ali.

"Don't think so." The bartender flashed her a wide smile. Diamonds slid up the lobe of her right ear. She offered her hand to Ali. "I'm Imari."

Ali finally let go of Jinx's shoulders—or, rather, let go of one of his shoulders—and she shook the offered hand. "Ali." Imari's handshake was firm.

Imari pulled back and raised a brow as she looked at Jinx. "So I'm guessing you're his girlfriend?"

Ali opened her mouth to agree, because that was the deal, after all—

"Hardly," Jinx said with a laugh.

What? Ali made sure her expression didn't alter. Was the man seriously changing the story on her *now?* Was he about to say she was just some flavor of the week and not his girl—

"Ali is the love of my life. My whole damn reason for being." He smiled at Ali. "She came back to me and made me the luckiest bastard in the world."

Ali felt her mouth part in surprise. He swooped in and kissed her again. A kiss that was hard and demanding and possessive. One that had her heart racing once more, her body tightening, and her nipples aching. No, had *her* aching because he was the only man who'd ever been able to kiss her and instantly make her want to rip off her clothes, his, and have sex right then and there.

"Well, okay, then. You two have fun tonight," Imari said. "Though obviously, you're off to a killer start."

Ali pushed back from Jinx in time to see Imari heading for other customers.

Jinx handed her another shot glass. "To the fun we'll have tonight." A devilish gleam was in his eyes.

She tapped his glass. "To the fun."

Ali tipped back her head and gulped down the liquid.

***

It was easy to disable the motorcycle. Fucking child's play. He just went up to the ride, crouched down next to it as if the bike was his, and he went to work. There was a long, winding crowd around Armageddon. But he didn't worry that anyone was looking his way. They were focused on the bar, focused on each other…

No one paid much attention to the guy wearing the helmet as he fiddled with his motorcycle.

A few twists, a few cuts with his knife, and he was sure that he'd done the job he needed to do. Not like this was his first time making a move like this one.

He was sure Jinx would get the point.

Death had a way of making a man understand.

CHAPTER SIX

His hands were on her hips. The music played in a slow and steady beat, and Jinx moved his body in time with Ali's. She was in his arms, her head pressed to his chest, and all he wanted to do was take her out of there. Take her home. Get her in his bed and—

Someone tapped him on the shoulder. "Problem."

It was a problem, all right. He'd just been interrupted mid-fantasy. Jinx turned his head and glared at War. "If this is about the whiskey, I totally mean to pay you back." Nah, he didn't.

War shook his head. "Upstairs. Now."

Uh, oh. Someone was using his I-mean-business tone. Never a good sign.

Without another word, Jinx and Ali followed War away from the crowd and up the private stairs that would take them to the building's second level. As soon as they were securely in the PI office, War locked the door behind them. "The fucker screwed with your bike."

"What?" Not his new ride. Hell, *no*. The scratch he'd gotten last night had been bad enough. "What did he do?"

"How do you know?" Ali demanded in the same instant.

"Because Odin was watching the security feed from the camera I have at the door. It caught the guy—he came up wearing a helmet, just crouched right down, and went to work. Smart SOB, I'll give him that. People who saw him in the helmet figured it was probably his bike. No one even looked twice at him."

Odin had. "What did the jerk do?" Jinx repeated.

"Screwed with your brakes. Odin said you probably would have gotten a few miles before they gave out completely."

Ali would have been on that bike with him. If he'd crashed, *she* would have crashed. "Sonofabitch." He lunged back for the door.

War stepped into his path. "Odin is searching for him. By the time Odin got to your ride, the perp was gone. Odin is scanning the area. We're looking for the joker. In the video, the bastard wore gloves, so he didn't leave prints behind—"

"He could have *killed* her." Low, lethal, and ice-cold.

War's stare was unwavering. "He could have killed you both. I think it's safe to say that you definitely have his attention."

Ali's hand touched Jinx's shoulder. He spun to face her. Horror was on her beautiful face. "The plan isn't working," Ali said. "I told you—"

"He's coming out of the dark, Ali. Making mistakes. We *will* get him."

But Ali asked, "Before or after he gets you?"

But it hadn't just been Jinx that the SOB had been trying to hurt. This time, Ali would have been in the crossfire, too. "Has he ever tried to hurt you before?"

Her brow furrowed.

"Has he ever come at you directly? Done anything that could have injured you in any way?" Jinx pushed.

"No."

"Has he ever *threatened* to hurt you? Told you to stay away from anyone or he would do—"

Her eyelids flickered.

Bingo. "Ali..."

"When I came back...the one time I went to that bar and saw you dancing with the redhead—"

"I don't even remember her," he growled automatically.

"Drama," War noted in a flat tone.

Jinx cut him an annoyed glance. Then he stared back at Ali. "You said he called you as you were leaving that place." And he'd made his BS taunt.

A nod from Ali. "Yes, and the next day, I got another call from him. He said it was better that I saw you for what you were because if I'd gone back to you, he would have made me sorry." She licked her lips. "I thought he meant that he would hurt you, but it's possible..." Her words trailed off.

He knew where her thoughts had gone. "It's possible he meant he would physically make you pay."

"I'm not anyone's punching bag. I don't belong to anyone but myself." Her shoulders straightened. "He's the one who is going to pay."

Her eyes were burning with a dark fire. "He could have hurt you, Jinx. If we'd hopped on that bike, took the twisting roads around here, then crashed, you could have been killed. We just got *lucky*."

"It wasn't luck," War clarified. "It was a big-ass Viking named Odin. We're a team. We're watching out for each other. That's how we're taking him down. He thinks he can isolate you. Make you weak."

He *had* isolated Ali, for far too long. "He might think he's upping the stakes, but all he is doing is digging his grave, one foot at a time." A grave that Jinx would be using to bury the bastard.

War tossed him a set of keys.

Surprise jolted through Jinx even as his fingers automatically fisted around the keys. "Are you actually going to let me drive the Impala?" That 67 classic was War's pride and joy.

War blinked. Squinted. "Hell, no, I'm not. You crazy? Those are keys to Odin's Jeep. You can drive that home, and we'll take care of switching you out with a new ride tomorrow." He huffed out a breath. "Am I letting you drive the Impala? Only when hell freezes over."

Right. That made more sense. No one touched War's ride.

War headed for the door. "You can sneak out the back—"

"No, thanks. I prefer to make a glorious exit via the front door."

War threw him a fast glance over his shoulder. "Are you kidding me right now?

Because I need you to be serious for like, five minutes."

"I am serious." Dead serious. "He was watching. He's probably still watching somewhere. I intend to make sure he has one hell of a show. The more we push him, the more of an advantage we have." Because if they could make the jerk lose control, he'd be weak.

War's gaze flickered to Ali. "You agree with this?"

"I don't like it." Her voice was crisp. "But I understand Jinx's reasoning."

A swift knock rattled the door. War jerked the door open to reveal a big, giant blond wall. Odin had joined the party.

One look at his face, and Jinx knew their bad guy had slipped away.

"No trace," Odin said. Just that, nothing more. That was typical Odin. A man of ever so few words. Even though his voice was flat, Jinx knew Odin was pissed. Odin fired a fast, worried glance at Ali.

Odin had always viewed Ali as a little sister, so that meant his protective instincts were definitely in overdrive when it came to her. Jinx had very much not viewed her as a sister, but his protective instincts were screaming at him, too. Demanding that he charge out, find the freak, and rip him apart.

And I will. It was all a matter of timing.

"I'll take care of the bike for you," War promised. "It will be fixed in no time."

Ali began to pace. "He sure does like playing with people's rides, doesn't he?"

Seemed that way.

"The plan still the same?" Odin asked as he crossed his arms over his massive chest. He didn't move out of the doorway.

Jinx watched Ali for a moment. Her steps were quick and obviously angry. It probably wasn't the time to tell her she was extra gorgeous when she was mad. "Still the same. We drive the guy to the edge and then push him over."

"Provided he doesn't push *you* over first," War noted.

Jinx rolled one shoulder. "That is the goal." And it was time to get moving. Odin might not have been able to find the guy on the streets, but Jinx knew he was going to be staying close.

All the more reason for my show.

He tossed the keys onto the desk. "Thanks for the offer of the Jeep, but I have a different idea for tonight. I'll take care of the ride." He pulled out his phone and fired off a quick text. He'd actually had this transport as a stand-by, anyway. Just in case.

"What's the idea?" War wanted to know. He slanted a suspicious glance Jinx's way.

"Why spoil the surprise?"

"You're kidding me."

He wasn't. And...Jinx snapped his fingers. "I almost forgot." No, he hadn't. He waved toward Ali. "Ali and I have a question for you, War." He braced his legs apart and kept his body deceptively loose and relaxed. "Why the hell do you have an undercover cop working at your bar?"

War's shoulders stiffened.

Jinx smiled at him. "I'm sure a guy like you wouldn't miss the tells that woman was sending out."

War shook his head.

"So, that means...you deliberately hired a cop."

"Imari's not a cop."

Odin was silent. Just watching.

Ali edged closer to Jinx's side. "If she's not a cop, then what is she?"

"She's an old college roommate of my wife's. Imari was looking for a fresh start, I gave her one."

Jinx brought his hand to his mouth and coughed. "*Bullshit.*"

Odin's head moved in the faintest of nods.

War's expression was hard. "That's the story she told me, and she *is* a friend of Rose's. Because of that, I couldn't throw her out on her ass. Someone wants to keep tabs on me. Don't know why, so I figured...hey, keep your friends close and keep the assholes who want to spy on you closer so you can spy on *them.*"

Jinx had figured it was something like that. "You're thinking it's the same off-the-book group we did some favors for?" The same group that had employed Ali.

"Either them or perhaps someone who is interested in the ties *you* have." War's gaze didn't waver.

Jinx didn't let his expression alter. He didn't even blink.

"You see, Imari came looking for the job right after I brought you on at Trouble. Interesting timing, am I right?"

He was certainly right. The timing was suspicious as hell. "It would have been helpful if you mentioned her to me sooner."

"It was on my to-do list."

"*What* are we talking about right now?" Ali demanded to know.

He'd probably have to get around to telling her. Sooner or later. Currently, Ali believed that she'd accessed his files and learned everything there was to know about him. Such a cute belief. One that was totally wrong. Most of his files were fake. Most of his life was fake.

But if Imari was there because of Jinx's ties, then someone knew the truth. Someone other than War and Odin. Because staring at his friends, it was obvious they knew about his skeletons.

When Ali wasn't watching and listening, he'd get around to figuring out how they'd discovered the truth—and just how long they'd known. But Ali had asked a question, and he had to give her some sort of response, so he disclosed, "I'm tight with some dangerous people."

She just stared at him.

"You know me, everyone wants to be my friend. Because of that, people in shady government agencies think they can use me and my connections for their own gains." He waited a beat. "They're wrong."

Her lashes lowered to conceal her gaze. Uh, oh. He'd said something that struck a chord with her. A bad chord. Now he needed to go back and figure out *what*. "Ali and I will be downstairs in a minute," he assured the others. "We'll make a grand and dramatic exit, and then I'll be taking her to our next stop. I'd say odds are good that we might pick up a tail along the way."

"I'll keep eyes on you," Odin assured him. "If you're followed, I'll be on your six to back you up."

He'd figured as much.

"I...thought you all had other cases." Ali's voice was halting. "Jinx did say he was the only PI available."

Yes. That had been a lie. A white lie. Tiny fib. "You know these two, they always hate to be left out. So we shifted things around a bit, and now they're doing secondary protection and investigation on this one."

Her brows lifted. "Are they?"

Which was her way of calling bullshit.

Jinx shrugged before looking meaningfully at War. Hadn't Jinx already said that he and Ali would be down in a minute?

War put his hands on his hips. "You're kicking me out of my office again?"

"Yes." It was good of War to notice. "How about you run downstairs and tell the bartender to be less obvious? She's never going to get good intel if she's screaming rookie cop at everyone she meets."

War's lips almost twitched. Almost. Such a near thing. At the last moment, he nodded and strode for the door. Odin was right on his heels.

"Odin..." Ali's voice was soft.

Odin stilled.

"When you arranged for me to take this little getaway, why didn't you mention to me that Jinx was down here?"

The question caught Jinx off-guard. As far as he knew, Odin hadn't known a damn thing about Jinx's personal relationship with Ali.

Not looking back, Odin replied, "If I'd told you, you wouldn't have come."

What? Well...*fuck me. He did know.*

Odin shot her a fast glance over his shoulder. "And I could hear the fear in your voice when we talked."

Ali took a step toward him. "You never said a word."

"Was waiting on you."

Odin had known Ali was scared and he hadn't passed that news on to Jinx? They'd be having a talk about *that* ASAP.

The door shut behind Odin. Ali frowned after him. Jinx kept his gaze on her. With an effort, he also managed to keep his hands *off* her. Major effort, though. Because he wanted to yank her close and hold her tight and make absolutely sure she was never hurt by anyone or anything.

She sighed out a long exhale. "I'm sorry."

Ali was apologizing to him? "What the hell for?"

"I'm one of those people that you mentioned." She bit her lower lip. Let it go. "I didn't intend to be. But here I am, using you, for my own gain."

Ah, so *that* comment had been the one to make her uncomfortable. Good to know. "Sweets..." he drawled.

Her gaze met his.

He motioned toward his body. "Use me all night long."

"Jinx..."

He closed in on her. Lifted his hand and lightly slid his knuckles over her cheek.

"I worked for the 'shady government' agency." Her voice was husky. "I'm one of the people using you."

"And I say to you again, use me all night long." Did it look like he was complaining? "I wasn't talking about you earlier." So she understood completely. "There is more at play. Stuff you don't know yet." Stuff he'd worked to keep secret. "Protecting you, pretending to be the lover who is so obsessed that he can't keep his hands off you..." His hand slid down to her neck. Curled around her nape. "That's a job I willingly volunteer for."

She was leaning toward him. Edging up onto her tiptoes. Did she realize it? He sure did.

"Why?" Ali breathed. "Why do this for me?"

"You didn't ask War and Odin why they were so willing to help."

She edged up a little higher. "They're my friends."

"And I'm not your friend?" He wanted her mouth. He'd be taking it. "That hurts. Wounds me deeply."

"Jinx, be serious."

Why was everyone always telling him that? The world was serious enough as it was. Besides, in this instance, he *had* been speaking honestly. "I can be your friend," he told her, "*and* be the man you want to fuck over and over again in the middle of the night." Or the middle of the day. Or every single moment.

Her eyes widened.

"I'm so willing to help because you need me right now. You need a friend. You need a partner. You need someone who won't hesitate to get rough and dangerous with the psycho messing with you. You need someone who will do *anything* necessary to make sure he's stopped." Jinx brought his head down. *Almost* kissed her. Almost. "Like I said...you need me."

Then he lifted his head.

She was still staring at his mouth. A good sign, he thought. Very promising.

"Jinx?"

He whistled. Reached for the door.

"Jinx, why didn't you just kiss me?"

His back was to her. The better to hide the big grin that swept over his face. "Because, love, you'll be the one who kisses *me* next time."

"Excuse me?"

"You'll be the one. You'll kiss me. Madly, frantically, desperately. And for the whole world to see." He swung open the door. "You'll know when the moment is right."

"You just—you want it to be for show?"

No, he wanted everything to be for keeps. But he was getting to that. He was playing a long game. "Isn't that the point?"

She stormed by him. "Right. Yes, of course."

His hand shot out and curled around her wrist. "Of course, if you want more than a show..."

Her head turned toward him. Her deep, dark stare met his.

"All you have to do..." *I want her mouth.* "Is say the magic words."

Her breathing hitched. "And what would those words be?"

Now he did let her see his smile. "Fuck me."

CHAPTER SEVEN

Armageddon was even busier when Ali headed back downstairs. She was far too conscious of Jinx behind her. When his hand lifted and his fingers pressed against the small of her back, Ali couldn't help but tense.

She'd *wanted* him to kiss her upstairs. It hadn't been about a cover or a show or anything else—she'd just wanted his mouth. But when Jinx kissed her, she tended to kiss her self-control goodbye. Not a good thing when they were dealing with a crazy stalker. A man who had apparently intended to hurt—and possibly kill—both her and Jinx that night.

"Head for the door," Jinx directed as his breath blew against the shell of her ear. "Time for our big exit."

A shiver slid over her as she began to maneuver through the crowd and for the door. Jinx shadowed her movements, and his fingers never left her back. She felt the touch like a brand burning through her shirt and sinking into her skin. She'd always been too hyper aware of Jinx.

Part of his charm?

Part of his danger?

Maybe a mix of both?

All too soon, they were nearly at the door. She risked a glance back and noticed that the bartender, Imari, had her eyes on Jinx.

More tension snaked through Ali. She didn't know what was happening with Imari, but she certainly intended to find out.

She shoved open the door and the thick night air wrapped around her. Plenty of people were still lined up to get inside. Actually, the line looked double the length that it had been earlier. Laughter and voices drifted in the air. So many people. So many faces.

And he could be in this crowd.

The guy had worn a helmet when he sabotaged Jinx's motorcycle. How easy would it have been to ditch the helmet in one of the alleys and to just stroll right back out to blend with the crowd?

She knew Jinx suspected the same thing. That was why he wanted their show. And if he wanted a show…

Ali turned and pressed her hand against Jinx's chest. They were a few feet away from the entrance to Armageddon, and a streetlamp glowed nearby.

Jinx had said she had to be the one to make the move. This seemed like the best spot to her. He waited and watched her as she slowly released a breath. Her fingers were trembling and her heart raced. Why she was so nervous about a simple kiss, Ali didn't know. Except maybe because…

No kiss with Jinx had ever been simple.

He had panty-dropping kisses. Body-melting kisses. Kisses that made you moan and ache.

Stop hesitating! She surged onto her toes. Locked both hands around his shoulders and tugged him down to meet her. Her mouth crashed into his, and she realized she was being too rough and awkward and this was—

His lips opened. His tongue darted into her mouth.

This was Jinx.

Her body seemed to soften against him. Her mouth parted more for him, and her tongue met his. She stopped wondering about who might be watching, and she just *felt*. Felt the reckless need that he could stir so easily. The desire that she couldn't hold in check when he was near.

His hands were sliding around her hips. Hauling her ever closer. And closer was exactly where she wanted to be. His mouth was warm and sensual, and it moved so expertly against hers. His fingers were at the edge of her ass, and she was pushing against him. Trying to get closer.

The unmistakable bulge of his erection thrust at her. Well, that was definitely not just for show.

His head lifted. "Our ride's here."

It was?

He laced his fingers with hers and tugged her toward a waiting limo.

A limo? How in the heck had he arranged for a limo on such short notice? It had literally been like ten, maybe fifteen minutes since he'd sent out his mystery text from upstairs.

"How?" she whispered.

He opened the back door of the limo. The driver had never exited. "I was owed a favor."

She slid inside. Glanced at the lush interior. The waiting champagne. Soft, romantic music played from speakers even as a faint, warm blue glow of light shone from the floor. "Must be some favor."

"Actually, it was a pretty small deal. Just saved a guy from dying." He shut the door and sprawled back on the seat. "You know how it is. You do one good deed and people start calling you hero. Saying things like... 'How can I ever repay you?' and 'I'll owe you until I die.' Stuff like that."

The limo pulled away from the curb. She stared at the privacy screen that separated her from the driver. "How does he know where we're going?"

"The destination was included in the text I sent." Jinx's gaze was hooded as he watched her. "You are an incredible actress. I mean, I've seen your skills in action on undercover cases, but the kiss...tell me, can you always fake a response that easily?"

"It wasn't faked," she responded immediately, annoyed.

"I know. Just wanted to hear you admit it."

He just... "*Jinx.*"

"Yes?"

"Stop it. Stop the games. Stop the teasing. Stop it all. It's you and it's me, and I want you to be real."

"I am hardly pretend."

She surged toward him. The limo hit a pothole, and she fell forward. He caught her easily, balanced her, and in a blink, she found herself straddling his hips. Her hand pressed to the leather on either side of him.

"That is much better," he murmured. "Don't you think?"

What she thought was that she could feel the thick, heavy length of his arousal pressing at the juncture of her thighs, and it took all that she had not to rub against him. "I think that you want me."

"Obviously."

She tried to search his gaze, but realized she saw only what he allowed her to see. "Not for show?"

"Nothing about my reaction to you is for show. It never has been." His fingers pressed lightly to her hips. "Can't you tell?"

She could tell that he was very big and full, and Ali found herself having to bite back those two magic words...

Fuck me.

"I wanted you the first time we met. You were all business, of course, barely glanced my way."

Surprise pulsed through her. She remembered their first meeting. She'd been pretty sure her jaw had dropped when she met him. Their hands had touched, and the flood of sensual awareness she'd felt had nearly knocked her off her feet. Later, when they'd been alone, he'd come close to her and whispered...

"I want you."

So direct. So straight-forward. And she'd been terrified because she had never responded so strongly to anyone before.

"Not going to happen."

Her body jerked.

"I believe those were the words that you gave me when I first told you how I felt. Of course, I respected that. I stayed away."

He had. He hadn't done or said anything sexual to her after that. She'd had plenty of fantasies about him, but she'd been sure that ship had sailed. Her own fear had made her miss out. Until...

The last night.

The night when she'd been tired of missing out and imagining what it would be like if she let go and gave herself to Jinx.

"You kept a careful wall between us until the very last mission. It was only then that you took me up on my ever-so-casual invitation for drinks. Spoiler alert, there was nothing casual about the invitation." His fingers pressed against her. "Satisfy me, will you?"

She sucked in a breath.

"Because I have been curious ever since that night. Just what was it that changed for you? What made you decide to have those shots with me?"

Where was the limo going? Why hadn't he told her this part of the plan? "Why are you keeping me in the dark?"

"There's plenty of light here. Don't know what you mean."

"You're hiding things from me."

His right hand rose. Brushed a lock of her hair behind her ear. His hand lingered near her cheek. "I hide things from everyone."

"I looked at your files. I know about your past service, your black ops work. I know how you transitioned to working with the agency on select missions. I know about the lives you've saved..."

"And the lives I took? I'm assuming you know all about those, too?"

She wet her lips. "You didn't have a choice."

"I did. I'm quite good at killing, and I chose to make that part of my life's work." His knuckles brushed over her cheek. "I've found that people are less terrified of me if I give them an easy grin or a mocking comment."

Her hips pushed down. She had not meant to do that small movement. "It...makes you seem less of a threat."

"When I'm underestimated, I work better. Just one of my quirks." His fingers slid under her hair. Cradled her nape. "You don't know everything about me, but it's precious that you think you do."

Her hips were trying to arch down against him. What was her problem? Why did she have zero control with this man? "You don't know everything about me, either."

"Obviously not, or I would have been aware you had a stalker. That pisses me off."

"That I have a stalker? It pisses me off, too." Her gaze was on his mouth. His sensual, sculpted lips.

"Yes, he makes me want to rip him apart, but I'm pissed that *you* didn't come to me as soon as you needed help." Anger hummed in his voice.

"You'd moved on. Not that we had anything together to begin with—"

"*Wrong.*"

Her gaze flew to meet his. Or, try to meet his. Too many shadows cloaked him.

"Whether we had something or not, I would help you. Understand that. Doesn't matter what goes down between us personally. You need me? I'm there for you. *Always.* You have someone you want me to hunt? I'll get to tracking. You have someone you want me to kill? Just point me at him."

"Jinx." Her nails bit into his shoulders. "It's not like that."

"Sure it is. You think I'd hesitate? I wouldn't. Not when it comes to you."

"I don't want to *use* you, dammit! That's not what this is about! And I certainly would never want you killing for me."

"But we already covered that I am very good at killing. Probably one of the best there is. I've always been exceptionally good with my hands."

Hands that he could use to kill or hands that he could use to bring pleasure.

"Does it bother you?" Jinx asked, voice roughening. "That the hands touching you have done so many bad things?"

"Stop it." The order burst from her. "You're playing some mind game with me—or trying to. You are a hero, Jinx. Like I said, I read your files. I know what you did was necessary. You saved lives. You helped people. You—"

"Like *I* said, you don't know everything about me. If you did, you'd be jumping off my lap and putting as much space between us as possible."

Her mouth had gone dry. "Why?"

"Because I want to fuck you right now. The driver can't hear a word we say. Can't see us. I want to strip those jeans off you, rip away your underwear, and thrust deep into you."

Her breaths came faster. "You said I needed to say the words."

"Indeed, I did. That's why I'm not in you already. Even though you keep rubbing against me. Even though your nipples are tight and hard. You know you want my mouth on them."

She was rubbing against him? Oh, crap, she was. She was rocking her hips against him over and over again. Helplessly.

"Don't stop," he growled. "I love the hell out of feeling you slide against my cock."

Ali loved the way he felt against her. Only she loved the way he felt *in* her even more. "This isn't the right time."

"Feels right to me."

"We're in a car, for goodness' sake."

"Who cares about goodness? Let's be bad."

He made her want to be bad and reckless and wild. "It will get complicated," she whispered.

"What's complicated about sex?"

Everything. "We're working as a team. If we have sex..."

"Ah, I see..." He leaned forward. His lips pressed against her throat. "You're still worried you'll fall in love with me. Thought we'd covered that one before."

He was joking. She wasn't. When it came to Jinx, her emotions made her too vulnerable. "There is no future for us."

"I'm not worried about the future. I was more concerned…" His tongue slid over her skin then he gave her a light nip. "About how I feel for you right now."

He was hard and strong. His mouth on her neck was sending little surges of electricity all through her body. Ali knew she shouldn't do this. Knew walking down this path was particularly dangerous. But she also knew how incredibly *good* they were together. Her eyes squeezed shut. She should not say… "*Fuck me.*"

She felt his body tense before he went motionless.

She'd kind of thought that if she gave him those words, he'd start stripping her. Or himself. Or both. He wasn't doing anything.

She cracked open her eyes. Even in the dim lighting, the electric fire in his gaze was undeniable.

"Say it again," Jinx ordered. "While you are looking at *me.*"

She wet her lips. "Fuck me?"

He yanked her shirt over her head. Twisted her around so that she was partially lying down on the seat as he lunged over her. His mouth went to the curve of her breast. He kissed her, teased, then shoved her bra out of his way so that he could tongue her nipple. He was hungry. Relentless. His mouth opened wide, and he sucked her inside. Even as he worked her with his mouth, his hand was sliding down her body. Hauling open the snap of her jeans. Hauling down the zipper. He jerked aside her panties, and she lifted her hips, trying to get the jeans and underwear out of his way. She'd kicked away her shoes and they were on the floor of the limo. Her jeans were half-on, her underwear was tangled around his hand and he was—

"You're wet." A hungry rumble. "Baby, you feel so *good*." He was strumming her clit with his thumb. Pushing his index finger into her. Stretching her, and Ali bit her lip because she wanted to moan with delight.

He'd said the driver couldn't hear them. She didn't want to take any chances.

Jinx withdrew his finger, only to thrust it back in—with another. Her hips surged up to meet him. Desire spiraled through her. He'd turned his mouth to her other breast and was licking and sucking on her nipple. Every sensual tug had her breath choking out. Need burned through her, and she grabbed desperately for his shoulders. "Your jeans need to *go*."

He didn't speak. But he pulled his mouth from her nipple. Stared down at her with glittering eyes. Then he yanked off her jeans. Took her panties with them. He knelt on the floor of the limo and pushed her legs apart.

His jeans were still in the way. Still needing to *go*.

Just like the time before...when he touched her, lust exploded. A craving for him that pushed her beyond all boundaries and control. She wanted him so badly. More than she could ever remember wanting anyone else.

But he wasn't taking off his damn jeans! "Jinx!"

His hands were on her thighs. "I have missed this." Almost savage. Then his mouth was on her. He stroked her with his tongue and lips, and her hips surged up against him. She was in the back of a limo. Cars buzzed past them. And she was going to come. There was no stopping the release. Ali could feel it building through her. She was too tuned, too primed, too *hungry* for him. When his tongue rasped over her clit, licking her again and again, Ali exploded.

"*Missed. This.*"

Her whole body jolted at his words. She couldn't suck in a deep breath and the frantic drumming of her heart echoed in her ears as it pounded and pounded and—

Pounded.

"The door is locked. Don't worry. He won't get in."

That wasn't just her heart pounding. Someone was pounding on the window. *Oh, no.*

Her mouth opened, but she didn't know what to say. Ali surged upright. She needed her shirt. Her bra was kind of on. Ali yanked it back to actually cover her breasts. Her shirt was behind Jinx. So were her jeans. She lunged for them.

Jinx caught her and pushed her back. "Don't regret it."

"I-I don't." She *would* regret the driver seeing her mostly naked if that door opened. And she... "You didn't..."

"Didn't what?"

"Didn't come, Jinx!" Heat burned in her cheeks.

"I'll come when I'm buried in you and your nails are leaving marks down my back." He pressed a kiss to her cheek. "In other words, as soon as I get you in my place. Because the first time I have you again, I *will* be taking my time."

That was...a lot. And hot. A hot lot.

"Don't put up walls." A low warning. "I have you again. Not planning to let go."

Her body was still doing little aftershock bursts of pleasure. She wasn't exactly planning to run anywhere. Except maybe to the nearest bed. His bed. Ali managed a quick nod.

He handed her the shirt. Her jeans. And her panties. She fumbled and twisted because getting *undressed* in a limo was way easier than getting dressed. But soon she was finally presentable. Mostly. Ali schooled her expression as Jinx opened the door.

The driver was waiting to the side. "Sure as hell took you long enough," he muttered.

A familiar mutter.

The burn in her cheeks flared red-hot. *Odin.* How the hell had Odin become their driver?

"Figured instead of tailing behind, it would be better for me to be watching from the front. Got the destination from the driver and sent him on his way as soon as the limo arrived." Odin had a ball cap pulled low over his face. Like that helped to disguise him in any way. There was a reason Odin hadn't ever been given much undercover work. The man was huge, and there was never any blending or hiding him.

"No one tailed us," he added. "We're good."

Good, and they were...*where*, exactly? She could hear the crash of waves. She could smell the salty air. They were at the beach, obviously, but when she turned her head and scanned the area, Ali gave a low whistle.

They were in front of a massive beach house. One perched high above the sand. Lights glowed from its many windows. Two levels. Three? The bottom seemed to be mostly a garage area, with heavy columns supporting the white structure. The second and third levels were big and sprawling, and the whole place just screamed money. A whole lot of money. "Who owns this place?"

"A friend," Jinx replied.

"The same friend who had the limo ready at a moment's notice?" she asked. Jinx certainly had interesting friends.

His fingers laced with hers. "How did you know?"

"Call it a lucky guess."

A soft laugh. "You know I love it when you get lucky with me."

She could only shake her head.

"The friend in question is out of the country right now, so I've been crashing here while he's away. Part of that whole 'how can I ever repay you' bit I mentioned earlier."

Odin was an immoveable wall near the vehicle. "It's got state-of-the-art security. This is the best place for you to stay."

She wasn't going to argue. Ali would be more than happy to stay in the million-dollar mansion with the awesome security, thank you very much. "Sounds good to me."

"I'll be close by tonight," Odin assured her. "Just in case he's better than we think and he managed to tail you here."

"Or…" Ali added as she stared up at the house. "If he's already aware that this is where Jinx has been staying. There may have been no need for a tail, not if he knew we would wind up at this location."

If this guy was as good as she feared, even the awesome security wouldn't be able to keep him out.

"It will seem like I'm leaving," Odin added quietly. "All for show." Then he headed for the front of the limo.

Jinx's fingers tightened around hers. "Ready?"

Ready to go in the house? Or ready for what would happen once she was inside and they were all alone? Her gaze slid from his and tracked down the beach. Far in the distance, she could see the glowing lights of what she suspected was a tall condo building. And there was one other house close by, but it appeared to be empty. No glowing lights, a shuttered look about it. It seemed that they would certainly have plenty of privacy. In terms of security, that was both good and bad.

"Ali?"

She released a quick breath. "I want to go inside." *I want you.* Just as she'd wanted him before. He'd asked why she'd agreed to those drinks with him on that last, fateful night. Simple…

She'd wanted Jinx from the first moment they'd met. Every time that she'd glanced into his eyes, she'd felt that same hot awareness but she'd tried to hide the truth from him. Every time she'd seen his slow smile, her stomach had done a little flip. Jinx had become a serious weakness for her.

She hadn't thought they would work together again. She'd heard rumbles that Jinx had been planning to stop the missions. War and Odin had already been out. The night he'd offered her the invitation for drinks, she'd decided...

Why not?

What could it hurt?

Turned out, it could hurt quite a lot.

They headed for the house. Climbed up the long line of stairs that led to the second level. He pulled keys from his pocket. Opened the door. Waited.

His words whispered through her mind as she crossed the threshold.

You're still worried you'll fall in love with me. Thought we'd covered that one before.

Jinx was so very wrong. She didn't worry at all that she would fall in love with him. How could she?

She'd *been* in love with him for a very long time. And *that* had been the real reason she'd agreed to drinks on that unforgettable night they'd had together.

CHAPTER EIGHT

Do not screw this up. Do not screw this up.

"If we're in the house, how does that bait the jerk after me? I thought our plan was to go out and catch his attention."

He finished setting the alarm. Turned toward her. Ali was staring out of the giant floor to ceiling windows that overlooked the beach. She couldn't see the waves, not in all that darkness, but come dawn, the view would be unforgettable.

The view was the whole reason he was in that house.

And *she* was the whole reason he'd gotten it in the first place. Not the time for that talk, though. Later. *After* he'd managed to get one whole night of fucking her repeatedly off his to-do list.

"We already caught his attention." His voice was low. A little too savage. That wouldn't do. He had to play this scene just the right way. Jinx tried again. "You know, what with the whole motorcycle sabotage bit? And then, to make sure I was waving a lovely red flag at him, I had the limo arrive at Armageddon. Because nothing says not-subtle like a big limo in the middle of the road."

She turned toward him. "I thought that might have been your intention."

Sneaking off in Odin's Jeep wouldn't have gotten him the attention he wanted. "A limo is easy to follow."

"But Odin doesn't think we *were* followed."

"Even if we weren't, I've been staying here for a while. It's likely he knows the location. When he realizes that you and I are here together—that we're staying here together all night long—that will make him crazy."

She swallowed. "How do you know that?"

"Because he wants you." *And he will never have you.* Jinx slowly crossed the room until he was standing right in front of her. "Because it would drive me insane if I thought you were spending the night fucking someone else."

She tensed. "Why would you care?"

Why the hell would she even ask that question? "Because it's you. And when it comes to you, I find that the idea of any other guy touching you..." His hand rose. Skimmed over her shoulder. Down her arm. "It pisses me off. I don't want somebody else making you wet." He caught her hand. Tugged her ever closer. "I don't want some jackass seeing you moan." Her head tipped back as she stared up at him. "And I damn well don't want him making you come."

When she came, when pleasure washed over, Ali was absolutely beautiful. And, yes, he was being a jealous, possessive bastard. Because he *was* a jealous, possessive bastard. At least where Ali was concerned. Probably time she realized that about him. He wondered if she would jerk away. Tell him to back the hell off.

But...

Ali nodded. "I get that."

His eyebrows rose. She did?

Her free hand rose to press to his chest. Right over his heart. "Because I don't want some bottle-made redhead—or any other chick who isn't me—making you hard."

He was so hard right then that he was about to burst out of his jeans.

Her fingers trailed down his chest. He could swear her touch was burning him through the t-shirt. Holding his gaze, she told him, "I don't want someone else hearing your voice when it gets all rough and low and extra sexy..."

"You don't?" A growl. Rough and low, and sure, she could call it sexy if she wanted.

Ali shook her head. She tugged free of his grip and both of her hands went to the top of his jeans. "And if someone is going to make you come, it's going to be me." She pulled down the zipper. His eager dick bobbed toward her.

And when she touched him—

He *almost* came right then and there. Like he was some freaking, no-control kid.

His teeth snapped together, and Jinx hissed out a breath as her fingers closed around him. Squeezed and pumped.

"If you don't stop," he warned her, "I'll be coming faster than you think." The plan had been to get her in bed. Get her naked. Make *her* come twice, then sink into her.

She offered him a slow smile. One that made her incredible eyes sparkle. "Promises, promises…"

Then Ali eased down to her knees in front of him.

Oh, hell, no. "*Ali.*"

"You've gotten to taste me—twice now—and I think it's only fair that I should have the same opportunities with you."

But she didn't get it. He'd had about a million fantasies that all began this same way, and finally having his dream in front of him? Oh, hell, no, there was no way his control would last. Not at all. Not at—

Her mouth closed around him.

His whole body shuddered.

He could not look away from her. Ali was the sexiest thing he'd ever seen in his life. She was being careful and slow, hesitant, and he was *done*. Just done. She was licking him, sucking him so sweetly, and he kissed his control goodbye.

He'd tried to warn her…

His hands were shaking as he reached for her. He pulled her up, lifted her into his arms, and took her mouth. His tongue thrust past her lips as her arms snaked around his neck—and her legs locked around his hips. He made it to the bedroom, moving pretty much blindly because he was not letting her go and he couldn't give up her mouth.

They fell onto the bed. Her shoes kicked to the floor. He ripped her clothes out of the way and sent them flying.

He grabbed a box of condoms from the nightstand and yanked one on. He'd tossed his own clothes away and didn't give a damn about where they were.

She pushed up onto her elbows and stared at him with her plump, red lips parted. "Jinx?"

He couldn't speak. He'd gone way past that point. He grabbed her legs. Hauled her to the edge of the bed. Leaned over her. *Took* her.

She gasped out his name, and Jinx worried that he was too rough. Need had ridden him for months and he should be more careful—

"Yes!" Her hands were curled around his shoulders, moving down. Her nails scratched over his back.

Fucking perfect. He hammered into her. Kissed and touched and stroked, and her hungry moans just drove him on all the more. He yanked her closer. Pushed her legs over his shoulders. Slammed deep and took and took and took.

She let loose a quick, startled scream of pleasure, and he felt her inner muscles clamp tightly around him. He kept thrusting through her orgasm, driving into her relentlessly. Her pleasure was making him wilder. He wanted her to come endlessly. To hold on to him and never let go.

The pleasure was wrecking him, too. His grip on her hips was too hard. Too tight. Her moans made him even more crazed. So desperate for more. For all of her.

The climax hit him. Blasted through his body and made his eyes want to roll back into his head. The pleasure was so intense, enough to obliterate the memory of any other lover he'd ever had. The orgasm stormed through him, filling every single cell of his body.

When it ended, he became aware of the hard drumming of his heartbeat. Of the fierce grip that he'd had on her hips. Of the fact that he'd been way too rough. He'd intended for the first time with her—*this* first time—to be different. He'd wanted to woo her. To give her so much pleasure that she forgot everything else.

Except, *he'd* been the one to forget.

And he'd been the one who should have exercised more freaking control with her.

"I can't move," Ali whispered.

Oh, hell. *What did I do?* Carefully, gently, he pulled her legs off his shoulders. He pulled *out* of her. "Baby..."

Her legs dangled off the bed, and Ali arched her back as she gave a long, delicate stretch. "Awesome."

He squinted at her. "Say again?"

Her long lashes lifted. "Why? We both know you heard me the first time."

"Not too rough?"

She eased back. Maneuvered herself so that she was on the pillows and her legs were fully on the mattress. "Not too rough at all." Her gaze raked over him. Lingered on a certain eager portion of his anatomy. "I don't mean to tell you your business, but you still look pretty, uh, intense..."

"I'm intense...again." But first he needed to ditch the old condom. "Do not move."

She nodded.

He spun away. Took two steps toward the bathroom. Then stopped. He peered back over his shoulder at her. "I'm serious. Last time, I left for five minutes, and you were gone. Took me months to get you back. I'm not in the mood to chase you down."

Her smile held a world of promise. Lots of sexy, sexy promise. "Where would I go?"

He wasn't going to toss out options. "Stay here."

Her gaze slid to the nightstand—and the open nightstand drawer. "Is that a box of condoms?" Her voice had gone carefully neutral.

"A full box, minus one."

"You...entertain a lot, I take it?"

"No." He waited for her gaze to come back to his. "Bought that box when I realized you were slipping back into my life. Figured this time, I'd be prepared. No runs to the gas station that give you a chance to vanish on me."

Her eyes widened. "You bought the box for me?"

Who the fuck else? But he held back that response. "Be here when I come back."

"There is no other place I would rather be."

Okay, yes, he liked that answer. He'd take it. He jerked his head in a nod and hurried for the bathroom. He'd ditch the condom, try to get more friggin' control before the next round, then he'd be back for his Ali.

***

She swore that she could still feel him, inside. Ali stared up at the ceiling and released a long breath. Her body was tingling. Aftershocks of release quivered through her sex, and...

Jinx wanted her again.

There was a box of condoms waiting. He was coming back, and they were going to have sex over and over again.

She had so experienced this fantasy before.

A phone let out a quick peal of sound.

Ali jerked. She'd had *this* reality before. She'd had—

No, no, that wasn't a phone ringing. *Not this time.* Instead, it was the warning peal of a text. When her head turned, she saw a light glowing from the pocket of Jinx's discarded jeans. The peal came again, followed by a vibration.

Jinx was getting a text. "Jinx!" she called.

Had he turned on the shower? Ali thought she could hear running water.

Another peal of sound. Another text. Whoever was texting Jinx—the person seemed very impatient.

She slipped from the bed. Hauled the sheet with her and tiptoed for the bathroom door. Her hand lifted and knocked against the wood. "Jinx? Someone is texting you. Someone is—"

A loud, shrieking alarm filled the house. A startled cry broke from her lips even as she whirled around. The alarm seemed to be coming from every single direction. It was blasting at her, and she knew an intruder had gotten into the house—or was *trying* to get inside. She needed a weapon!

"What the fuck?" Jinx yanked open the door. He was dripping wet and naked. He grabbed for her.

The alarm stopped as abruptly as it had begun. The alarm *shouldn't* have stopped, though, not unless someone had disengaged it.

Jinx pushed her toward the bathroom. "Lock the door." Still naked, he shot across the room. Yanked open the top drawer of his dresser and hauled out a gun.

"Tell me you have two of those." She wasn't hiding in the bathroom. She was staying with him. Watching his six. *Helping* him.

His head whipped toward her.

"*Jinx.*" A snarling voice spat his name. A hulking figure stood in the doorway. "I am so going to kick your ass."

The hell he would.

CHAPTER NINE

Jinx aimed his gun at the man who'd just broken into the house and kicked his way through the bedroom door. "I do not have time for this shit." He was far too conscious of Ali's frozen form near the bathroom.

"Make time for it," the intruder snapped back as he stalked toward Jinx—and showed no fear of the weapon pointed at him. "And while you're at it, put on some clothes so that I don't have to stare at your naked junk all night, would you?"

Ali took a step forward.

The jerk finally noticed her. "Hell."

Jinx nodded. Hell, indeed.

"That would be the reason your ass is naked," the jerk realized.

"She would be the reason." She was also the reason he still had his gun up and aimed. Because *no one*—not even family—would jeopardize Ali. "You don't break into my place when she's here. You don't scare her." Each word was hard. Brutal. Cold. "You don't come anywhere *near* her, you got me?"

The intruder narrowed his eyes.

"And you don't *look* at her when she's just wearing a damn sheet. Keep your gaze on me, got it?"

A muscle flexed along the other man's jaw. "At least she *has* a sheet on. You're still buck-ass naked."

Ali cleared her throat. "I believe he's armed," she announced to Jinx. "I can see the bulge of his weapon tucked into the back of his jeans. Perhaps you should tell him to put his hands up and then to remain in that position while I take his gun?"

"No one is taking my gun." Low. Rough.

"The alarm was quite loud and shrieking," Ali continued in a surprisingly cool voice. "I'm sure Odin will be bursting in any moment. The cops, too. I have no doubt that an instant signal was sent to the authorities. That is typically the way security systems operate."

Their unwelcome guest swore. "Cancel that shit, Jinx. Now."

"Are you giving *him* orders?" Ali asked. "Bad move when he's the one with the weapon pointed at you."

"*Jinx...*"

"Ali, come take my gun. Keep it aimed at him."

She quickly nodded.

The intruder shook his head in disgust. "What the fuck, man?"

Ali hurried closer. The sheet trailed behind her like a wedding train. Luckily, the sheet also covered most of her body. She took the gun from him. Held it in a steady grip. Jinx backed up. Grabbed for his jeans and jerked them on.

"I will shoot you," Ali said crisply as she held the gun in position. Jinx snagged his phone. Saw that he'd missed some texts. Quickly, he read through them...

Are you in trouble?

Then...

What the hell is going on?

And...

Fuck it. I'm worried. I'm coming in.

He'd been in the shower and missed the texts. If he'd seen them, he could have prevented the break-in. Oh, well, time for damage control.

He dialed Odin. Put the phone to his ear.

"You all right?" An instant bark from Odin. "Right outside now—"

"Everything is fine here. Make sure the cops don't come in, got me? It was a false alarm. I accidentally triggered it."

Silence.

"Make *sure* the cops don't come," he repeated. "Everything is clear here. You can relax."

"Ok." And that was all. Odin ended the call.

"Done." Jinx rolled back his shoulders and shoved the phone into the back pocket of his jeans. "No cops will be busting in to arrest your sorry self and haul you off to jail." He crossed his arms over his chest. "You are most welcome."

The guy kept glaring.

"So..." Ali's voice was still all calm and cool and collected. "Someone want to tell me why Ramsey just broke into the house? Because it looks suspicious and scary as all hell to me, but, Jinx, *you* just canceled the cavalry."

Ramsey began to lower his hands. "It's because—"

"Do *not* lower your hands," Ali ordered. "If I think you are reaching for your gun, I will shoot you."

Okay, obviously, things were tense. And Ali was still in a sheet. A situation that needed to be corrected. He slipped between her and Ramsey.

A furrow immediately appeared between her eyebrows. "What are you doing? Why are you in my line of fire?"

"Because I suddenly got worried that your finger might get twitchy, and it would be awkward as hell if you shot my brother."

Her eyes flared. "What?"

"*Jinx.*" A snarl from behind him. "What are you *thinking?*"

"I'm thinking that Ali just learned one of my secrets." He never took his gaze off her. "I'm thinking that now, she'll be comfortable leaving me alone in the room with you *while she gets her sweet ass dressed.*" He offered her a quick smile. "Because he might be pissed at me—he usually is—but Ram won't hurt me."

"Don't be too sure about that," Ramsey groused. "At the moment, I feel like killing you."

Ali hadn't lowered the gun. "If he's your brother, why go through the show of giving me your gun and having me hold it on him?"

"Well, obviously, because I wanted him to know he couldn't mess with you." His head turned toward Ramsey. "She never gets caught in the crossfire, understand? Ali is always off-limits. You don't touch her, you don't threaten her, and you don't let your world come near her."

Ramsey's mouth thinned. "Message received. Loud and clear."

Good.

"Oh. I get it." Ali grabbed Jinx's arm and pushed the gun into his hand. "You're both crazy. Should have just said that from the beginning." She frowned up at him. "Do *not* let your brother leave before I get back. It will take me less than a minute to dress, and then I want a full explanation as to why one of the most notorious criminals in the area decided to pay us a late-night visit—and the answer had better be more than just...he's family."

Well, he had been planning to lead with that...

Ali scooped up her clothing and hurried for the bathroom. The door shut on the end of her sheet.

Jinx looked down at the gun.

"You can put that away, don't you think?" Angry. Rough.

He put the gun back in the drawer. Tension still tightened his shoulders. "I didn't get your texts. I was busy at the time."

"Busy—fucking the new girl?"

His head snapped up. "Off-limits." Hadn't they covered that? He stalked toward his brother. Ramsey held his ground. "Everything about her is off-limits to you."

"Sure. Because you get to poke your nose into my life, try to tell me how to handle my lady—"

"You don't have a lady!" Jinx exploded. "You let her go. The best thing to ever happen to you, the first *good* thing that I can remember—and you let her just slip away!"

Ramsey lunged toward him. "I didn't let her slip anywhere. She was taken."

"But she came back," he snarled.

"And she doesn't remember a damn thing about me!" Low. Guttural. Pain-filled.

The bathroom door opened.

Jinx realized that it probably appeared as if he and his brother were about to rip each other's throats out. Fair enough. They both turned and looked toward Ali.

She raised one eyebrow. "Family issue?"

She was dressed. Good. Great.

"How about we take this conversation out of the bedroom and say...to the den? That good with you two? Then we can all sit down and have a nice, civilized discussion that doesn't involve the two of you attacking each other." With that, she headed for the bedroom doorway.

Ramsey straightened his shoulders and kept glaring at Jinx. "I won't be staying. No need for a civilized discussion about anything. Not like you and I have ever been *civilized* a day in our lives. That shit is for losers." He stomped after Ali.

Sighing—because his brother was actually right, being civilized was not a strong suit for either of them—Jinx followed in his wake.

But when he got into the den, he saw that Ali was blocking the door—and Ramsey's obvious intent to exit.

"Nope," she said ever-so-sweetly with a flutter of her lashes. "Not until I get answers."

Ramsey's hands went to his hips. "I'm not super fond of you."

Jinx tensed. "*Ramsey.*"

His brother ignored him. "You pop up out of nowhere, and suddenly, Jinx is in danger. Danger that I am sure is tied to you. So, how about you do us all a favor and maybe just pop *out* of his life?"

Jinx grabbed him. Spun him around. "What the actual fuck?"

"It's her, isn't it? I get it now. When you called and said the guy was coming for you, that he was trying to hurt something that was *yours*, I didn't put the pieces together. Now, it's all fitting for me. You know, since I walked in on the aftermath of the two of you and your obvious fuck scene, it's all fitting into place for—"

Jinx shoved Ramsey against the nearest wall. His forearm pressed to Ramsey's throat. "Not another word." Savage. Jinx glared at him. "Blood or not, I will kick your ass. Everyone else in the area might think you're the boogeyman, but I'm still bigger, still badder, and I will make you cry just like I did when we were kids."

Ali tapped him on the shoulder. "He's not wrong."

"Damn right, I'm not wrong," Jinx snarled as he shoved his forearm even harder against Ramsey's throat. "I will make him cry, I will make him beg—"

Ramsey rolled his eyes.

"No, I mean *he* isn't wrong. Ramsey isn't. I did pop back into your life, and now you're in danger because of me. He also did walk in right after we had sex. I mean, I was wrapped in a sheet.

You were naked. All very obvious tells." Another tap on the shoulder. "So I don't see why you are attacking him when all the man is trying to do is protect his brother. Seems unnecessary."

It felt very necessary.

Dammit.

And then—

The front door swung open. No alarm sounded. No beep. Nothing.

Odin stood in the doorway—filled the doorway—and glared at them.

"So much for this place being secure," Ali mumbled. "I'm thinking we should have just stayed at my condo."

"I remotely disabled the alarm so I could get in. And I have a key." Odin shut the door. Took in Jinx and Ramsey. "Figured it had to be him, when you called and wanted the cops to stay back."

Terrific. Now they were in full-on cluster-fuck mode. "I wanted the cops *and* you away." Just for clarification.

Odin inclined his head. "You were protecting your brother. I get it."

Ramsey swore. "What have you done, Jinx? Hired a skywriter or some shit? Does everyone know about our relationship?"

No, he hadn't hired a freaking skywriter. "Odin is a PI. He figures stuff out. Uncovers clues. It's in his job description."

"I knew long before I started working at Trouble for Hire," Odin told him. "I trailed you once when you cut away from everyone. Was worried you needed someone to watch your six." He motioned to Ramsey. "Saw you two meet up."

"Well, mystery solved." It hadn't even taken the Scooby gang to close the case.

"Once I saw you two together, I was even *more* worried that you needed someone to watch your back," Odin continued. "Because sometimes, when it comes to family, we can be blinded to their faults."

Odin's concern was sweet, but unnecessary. "Oh, I am quite aware that Ram is a psychopath with a trail of chaos in his wake. Not blinded to that at all."

Ramsey shot him a dirty glare. "Do not get me started on *your* life."

Probably better not to go there. Jinx peered expectantly at Odin. "Are more people about to burst inside? War, perhaps? Or your lovely lady, Maisey?"

"Just me."

"Great to know." He released his brother and stepped back. "Now how about you and Ram get out? The visit has been fun, but it's over."

Ali let out a quick gasp. "That is not a nice way to talk to your brother or your best friend!"

Was she for real? "Newsflash. Ramsey *isn't* nice, and Odin is only semi-nice. Do not let him fool you." And, bigger picture... "We're supposed to be baiting a trap, remember? If our perp sees the whole party we have going on, he's hardly likely to come and get me."

Ramsey narrowed his eyes. "So that's what you're doing. Trying to draw him in? Get him to come after you and not her?"

Jinx opened his mouth to respond—

But Odin beat him to the punch. "Unfortunately, the perp came after them both tonight. Sabotaged the brakes on Jinx's ride. If I hadn't seen it, they would have smashed all over the road."

Ramsey's jaw hardened. His nostrils flared. "Give me a name."

Jinx had to roll his eyes. "If I had a name, I wouldn't be playing bait now, would I?" Obviously. Also... "My problem. Not yours. You're the one who kicked me out of your life—"

"Because you're an interfering asshole."

"And you're being an interfering asshole right now. I've got this. I have backup."

Ramsey's gaze slid to Odin. "Right. You've always had him and War."

Was that anger? Jealousy? WTF? Brothers could be such a freaking pain.

"You don't have to take the family you were given." Ramsey's voice was grating. "You could pick your own. How lucky for you. But then, you always were the lucky one, weren't you?"

No, sometimes, his luck was pure shit. He surged toward his brother again. Only this time, Jinx didn't pin him to the wall. "You'll always be my family." Just so they were clear. "I don't care what you do, you're still family. You always matter. Haven't I proven that, over and over? I'm always there for you." They'd been ripped out of each other's lives long ago, but Jinx had clawed his way back to Ramsey. Jinx hadn't turned his back on the guy, no matter what twisted truths he'd found.

Jinx was aware of Ali and Odin watching him.

Ramsey's eyes blazed, but he didn't speak.

"Appreciate you checking on me," Jinx added softly as he tried to defuse a way tense situation. "Makes me feel all warm and tingly. Nice to know you care."

"Screw off." Ramsey shouldered past him. Then he stopped right before Odin. "You're in my way."

He was. Odin was a wall between Ram and the door.

"Am I?" Odin asked. He didn't move. "Maybe you should remember that. Because Jinx might think he can trust you, but I don't exactly feel the same way. I know how dangerous you are."

"Good for you. Get the hell out of the way."

Odin glanced at Jinx.

Jinx inclined his head. Odin got out of the way.

And just like that, his brother slipped from the house.

"So, I hate to point out the obvious," Ali began as she delicately cleared her throat. "But, uh, here we go. Anyone watching the house will just have seen Ramsey leave. That could potentially make him a target."

A possibility but... "As long as he isn't fucking you, he shouldn't be a target."

Her eyes widened. "Well, there's that."

And he won't be fucking you.

"We clear here?" Odin rumbled.

Jinx nodded. Tension twisted at the nape of his neck. He knew that as soon as Odin left, he'd have to explain to Ali about Ramsey. Like that was going to be fun.

Odin slipped away, too, but Jinx was sure Odin made certain not to be spotted. Despite his size, Odin was surprisingly good at blending into shadows.

Then it was just him and Ali. Her feet were bare. She hadn't bothered to put on her shoes. Her toes curled against the marble tile of the floor. The atmosphere was uncomfortable. Way too tense.

Hell. "Guessing that was a mood killer, huh?" He'd gone from tasting heaven to being back in the cold. "You want a drink?" Because telling this story over drinks would be way easier.

But when he moved toward the well-stocked bar, Ali caught his hand. "That's why you were at Ramsey's the other night. You were there to see your brother."

Yes. His brother had a tangled web going on with his life at the moment. "Ramsey wants me to stay out of his business. I want him to stop being a dumbass. I went to the bar in order to make my case again." Her fingers were so soft against him. "He didn't take my advice. The fool."

"He cares about you."

"Ramsey likes for the world to think he doesn't care about anyone or anything."

"But it's a lie. Or he wouldn't have come here tonight. He was checking on you. He was mad because I put you in danger."

He reached for her hand. Lifted it to his lips. Kissed her knuckles. "That's where you are wrong. Again."

Ali shook her head. "No, no, I am sure he cares—"

"You didn't put me in danger. The creep stalking you did that, and like I've told you before, I don't mind danger. Hell, I thrive on it. Makes me feel alive."

If anything, the shadows in her eyes deepened. "Ramsey is one of your secrets."

One of many.

"There was no mention of any family in your files."

Another kiss to her knuckles. Then he turned her hand over. Pressed his lips to her palm. "That's because Jinx doesn't have family."

But he was more than just *Jinx*. That wasn't even his real name. Not that he used the other name. Ever. That man was dead. He had the death certificate to prove it. For a while, even Ramsey had thought he was dead. The first time he'd walked back into Ram's life, the guy had looked at him as if seeing a ghost.

Because that was exactly what Jinx had been.

"Know what happens when everyone else on your team dies but you keep going?" He shoved back memories. "Some folks say you're lucky, but when you're watching their families cry, when you're watching friends get buried, lucky is the last thing you feel."

He could see tears gathering in her beautiful eyes.

"Don't," Jinx ordered gruffly. "Don't cry for me. I kept going. Found myself in a group slammed together by Uncle Sam. One that included Odin and War—those two had known each other long before that team was formed. They welcomed me, though, like I was a long-lost friend. Brought me in and never hesitated to protect my back." They still didn't hesitate. "Then you came along, and our team was set. I was determined to make sure that nothing happened to any of you. No one was going to take any of you from me." Another kiss to her palm. *No one was going to take my family.*

The way his family had been taken before. "I was sixteen when my dad went to jail for the third and final time. He died in his cell two weeks later. My mom had passed a few years before." He didn't like walking down this path. For her, he was doing it. "My brother was a year younger than me. I wanted to stay with him. Told the lady from DHR over and over again not to separate us but..." But in the end, it hadn't mattered. "It's hard to place older kids." Hard was an understatement. "Do you know how many older kids just sit in foster care? Everyone wants the younger ones. Two tough-ass teens aren't exactly cute." Maybe that was when he'd first learned how the world responded differently to smiles. To jokes. To charm. But Ramsey hadn't played the same game. He'd never hidden his darkness. "They said my brother had anger issues. Attachment issues." He remembered that designation so clearly. The counselors and the paper pushers had been so fast to label Ram. "Said he'd never connect with another family, but that I had a chance. If I would just agree to be permanently separated from him, they could place me." His hand tightened around her fingers.

"But you didn't agree."

Surprised, he looked into her eyes. Tears still swam in her dark gaze.

"You didn't agree to give up your brother. That's not how the two of you became separated."

"How do you know?" He forced his smile. "It's my story."

"Because I know *you* better than you realize. You didn't walk away from him. You aren't doing it now, and I don't think you did it when you were sixteen."

No, he hadn't. "You're right. He left me." A pain that still gutted Jinx. "Found a note. It said that I'd be better off without him. Said he knew he was holding me back." His chest burned. "Guess people like leaving me notes."

Her thick lashes flickered. "Jinx..."

"I took off, trying to find him, but he was gone." *Too late*. "Couldn't find a trace of him. Not until years later when I discovered just what he'd become."

Crime boss.

"Then I had to try and save him." He was going to stop the story there. Enough secrets had been exposed. He let go of her hand. "About those drinks..." He made it to the bar. Flattened his hands on the gleaming top.

"Now I know why you did it."

He had reached for a bottle of whiskey. Not the fancy-ass whiskey that War kept stocked, but a passable bottle. "Did what?"

"The agency. Odin and War cut out early. They retired and found a different path sooner, but you took more cases. I always wondered why. Especially when I looked at your files and saw that a lot of your solo runs, they could have counted as suicide missions...if anyone but *you* had taken them. See, I thought you were called Jinx because you got lucky on so many dangerous missions. You know, one of those opposite nickname things that service guys like to use. Jinx—not for bad luck, but for good."

He didn't speak.

"You took those cases for him, didn't you?"

He would not look back at her. "I have no idea what you're talking about, sweets. We already covered that I live for danger." He put the bottle back down.

But she was determined. "You worked out some kind of deal, didn't you? What is Ramsey going to get for all the cases you took? A new identity? His sins erased? And does he even *know* what all you risked for him?"

CHAPTER TEN

Jinx's broad back tensed. The light spilled onto him, showing the powerful muscles and strength of his body. He still wore just his jeans, jeans that clung loosely to his hips. His hands were flat on the bar, and it took all of her control to hold back and not rush toward him.

And then, he laughed.

Laughed?

What was funny? Ali didn't remember telling a joke. Actually, nothing about the night had been funny. Very unamusing so far.

"Erasing his sins..." Jinx turned toward her. Leaned back against the bar. Gave her an amazing view of his chest, his million abs, and his Adonis belt that just zinged down like the badass that it was. She'd never seen a real Adonis belt before Jinx. Sure, she'd seen them on seriously cut celebrities in the movies, but not in real-life. That sexy, V-shaped muscle slid diagonally from his hip bones and worked on down to his—

"I'm not trying to erase anyone's sins. Not even my own. But cute idea."

Cute? Her brows shot up. Her eyes also shot away from his distracting Adonis belt. "You're trying to save him."

"Ramsey doesn't need saving."

"You try to save everyone." She took a quick step toward him. "Case in point—look at me."

His gaze raked her. Heated. "I am looking at you."

Do not get distracted. A little late for that mental warning, though. She'd already been distracted. "One of the reasons I didn't come to you sooner was because I knew you'd risk everything to save me."

His lips thinned. "Just how did you know that?"

"Because it is what you *always* do. In the field, over and over, you take the riskier assignments to protect everyone else. You take the danger before anyone else can. You have more of a hero complex than anyone else I've ever met." Only now, she understood it. Jinx blamed himself for the team that hadn't survived. Was he determined to make sure no one else was lost on his watch?

"I'm not a hero. Don't make that mistake about me."

"Oh, really?" She closed the last bit of distance between them. "Then enlighten me. Why do you take the risks? The most dangerous missions?"

"Told you, I like the thrill of danger."

Ali was gonna call BS. "I have met adrenaline junkies. You are not an adrenaline junkie."

"You're right." His hand curled around her hip. "I'm not addicted to adrenaline. Though there is something I *could* become addicted to..." He tugged her ever closer.

Her head tipped back automatically.

His mouth lowered toward hers.

"You," he whispered right before their mouths touched. "I could sure as hell become addicted to *you*."

***

Paydirt.

He'd known that if he just kept to the shadows, if he watched long enough, closely enough, he'd find the perfect opportunity to strike.

That fancy house on the beach? It was his goal. The people inside? They were the targets he'd attack. He rocked back onto his heels as he watched the house.

This was gonna be so easy. They would never see him coming.

And when he was done…

No one would *ever* forget him again.

He just had to wait. Pick the right moment…

Then go in for the kill.

***

The kiss was drugging. Deep. Sensual. Her toes curled and her knees wanted to do a little jiggle as Ali leaned into Jinx. He kissed her with a languid passion, with a smooth possession—as if he had all the time in the world to savor her.

And…yes, guilty, she was kissing him back the same way.

Why do I feel like he belongs to me?

Jinx…and all his secrets.

"I think I could fuck you a thousand times," he growled as his mouth moved to press kisses along her jaw. Then down her throat. "And still want you a thousand more."

She felt the same way. As if she could never get tired of him. As if she'd want him forever, and that thought terrified her. She'd never imagined a forever with anyone. Not with anyone but...Jinx. Jinx slipped through her mind so often, and he wasn't the type of person who did forever. She knew that. He'd just told her he loved danger. Told her—

He nibbled on her lower lip.

The sensual bite had her sex heating with hungry desire.

He lifted her up, and her legs wrapped around his hips. He held her with such an easy strength. Raw power.

"Ready to pick up where we left off?" Jinx rasped the words as he pushed her back against the wall.

Where they'd left off...in bed. After an insane orgasm.

"Because it's been too long for me." His heavy cock shoved against her. "Too many nights of wanting you and not having you."

He didn't mean that, surely. Not like he'd fantasized about her. Or...had he? *Because I fantasized so often about him.*

"You'd slip into my dreams." His head lifted. His gaze burned down at her. "Taunting me with what I couldn't have."

She could not look away from his bright stare.

"But I have you now, don't I, Ali? I have you, and you won't vanish again."

She didn't plan to vanish. Her mouth pressed to his neck. Licked.

He shuddered.

She sucked his skin. Felt his racing pulse beneath her mouth.

His body was so hot and hard against her. The jeans did nothing to disguise his heavy arousal.

"You *won't* vanish."

He wasn't asking a question, but she gave him an answer anyway. "I don't plan to go anywhere. Except back to bed. With you."

"Hell, yes."

He carried her back to the bedroom. Stripped her. Was touching her with such careful control. He licked and kissed and caressed every single inch of her. Her body was hungry and taut and all she wanted was for him to plunge deep into her and send them spiraling into madness. Sweet, sweet madness.

Was that so much to ask? She didn't think so.

"*Jinx!*" He was torturing her. Her nipples thrust toward him. Her hips squirmed on the mattress. "Now, Jinx. *Now*."

He caught her hips. Lifted her up even as he rolled on the bed. In a flash, he was on his back, and she was straddling his hips.

"Put the condom on me," he ordered.

Ali grabbed for a condom. She ripped open the foil packet. Reached down for his cock—

His breath hissed out. "Love it when you touch me."

So she just had to touch more. To stroke. To caress.

"Put on the condom."

She rolled it over him.

"Ride me, baby."

Her knees pushed against the mattress on either side of his hips. Her hands pressed to his chest as she lifted up her body, then slowly eased down on him. One inch at a time. There were a whole lot of inches to handle.

And every slow glide had her heart racing faster.

"Don't fucking tease."

Was that what she was doing? She didn't think so. She was taking him. Just slowly.

He thrust hard. Deep. Settled all the way inside and it felt *amazing*.

A throaty moan slipped from her.

"You're the most beautiful thing I've ever seen." Rough. Savage. "And you are mine."

She stared at him. "You're mine." Only fair, wasn't it?

Then...as their gazes held, something seemed to break. Control? Was that it? Because suddenly, she was lifting her hips and shoving them down in a frantic rhythm. His hands were clamped around her hips, and he was moving her up and down, up and down, even as he pistoned his hips against her.

There was no slow. There was no careful. Her orgasm slammed into Ali with so much force that everything around her seemed to dim. Everything but Jinx. He was her only focus. His bright eyes were blazing. Staring straight at her. Seeming to stare *into* her. There was no hiding. No shielding from him. She came so hard that her body quaked.

He kept thrusting while her sex contracted around him. Kept driving deep until she was a limp mass on top of him, then he shot upward. Tumbled her back. Drove even harder into her. Her legs were spread wide, her hands had fallen to the bed, and he took. And took.

When he came, the whole bed seemed to shudder around them.

His hands slammed down on either side of her head as he loomed over her. His eyes were lit with an emotion that she couldn't quite name.

After that explosive pleasure, she'd expected him to appear sated.

He didn't. If anything, he looked hungry for more.

"A thousand damn times more," he gritted out. "Always." Then he took her mouth again.

***

Sunlight crept through the blinds. Ali cracked open one eye. She didn't even remember when she'd fallen asleep. The night had been...busy.

Each time that she'd thought they were done, Jinx had reached for her again. She'd reached back for him just as eagerly.

Her head turned. His arm was still around her. Thrown over her stomach and his fingers curled to her side. Holding her, even though she'd assured him that she had no plans to disappear.

Not this time.

For a moment, she studied him. His dark hair was tousled, and his long, thick lashes covered the brilliance of his eyes. Stubble slid over his jaw, and the stubble just made him look all the sexier. The sheets and bedding were shoved down to his hips, and as her gaze slid down over him...

Someone sure looks good in the morning.

No, actually, he always looked good.

Carefully, she lifted his hand, his arm, and shimmied from beneath his hold. She slid off the bed and darted for a nearby chair. He'd put a robe for her on the back of that chair. A lush, white robe that she pulled around her body.

She had plenty of clothes available in the nearby closet. Apparently, Jinx had taken the liberty of picking up some things for her the previous day. He'd assured her that everything was in her size. Workout clothes, jeans, shirts, underwear, even shoes—the man had covered everything.

She *could* have just brought along her own clothes, if he'd told her of his plans. Not that she was gonna turn away the new gear. He'd dropped his little bombshell about having everything she needed at one of the, ah, temporary resting points they'd had during the night.

"You are adorable when you tiptoe in the mornings."

She spun around. "You're awake."

"Um. Was awake the moment you touched my hand and tried to flee from my bed."

"I wasn't fleeing." Her hands shoved into the robe's pockets. "I was being considerate. Thoughtful. Letting you sleep." Now her lips pursed. "After your big night, I thought you might need to rest."

He sat up. Laughed.

His rich laugh sent a surge of heat through her. *Down, girl.* After last night, she should have been sated.

Except...

I want a thousand more, too.

"I-I was going for a run." The words rushed out of her. "You mentioned that I had workout gear here, so I thought I'd get dressed and do my morning exercise."

His eyes narrowed.

"I always start each day with a run. Helps me clear my head."

He rose from the bed. *Wow.* Hello, morning woo—

"You know you should vary your routine. If someone is watching you—and we damn well know someone is—having your schedule down gives him plenty of chances to attack."

She would not just stare at his dick. Wait, she *was* just staring. Her gaze flew up. "I vary my jogging path. Always do. Don't go the same way more than once in a week."

"But if you run first thing, he knows that. He could be waiting outside for you." Jinx strode toward the chest of drawers and pulled out a pair of black jogging shorts. "He could be waiting for you right now."

It was barely dawn. "The beach will be deserted. If he's out there, I'll certainly have plenty of time to see him coming."

"You mean *we'll* have plenty of time. Because I'll be with you. Bait, remember?"

Her lips tightened. "I would prefer that you stopped calling yourself that."

His gaze raked over her. "Are you going to run in that robe? Sexy choice."

"Smartass. I will be changing."

"Excellent. You change, and I'll wait for you outside. *After* I brush my teeth. Got to have fresh breath for running, especially if we're halfway down the beach and you get so overwhelmed by my body that you just jump me. When you throw yourself into my arms, I have got to have fresh breath." He headed for the bathroom.

Ali just shook her head.

Jinx.

What was she going to do with him?

And a little voice whispered...*Keep him, forever.*

***

She wanted to run at the crack of dawn? Jeez. Why? Who *chose* to do things like that? Jinx would have much preferred to drag Ali back into bed and go for round twenty-four or, well, whatever round they were on. He'd stopped counting.

Yet, after being pretty much insatiable for her last night, he was trying to show Ali that he had a little control.

Some.

Maybe.

Hell. Where she was concerned, he had more like five percent control? If that?

His running shoes kicked up a little sand as he paced in front of the beach house. Ali would be down soon, he knew that, but he'd gone out first because he wanted to make sure—

"Don't fucking move."

Because he'd wanted to make sure there were no unexpected surprises waiting for him. Jinx stifled a sigh.

Good morning, surprise number one.

The low voice snarled, "Put your hands up!" A voice that was coming from the right, on the side of the beach house that faced the Gulf.

Jinx took note of the position and had to give the guy points. He'd been hiding with his body pressed against the house. When someone looked down from above—as Jinx had done—he hadn't been able to see the man.

"If I put my hands up," Jinx said as he did *not* put up his hands, "then I'll be moving. You just very clearly told me that I was not to move. You should make up your mind and give better instructions."

"Asshole! Put your hands up! I want to make sure you don't have a weapon!"

Jinx laughed. "I'm wearing running shorts. No shirt. Where the hell would I hide a weapon?" A deliberate choice. He'd wanted anyone watching to think that he was vulnerable. It had seemed like the perfect time to step up his bait game.

Ali might not like the word *bait*, but it was exactly what he was, and it seemed his strategy had worked.

"Face me!"

Jinx turned toward him. He expected to come face to face with the bastard who'd been making Ali's life hell—

"What the fuck?" Jinx frowned at the kid who was gripping a gun. A *shaking* gun. The guy barely looked eighteen. "Who the hell are you?"

"Someone who won't be forgotten." Sweat covered his face.

That was a lot of sweat. *How long had he been waiting near the house?*

"You're a p-problem," he told Jinx, the gun bobbing up and down. "One I'll take care of, and then he'll see how good I am."

Jinx heard a door creak open from above. Then the pad of steps on the stairs that led down to the beach. "Ali," Jinx snarled. "Get back inside. *Now!*"

She stilled, but he didn't hear the sound of retreating footsteps.

"Go back inside!" the kid yelled. He swiped his free hand over his sweaty forehead. "This doesn't concern you, lady!"

Wait...it didn't?

Jinx tilted his head. "Who are you?"

A sniff. "The guy who is solving a problem for the boss, that's who I am. I heard him telling you to stay away. He didn't want you in his place. Didn't want you anywhere near him. Then he came here last night, and I know he must have put the fear of God into you—"

Shit. This wasn't the perp they were after. This wasn't Ali's stalker. This was one of Ramsey's wannabe thugs who thought he could get an in with the boss if he eliminated a problem.

I'm the problem.

"But I'm gonna do more than make you scared," the punk promised. "I am going to end you."

"The hell you are." From Ali. Hard and unyielding. Jinx hadn't heard her descend the remaining steps, but her voice had come from right behind the perp.

Jinx had forgotten how very light she could be on her feet.

"I have a gun pointed at your back," Ali informed the jerk in a steely voice. "If you don't drop your weapon, right now, I will shoot you. This close, there is no way I will miss."

Fear flashed in the kid's eyes.

"The bullet will go straight into your spine," Ali continued grimly.

Jinx took a quick step forward.

"It will sever your spinal cord. You'll be on the ground in moments—"

"Gah!" A guttural scream broke from the punk as he started to whirl toward Ali. Only he *hadn't* dropped his gun as she'd instructed.

There was no way he'd be pointing that weapon at Ali. Jinx launched at him. His body slammed into the kid's, and they hit the sand.

CHAPTER ELEVEN

Jinx yanked the gun from the kid and tossed it toward the stairs. Ali grabbed it because—yep, she'd been lying. She had no weapon. As he'd suspected. There'd been no time for her to go back into the house and snag the gun up there. She *had* kicked off her shoes and tiptoed down so she could get the drop on the would-be shooter.

Now Jinx had him pinned to the ground. Jinx was drawing back his fist to plow it into the guy's face—

His very *young* face. Jinx hesitated.

"That can't be him," Ali said as she gripped the gun and hurried forward.

"This guy isn't your stalker." Rage simmered in Jinx's voice. "He's a wannabe for Ramsey. Thought he'd break through the ranks if he did something to impress the boss." Instead of slamming his fist into the jerk's face, Jinx grabbed the kid's shirtfront and hauled the asshat to his feet. "You have no idea what a fatal mistake you just made."

The punk twisted and squirmed, but Jinx didn't let him go.

"I-I was doing the boss a favor! When I was sweeping up, I heard him say you weren't to come around again! Then he came after—after you—"

Jinx let out a disgusted sigh. "Did he ever say for anyone to so much as touch me?"

A negative shake of the guy's sandy hair.

"Okay, genius, if he didn't say for anyone to touch me, why the hell would you think he wanted someone to kill me?"

"I was just gonna shoot you in the leg. Maybe the arm. Not kill you."

Jinx's gaze drifted to Ali, but he didn't let go of his prey. "You think this kid can aim for shit?"

Ali shook her head.

"Yeah. Me, too." His stare slid back to his prey. "Your hand was shaking so hard I thought a bullet would come flying out at any moment, jackass, and you were pointing the weapon at my heart."

"I've never shot anyone before!"

Are you kidding me? This was just getting worse and worse. "Why do I get to be lucky victim number one for you?"

Jinx saw Ali examining the gun. "Uh, Jinx?" she called.

But he'd turned his glare back on the kid. "You've never shot anyone. And you thought you'd just start with big game?"

"Jinx." Ali cleared her throat. "It's not even loaded."

"*What?*" Both Jinx and his prey whipped their heads to look at her.

"Not loaded," Ali repeated. She frowned at the boy. "You didn't even check for bullets?"

"I bought it last night. Figured it came with them?"

Save me from idiots. "No, guns and bullets are not always a package deal," Jinx informed him. "Here's some advice. The next time you bring a gun to a battle, make sure it's loaded."

Hell. The kid looked as if he might pass out.

"Better advice," Jinx snapped. "*Don't* bring the gun in the first place. What are you? Eighteen? Nineteen?"

His thin shoulders straightened. "Sixteen."

Sixteen. Rage burned in Jinx. "Why the hell is Ramsey employing kids to do his dirty work?"

"He's not, he's—look, he said I could clean up the bar for some extra cash, okay? I wanted to impress him. He's a big deal, you know."

Jinx could only shake his head. "This is not going to make Ramsey happy. You have read the scene very, very wrong." He blew out a breath. The sun was rising higher as the waves rushed to the shore. "Get your dumbass back home. Get in school. Go tell your mama you love her."

The teen's pointed chin rose. "I don't have a home. Or a mama. So why would I go back? Now get your damn hands off me before I—" He broke off.

Jinx waited.

And waited some more.

"Before you...what?" Jinx finally prompted, truly curious about what this threat would be.

"Before I mess you up!"

Jinx quirked one brow. "I would love to see you try."

"Jinx," Ali warned. She shook her head and mouthed, *No.*

"Just call the cops already!" the wannabe criminal cried out.

"Oh, no, that would be too easy. I'm not letting them handle you. I'll let Ramsey settle things. We'll see what happens when he finds out you went off book and didn't follow orders."

The kid in his grip started shaking all the more.

"Jinx, stop playing with him."

Did it look like he was playing? "It's called teaching a life lesson. He needs it." He lowered his voice. "The next time you aim a gun at someone, be prepared that you might be the one to die. Because as easily as I am holding you now..."

The boy's Adam's apple bobbed.

"I could kill you in a heartbeat. You wouldn't even have time to scream."

"Oh, God!" The kid swayed, seemingly on the verge of passing out.

Jinx smiled at him. "Good talk, am I right?"

***

"Maybe the punk kid was the one who sabotaged your ride." War stared down at the street below.

The would-be thug had been hauled away, and Jinx was certain that Ramsey would deal with him. *Sixteen.* No family. No home...

I was you once, kid. Except Jinx hadn't tried to get the jump on a much bigger, tougher bastard...with an empty gun.

Though if the kid *had* used a loaded weapon...
It could have proven to be a fatal mistake.

"Jinx?" War prompted. They were in his office above Armageddon. "Did you hear me? Do you think the kid could be the one who screwed with your brakes?"

"It's a possibility. I'm sure Ramsey will get to the bottom of things and let us know." And about Ramsey...

Jinx steepled his fingers beneath his chin as he studied War. Jinx was in the desk chair, leaning back, propping his feet on the edge of the desk as he assessed his friend. "You and Odin think you're extra clever, huh? Knowing my business but not saying a word."

War shrugged. "Was waiting on *you* to say the word. Figured when you wanted us to know, you'd tell us."

"Uh, huh. You just want to flex that you're good at uncovering secrets. I get it."

"I am a PI," War replied, voice modest.

"You're a pain in the ass." A pain who was also a damn good PI. "Right now, though, I really want to know why the hell you insisted I come up here and talk to you, *without Ali*, when you know my whole goal is to stay close to her." It was step one of his plan. *Stay close to Ali.*

"Relax."

For real? *Uh, no.*

"Odin is at the beach house with her. He's not going to let anything happen to her. And, before you get all extra pissy, know that I'm not the one who wanted this meeting. If I'd had my way, you'd still be close to her."

Wait...what?

The door to the office swung open.

"I didn't schedule the meeting. *He* did," War added softly.

Jinx didn't move. He kept his feet propped on the desk. Kept his hands steepled beneath his chin as the SOB he'd never hoped to see again stood in the doorway.

Landon Hatcher wore gleaming loafers, pressed khakis, and a spiffy polo. He also had a wary expression on his pretty-boy face. An expression that said he was more than a little bit concerned about the reception he'd be getting.

Good. The man wasn't a total idiot. *Oh, wait, he is.* "I can give you a two-minute head start," Jinx offered as he considered the matter.

Landon's jaw tightened. "We need to talk."

Jinx reevaluated. "One minute. Just one. Because I'm feeling pissy." That had been War's word, and he decided it fit. "I had a gun shoved at me today. Granted, it wasn't loaded, but it still pissed me off." Slowly, deliberately, he lowered his feet to the floor. "One minute, Landing Zone." He deliberately used the nickname that he *knew* Landon hated. "Then I'm kicking your ass."

"You can't threaten me." But Landon's expression had tightened. "I'm your boss!"

"Didn't you get the memo?" Jinx jerked his thumb toward War. "I'm working for him now. Sure, the pay is crap, but I happen to like him about a million times more than I like you." He rose. "No, come to think of it, I just don't like you at all."

"It wasn't my place to tell you," Landon said quickly. "How would I know that Ali was going to share with you? How would I know that she'd want to share anything personal at all with you about—"

"I offered you a one-minute head start. You should have taken it." He stalked forward. His hands were flexing and clenching. Flexing. Clenching. He came to a stop right in front of the bastard he'd dubbed Landing Zone long ago...because Landon Hatcher never got into the middle of battle. He was one of those pencil pushers who liked to stay back in the safe spots.

You'd find him at the end of a mission. Waiting to take credit.

Grinning his smug ass off from the Landing Zone as the chopper descended.

Jinx swung up his fist.

Landon flinched and squeezed his eyes shut. Jinx hadn't actually connected with the guy, tempting though the idea certainly was. Instead, he'd stopped his swing at the last moment because Landon wasn't even trying to fight back. "Are you freaking kidding me?"

Landon opened the eyes he'd shut. "I...thought I deserved at least one hit."

"You deserve a whole lot more than that. *Ali was in danger!*"

"Ali has worked ops for a long time. She's used to danger." Landon's gaze darted to the fist that still lingered near his face. "If you aren't going to punch me, would you please lower your hand?"

He didn't lower it, not yet. "I'm thinking about punching you. Over and over again."

A wince from Landon. Then a beseeching glance toward War. "You're just gonna stand there?"

"Yes."

Good to know War had Jinx's back. *As always.* "He's pissed, too," Jinx informed Landon. "See, we both happen to *like* Ali. And if someone—someone like, oh, say her *handler*—had bothered to mention to us that she was in danger, we would have moved in to protect her. We protect our own, you know that. Ali is part of our team. We'd do anything for her."

Landon took a quick step away from Jinx's fist. The space seemed to make him brave because he gave a little laugh. "Right. Like you want to protect her because she's part of the *team.*"

What was that supposed to mean? Jinx lowered his fist. *Don't beat the crap out of him...not yet, anyway. Get your intel, then you can kick his ass.*

"I was there that night," Landon revealed. He smoothed his shirt. It was a freaking wrinkle-free shirt. Why did he think it needed smoothing? "Don't have to be a genius to figure out what was happening in that cheap motel room with you two."

Every muscle in Jinx's body tightened. "I have never liked you." Just so they were clear. "You've never stepped away from the safety of your job, never gone into the field to help anyone, but you love taking credit for the work we do." There were plenty of other reasons why Landon enraged Jinx, but he couldn't go into them, not with War watching him.

"I wasn't supposed to be in the field." A sniff. "Someone had to stay back, you know that. I got the orders from above. I delivered them to you all. We—"

"Can we get back to Ali?" War demanded. "Because I've got shit to do and listening to you ramble isn't high on my priority list."

"Thank you," Jinx murmured. "Couldn't have said it better myself." His gaze swept over Landon in disgust. "You watched us at the motel."

"I wasn't *watching* you. Not like I'm some kind of voyeur." A nervous laugh slid from him.

Jinx shook his head. "Don't." The only warning he'd give. Landon had no clue how close he was to getting that straight nose of his broken.

Landon wet his lips. "I had an assignment for Ali. When I saw you leave, I knew it was safe to contact her."

The creep really had just been lurking outside? *Red flag.* "Then you took her away from me."

Another nervous laugh. "Come on. It's you. Figured you were done."

"With Ali? *Never.*"

Landon's gray eyes widened. "You...you don't make permanent commitments to anyone. Ali wasn't looking for that, either. It was a hookup, then you both moved on. That's one of the reasons why I didn't tell you about what was happening with her. Didn't think it mattered to you."

"That's where you were exceptionally wrong. It matters." His feet were braced apart, his hands clenched at his sides. "Ali matters a great deal to me. Just as I matter to her."

Landon's shock was clear.

"We're making plans for a future together," Jinx continued silkily. "So how about you stop being a dick and you offer me congratulations?"

"C-congratulations?"

"Yes, because Ali and I are planning to get married."

Landon's eyes bulged. "*What?*"

"Married." He savored the word. "You know, when two people swear to be together forever and ever. That whole bit. I think I'll propose to Ali soon. Figure we'll have a house full of dogs and kids and go to lots of PTA meetings."

Landon's bulging eyes darted to War. "He's joking."

War shrugged.

The bulging eyes flickered back to Jinx. "You're joking." A little more confident. "You're not looking to settle down."

Not looking. Already have.

"And the PTA?" Landon's lips twisted. "No way. But you had me going there..."

"Really? Because it looks like you're standing in front of me," *going nowhere,* "and you still haven't told me why the hell you called this meeting when I should be with my soon to-be fiancée right now." Jinx tapped his foot meaningfully. "How about you get on with it?"

Landon shook his head. "Right. Ah...*right.*" His shoulders squared. "Well, now that Ali has brought you up to date on the events happening in her life..."

Events? That's how he talks about the stalking?

"I thought you'd want to know what sort of material I've managed to uncover so far. Obviously, the subject is obsessed with Ali. He's keeping a very close watch on her, and the last three times that she's switched the location of her home, he's followed her immediately."

"Hold up." Jinx stopped tapping his foot. "The last three times," he repeated. "She's already had to move *three times* since this jerk started harassing her?"

"I-I thought you'd been told..." Landon clamped his lips together. Seemed to gather his thoughts. Then asked, "What *do* you know about the situation with Ali?"

Jinx didn't respond. Because he was staring at a man who happened to be very, very high on his suspect list.

Someone in the organization. Check.

Someone who knew how to play dirty. Double check. As far as Jinx was concerned, Landing Zone was damn dirty.

Someone who had worked with Ali. Someone who knew how she worked. Three checks equaled a man looking extra damn guilty. And the fact that Landon had just popped up out of the blue?

"Come on." Landon ran a hand through his hair. An agitated gesture for a guy normally much more controlled. "If you don't work with me, you're just hurting *her*."

"I would never hurt Ali." *But would you?* "How did you know she was down here?"

Landon blinked. "Excuse me?"

"How did you know she was here?" And…
"Why are *you* here?"

"I knew she was here because I've been trying
to keep tabs on her. Ali is my friend, too, you
know. Not like I just want her to wind up dead."
What could have been real heat entered Landon's
voice. "I get that you all think I'm heartless…"

"Not arguing." Jinx risked a glance at War.
"Are we arguing?"

"I don't think we are," War assured him. "I
was just sitting here, listening all quiet and
patient-like."

Landon growled. "On missions, I have
actually watched your backs. I care about the
people who work with me. I *care* about Ali."

How much?

"I've been digging. I've been trying to help
her. She believes this guy is someone that works—
or *worked*—in the government, and I think she
may be right." He motioned to War and Jinx.
"We're talking about someone who handled the
same kind of cases that you did. Someone with a
skill set that makes him exceedingly dangerous."
His tone turned wistful as he said, "Before all of
this happened, Ali was amazing in the field. She
was the light touch, the tech expert we needed,
and the woman could always play a character so
easily. She could blink and nearly become
someone else. Her skills were exceedingly useful."

And you used her plenty, didn't you? "If you
have a name, you should be meeting with Ali right
now and telling her about him. I am *still* not
getting why you insisted I meet with you here,
without Ali."

A muscle flexed in Landon's weak jaw. Then he surprised Jinx by surging forward.

You're seriously coming at me?

"Because I am trying to protect you!"

He was wasting Jinx's time, that's what he was—

"She never told you about her past, did she?" Landon's gaze cut to War. "Not either of you."

No, they hadn't exactly shared deep, dark secrets. Except for last night, when he'd told her one of his secrets. But Jinx didn't care that Ali hadn't revealed all to him. How could he expect her to share her past when he'd been hiding the truth about himself, too?

"You and War were brought onto the ops team because of the work that you did when you were enlisted. You each had special strengths that made you perfect for the job."

Right. War had been a SEAL, and Jinx had spent a little time in the air. Not that he talked about that service much. He preferred to think of it as his ace in the hole. And, not to brag, but he was pretty much the best damn fighter pilot in the—

Landing Zone exhaled on a long sigh. "You both joined the group because you wanted to protect your country. You were the good guys, doing work to help others."

Not one hundred percent true, and Landon knew it. At the end, Jinx had made a deal to help Ramsey...

"That wasn't the case with the woman you call Ali." He crossed the room. Stared out the window.

"She isn't former military, though you both figured that out early on."

Sure, they had. The same way he'd pegged the new bartender as being current law enforcement. Some things, you could just see. Former military personnel carried themselves differently. They *acted* differently in high stress situations.

The first case he'd worked with Ali...

She'd been terrified. But working damn hard to hide her fear.

"Ali was brought in because she had special skills."

"We know she's a tech whiz," War said with a wave of his hand. "How about you just get on with the story? We don't have all day."

Landon's lips thinned. "Prodigy is a better term. She's quite gifted. She's also...quite the criminal."

Jinx raised one eyebrow. "You don't say?"

Obviously, that wasn't the reaction Landon expected. His hands immediately went to his hips. "Yes, I do say. That's how Ali came to the attention of my previous supervisor. She'd broken the law. Numerous times. She—and her partner—were given options. Jail or—"

"Or they could work out their time." A very similar deal to what he'd been given for his brother, only things were a wee bit more complex when it came to Ramsey. "How old was she back then?"

"Seventeen."

Fuck. "And what did her parents have to say about this?"

"They didn't want their daughter going to jail. They encouraged her to do the right thing."

Ali had never mentioned parents to him. He got a twist in his gut, a foreshadowing that something very, very bad had happened.

"Ali took the deal. Discovered that she had quite a knack for the work. She did it for years without a problem."

War closed in on them. "You mentioned her partner..."

A jerky nod. "Yes, I did."

"Who was the partner?" Jinx wanted to know.

"Ali's boyfriend."

His shoulders tensed.

"He took the deal, too. For a time, he was quite good as well. For a time." Landon rocked back onto the soles of his feet. "Then, I suppose you could say he...went off the rails."

"Define that," Jinx ordered. "Explicitly."

"He vanished. Disappeared in the middle of an op. Only he took a great deal of intel with him. Intel that we now know has been sold to enemies around the world. He appears to have been working as a mole for an extended period of time before he pulled his disappearing act."

"Does Ali know this?" Jinx wanted to know. His instincts said she didn't.

A shake of Landon's head. "We made sure they were never paired together. It was decided that it was better for them to stay apart, that was even a condition of the offer that was made to them. And I believe they complied. Or, at least, it would appear that Ali did." He cleared his throat. "There were...a few times when I learned that

Cyrus had acquired Ali's location and gone to watch her."

"Watch her?" Jinx repeated as rage burned in him. *Cyrus.* The name had him seeing red.

A miserable nod. "He didn't make contact. At least, I didn't think he had, so I saw no point in telling Ali about the situation back then."

Jinx glanced at War. "Are you listening to this crap?"

"Listening and not believing Landon could be so idiotic." Disgusted, War snapped, "Her ex is stalking her, and you don't *tell* Ali?"

"It wasn't stalking. Or at least, I didn't think it was at the time. When I questioned him in those days, Cyrus assured me that he just wanted to make certain Ali was safe—"

"Fucking moron," Jinx growled.

Landon's chin jerked up. "We needed him. You don't understand just what the man can do."

"Let's see…" Jinx tapped his chin. "Ali told me her last target was murdered, and the killer left zero evidence behind. He disabled the security for miles and stumped all the authorities." A nod. "Yes, trust me, I think I am understanding quite clearly what he can do. Ali might have just been an asset that you used for tech skills and undercover missions, but this Cyrus—he was different, wasn't he? You used him for plenty more."

"Cyrus had an aptitude," Landon muttered. "Not like it was my decision. All of this was in place long before I arrived. I just followed the orders I was given." He pointed to War and Jinx. "Basically, Cyrus is a combination of you two. He has lethal skills that were honed by our government, and he has Ali's tech gifts. He was perfect."

"Oh, yes, perfect," Jinx agreed with a shake of his head. "Right up until the point when he went rogue and started killing people and hunting Ali. Right up until then, he was just an absolute rock star."

Another loud clearing of Landon's throat. "Yes, until then...though, we do not have concrete proof that he is the man behind—"

"Why the hell haven't you told Ali?" Jinx cut through Landon's words. "Why are you standing here telling us instead of her?" This bastard was driving him crazy. "Ali's got a stalker. A man who has *killed*. You seem to know exactly who he is, only instead of telling Ali this rather important intel, you are deliberately keeping her in the dark. Makes zero sense to me." He shouldered past Landon, a *hard* hit with his shoulder against the other man's body because he was done with this BS.

"It makes sense..." War's low voice stopped him just as Jinx was about to storm from the office. "If Landon doesn't trust Ali."

Jinx swung back around. "What in the hell? Are you kidding me?" War had better be kidding. Sure, he wasn't normally a kidder, but this time, *he'd better be.* "Ali is the victim! She needs protection. She needs her team. She needs—"

"If Ali finds out the identity of this man, there is concern—from my supervisors," Landon rushed to clarify. "There is concern from them that she might...join him."

"Join him?" Jinx's temples throbbed. "As in...what? Cross over to the dark side?" He laughed, but the sound was mocking. "This is Ali. She doesn't go dark. She doesn't do shit like that."

"She loved him when she was seventeen. Loved him so much that she broke the law for him, several times. I believe that Ali didn't have contact with him when she started working for the government, but I have no actual proof of that. She's very good, and if Ali wanted to hide her interactions with him, I suspect that she could have done so."

He wasn't believing this—

"And Ali *says* that she is being stalked but...again, I don't have concrete proof. I do know that the target who was killed on her last mission—he should have been safe. *Ali* knew how to get to him. Ali was the one with that intel. And then, in a blink, he was dead."

War swore. Low and viciously.

Jinx didn't say a word. He was too busy choking down rage.

"It's a possibility that I—and my supervisors—could not overlook." Landon's spine was as stiff as his voice. "So we thought it prudent to wait and watch to see what would happen next."

Jinx charged back to him. "Ali was being terrorized. Instead of helping her, you left her on her own because you thought you could pull in your missing agent." Yeah, he could connect the dots, no problem. *She'd* been the lure. "Didn't matter the danger to her, you thought you could use her to get back what you'd lost."

"*I* did not specifically lose him," Landon blustered.

He wanted to knock out the asshole. "You still want to use her." *Now* it all made sense. "That's why you're here telling me and War this crap. You think we'll side with you. You think we'll say, sure, yes, let's take down this mysterious big, bad wolf. You think we'll help you—"

"You *did* work for the organization—"

"Go screw yourself. Long and hard. Or short and fast. I don't really care which. Just go screw yourself. I am helping Ali. I'm telling her about this Cyrus jackass. I am not hanging her out to dry."

"Then you'll be hanging your brother out to dry, Jinx. I've learned that the Feds are about to close in on him. They have enough evidence to send Ramsey away for a very long time."

The throbbing in Jinx's temples got worse. A thousand times worse.

"Of course, I could help out with that. I mean, my supervisors could. They are the ones who told me to come to you with this offer. You work with me—keep this quiet for a little bit longer—and your brother will be given that second shot that you wanted. He'll have to make some concessions, you know. Provide evidence, turn on his associates. But we both know a suitable arrangement can be reached...and all you have to do is—"

Lie to Ali.

Turn on Ali.

Use Ali.

Fuck.

CHAPTER TWELVE

"Tell me again why the hell we're doing this." Odin's face was locked in especially tense lines, and his voice had gone even harder than normal.

Ali sighed. "I told you that you did not need to tag along with me."

"I'm supposed to be your protection for the day. You know that."

What she *knew* was that Jinx had left her high and dry at the fancy beach house. She'd been less than pleased, to put it mildly. "He and War cut me out of my own case."

Odin didn't deny the charge. "A development came up. You know Jinx will update you as soon as—"

A door opened beside them. A door that led to the shady bar that was owned by Ramsey.

"What in the hell are you doing here?" A rough, angry voice.

And it's the devil himself.

"I'm trying to figure out why we're here, too," Odin muttered.

Ali squared her shoulders and turned to face the man who stood glaring in the doorway of the bar. "Ramsey! Just the person I was hoping to see."

His gaze tracked over her, then to Odin. Then back to her. "Where is Jinx?"

Cutting me out of the case. But I have some work to do myself so... "You know, around." She motioned vaguely. "I was hoping to catch you at a non-busy time." She'd figured the place would be deserted so early in the day.

His eyes narrowed on her. "How the hell did you know I was even here?"

Technically, she hadn't known. She *had* planned for a small bit of B&E in order to get inside and do a little recon work. But since the bar wasn't as empty as she'd hoped, she'd settle for talking to Ramsey.

"Told you this was a bad idea," Odin grumbled.

"It's not nice to say 'I told you so,'" Ali chided him. "We've been over this before." She didn't let her gaze shift from Ramsey. Now that she studied him closely, she did notice some similarities to Jinx. Their eyes were different—his were dark while Jinx had that bright, bright blue. Same hair, though. Thick and black. Same hard jaw. Same—

"There a reason you're staring so hard at me?"

Her chin notched. "I'd like to speak privately with you."

"Yeah, that's cute. See...Jinx made it clear I wasn't supposed to do *anything* with you. Not supposed to look at you, not supposed to touch you, not supposed to let any of my big, bad world near you." He shrugged. "So how about you load up with Odin, and get the hell off my property?"

"Good idea," Odin rumbled. "Let's go, Ali."

She didn't go. "I need to speak with you, Ramsey. There are some facts that I think you need to be aware of."

He didn't even look mildly curious. "I'm generally aware of most facts."

How wonderful for you. "You're not aware of this, and you're not aware of what Jinx has been risking."

His eyelids flickered. His expression didn't change, but she suddenly felt the sharp surge of his attention.

That did it. Now he'll talk to me.

"Odin, don't take it personally, but keep your ass out here," Ramsey directed. "As for you..." He pointed at her. "Five minutes. That's all you get."

"Thanks ever so much for the gracious invitation," Ali murmured as she hurried forward and entered the bar.

"It wasn't gracious."

"I know."

***

"Well?" Landon pushed. "Do we have a deal?"

"This is bullshit!" War burst out before Jinx could say a word. "You don't threaten Jinx. And you don't blackmail him."

Landon rocked forward. "Blackmail is an ugly word."

"Yeah, and it's an ugly deed," War charged. "So how about you stop that shit and get out of my place?"

Jinx's phone vibrated. He pulled it out of his pocket and glanced at the screen. Just in case it was about Ali or it *was* Ali texting him—

But the text wasn't from Ali. It was from Ramsey.

Why the hell is your girlfriend at my bar?

Jinx stared at the text. Shook his head.

"No?" Landon said, sounding stunned. "You're telling me that we have no deal, Jinx? You're really going to let you brother be thrown to the wolves...or, in this case, thrown into a prison cell for the rest of his life? You're going to do that when you have the power to save him?"

To save Ramsey, all Jinx had to do was put Ali at risk.

He looked up at Landon. Landon had pulled out his phone.

"I can make one phone call to protect him," Landon promised him. "All you have to do is say the word."

Jinx swallowed. "This Cyrus...you want him that badly?"

"So badly that I would give your brother a deal? Yes. Though, please note, it's not that *I* want him." His face darkened. "I'm following orders from above. This is above my pay grade, and— look, it's not personal. I *like* Ali. I want her safe, too, and believe me, I will do everything I can to help her. But we need to spring this trap. She's our best bet of catching Cyrus." His fingers slid over the surface of his phone. "Do we have a deal?"

***

"Are you as bad as they say?"

The bar seemed big, cavernous, without any of the usual people inside. Ali sat on a stool while Ramsey stood near her. His arms were folded over his chest, and he certainly looked less than pleased to see her.

"Worse," he assured her. "I'm much, much worse than everyone says."

She considered the situation. "If that's the case, then why is Jinx working so hard to save you?"

His expression didn't change, but she could almost feel his surprise. "What are you talking about?"

"You may think Jinx turned his back on you, but he didn't. He's always fought for you. Maybe you need to cut him some slack and stop being such an asshole." Because she didn't like that this guy was hurting Jinx. Family or not, he needed to get his act together.

Ramsey squinted at her. "Did you come here today just so you could tell me—to my face—that I'm an asshole?"

She tapped her chin. "That is one of the reasons. You've hurt Jinx. It's not fair for you to do that."

Now he appeared almost...fascinated. "Do tell me more."

Her lips thinned. She couldn't tell Ramsey that Jinx had taken plenty of those dangerous cases *for* him. That story wasn't hers to share. But she could say... "Jinx is one of the best men I've ever met. I've never seen him turn his back on anyone. He fights hard, and he doesn't give up on the people who matter to him."

"Um…" He turned his back and took a few steps away from her. "If that's the case, then why didn't you go to him when your little problem first developed?"

Her chest squeezed. "What do you know what about my problem?"

"I know it impacts my brother, so I did some digging. Asked around in the right places, or, in the wrong ones, as it were." He looked back at her. "It would be helpful if you stopped pretending with me. I know you're a very intelligent woman. You'd have to be in order for the government to make deals so that your crimes vanished. They wanted you very badly, didn't they?"

She licked her lips. *This is another reason why I came here.* "Fine. I'll stop pretending." She jumped off the stool. She didn't want to waste her five minutes. "I figured that once you knew Jinx was working with me—and once you learned about the sabotage of his motorcycle—that you'd get involved. I knew you would research me, turn up my past, and then I knew you'd also start digging to see just who had dared to threaten your brother." She bit her lip and couldn't help but glance around. "Speaking of threats to your brother, what happened to the kid who had the empty gun?"

"He's been handled." Clipped. Cold.

She bounded toward him. Grabbed his arm and spun him fully toward her. "You didn't kill him!"

He looked down at her hand. "Does it matter?"

"Yes! It matters! It matters a whole lot, and you know it! He was just like you and Jinx. Just like—" She stopped before she said *me*.

"I don't remember Jinx ever pulling a gun on anyone at that age." He was still staring at her hand. "He was the one who went off to be all he could be. Wanted to save the world."

"He wanted to save *you*." *He still does*.

Ramsey's gaze rose to her face.

"You're the one who left him," she added.

"Because I wanted to save him." Soft.

She let him go. "And the reason you still push him away?"

His lips pulled down. "Not much has changed since those days. My reason is the same." He looked at his wrist. At a watch that wasn't there. "I'm sure five minutes have passed. I've learned nothing important or new from this conversation."

She wasn't leaving. "You dug into my past because you're worried about Jinx. You also immediately sent word through your contacts to learn about who might be targeting Jinx because he's helping me."

He neither confirmed nor denied her suspicions.

Whatever. She didn't need his response—she knew this was all true. "I want to know what you've learned about the stalker."

"It's only been a few hours. How could I have learned a lot by now? You overestimate my skills."

Fine. Maybe he didn't have new info...yet. "When you get intel, I want you to share it with me. And with Jinx. This guy that we're after—he's not your typical criminal."

"*I* am not your typical criminal."

He wasn't getting what she was saying. Her hold tightened on him. "This man may have all the same training that Jinx has—that Odin has. He's not some street thug."

"Now you are just insulting me." His brows rose. "Do *I* look like some street thug?"

"This man has access to classified intel. Intel on me. On Jinx."

"And me? Is that what you're implying?"

She was implying it, yes. Even if her stalker did not know that Jinx and Ramsey were related, he would have been able to access what the government *did* have on file about Ramsey. "He'll know your weak spots, just as he knows ours. If you have something that makes you vulnerable, he will go after that."

His gaze became shuttered. "It's time for you to go."

Dammit. "Don't go after him without me and Jinx! That's what I'm saying! That's the point of this visit! Jinx cares about you, and if something happens to you, he'll be gutted."

Ramsey backed up a step. "*You* care about Jinx."

She'd never denied that. "So do you. Now how about we work together so that everyone can stay safe?"

Silence. Ali held her breath because it seemed that he might be considering her offer—

"I'm not much of a team player."

He was refusing her. Seriously? "Why not?"

"I don't play well with others."

"You are an asshole."

He smiled, a smile that reminded her far too much of Jinx. "See, I was right. You *did* come here just because you wanted to call me an asshole to my face."

Loud knocking shook the front door.

"Ah, looks like Odin is growing impatient," Ramsey noted. "Better go and find your teammate."

She started to hurry past him.

The door swung open before she could reach it. Odin was there, all right, but he wasn't alone. In fact, there seemed to be a whole group of people behind him.

"Um, Odin?" Ali began, nervous.

Ramsey curled his hand over her shoulder and pulled her back.

But the group was already moving in—and the person leading the swarm? It was the bartender that she'd seen at Armageddon the other night. Imari. The bartender with the eyes of a cop.

Only this time, she didn't just have cop eyes. She was flashing a badge and pointing a gun. A gun that she aimed straight at Ramsey.

"FBI," she snarled. "Ramsey Hyde, you're under arrest for murder, conspiracy, racketeering, and—"

"I'm sure you have quite the list," Ramsey said as he better positioned his body in front of Ali's. "But my friends here are quite innocent, so how about you let them both go, hmm?"

"If they are friends of yours, I highly doubt they are innocent," Imari fired back.

"You might be surprised," he murmured.

But Imari had already given a quick signal to her team. They swarmed, and Ali found herself being handcuffed. No one told her why she was being arrested. No one read her rights to her. Odin appeared to be in the same boat. As Ali was pushed outside, she saw the cuffs around his wrists, too.

"Exactly what am I being charged with?" Ali asked, raising her voice to be heard above the noise. Half of the team had stayed inside. No doubt, they were probably tearing through the bar. Looking for evidence. Or bodies. Or maybe both.

Imari moved to stand right in front of Ali. "Accessory." The sunlight glinted off the diamonds that circled up her left earlobe.

"Accessory to...what?" Ali tilted her head. "I just stopped here to get directions. I'm new to town. I got lost."

Imari pointed to a watchful—and silent—Odin. "He's not new."

"Um, no, he's not. But Odin is friends with your boss at Armageddon, and between us..." Ali leaned toward Imari. "I think you are so about to get fired."

Imari's lips parted. But before Imari could fire off a retort, her phone rang. Imari's eyes narrowed. She took a step back from Ali.

Ali glanced around the parking lot. She saw that Ramsey had already been shoved into the back of a black SUV.

A black SUV...how very typical. In her experience, the FBI was always so predictable. When they'd come to haul her away years before, they'd swarmed in similar black SUVs.

She would say one thing for them, though. They certainly knew how to arrive silently at a scene.

Odin moved next to her. No one *pushed* him next to her. Probably because even cuffed he was super big and scary. He just sort of ambled next to her on his own.

"Didn't feel like giving a word of warning when they appeared?" Ali muttered.

"Didn't have time."

She cut him a hard glance.

"*What?*" Imari's furious snarl captured Ali's attention before she could say anything else to Odin.

"You have got to be joking me." Imari gripped the phone and held it to her ear. "But we've got him. He's in custody right now. Him and two of his so-called friends..."

"We're actually not very good friends," Ali called out. "More like acquaintances."

Imari's gaze shot to her.

Frustrated fury burned in the other woman's stare.

Ali clamped her lips together.

"I understand," Imari gritted out. "Yes. Doing it now." She ended the call. Shoved the phone back into her pocket. The bulletproof vest she wore flexed with her movements. "Uncuff them," she barked. "*Now.*"

Uncuff them? Ali eagerly lifted her hands. In a moment, she was free. And so was Odin. As for Ramsey...

"Get him out of the SUV." Rage seethed in Imari's voice. "And get the crew out of his place. Take nothing. We're leaving."

They were leaving? After coming in with guns blazing?

One of the Feds had opened the rear door of the SUV. Ramsey took his time sliding out. He lifted his hands, showing off the cuffs that still bound his wrists. Then, with the cuffs still on, he sauntered toward Imari.

"Change of plans?" he asked her, voice droll.

"Who did you bribe, bastard?" she demanded.

"Bribery is a crime. Do I look like a criminal?" He peered at his cuffs. "Oh, wait..."

No one rushed forward to remove his cuffs. No one had to. With a flourish of his hands that Ali thought would do a magician proud, Ramsey freed himself.

She'd seen Jinx pull sleight of hand tricks like that before. Had the two of them practiced those tricks when they'd been boys? Before life had pulled them apart?

Ramsey dangled the cuffs toward Imari. "Thanks for visiting. I would not recommend that you come back."

Imari snatched the cuffs. "She's lucky that she doesn't remember you."

Ali sucked in a quick breath. Before coming down to the area, she'd worked a long-distance case for Odin—one that had involved Ramsey in a roundabout way.

Or rather, it had involved the woman that Ramsey had once been involved with—Dr. Whitney Augustine. She'd been thought to be dead. Her killers had even confessed to the crime. They'd hit Whitney over the head. Left her to drown in the Gulf of Mexico.

Except, she'd survived.

She'd made it back to the coastal town, but Whitney didn't remember the last six months of her life. A very significant amount of time that she'd spent...being the lover of Ramsey Hyde.

At the mention of Whitney, Ramsey's face changed. A subtle change, at first. A tightening around his mouth. His eyes. A hardening of his jaw. A hollowing of his cheekbones. His eyes glittered with a barely banked fury. "You'll want to watch yourself," he advised Imari in a voice that had gone low and lethal. "And you'll want to make sure you stay the hell away from her. She had *nothing* to do with my life."

"Are you threatening me?" Imari seethed.

He put his hands on his hips. "I'm actually wondering...why the hell are you still on my property? You keep lingering like this—staying where you are not wanted—and I just might have to call the cops on you."

Imari stormed away. All of the other FBI agents fell in line quickly. Tires screeched as the SUVs flew from the lot. They were definitely not worried about making a loud exit.

No one spoke until the SUVs were gone.

"They probably bugged your place," Ali finally said.

"Don't worry, I'll be sure to do a sweep." Ramsey still had his hands on his hips. His gaze was focused on the road—where the SUVS *had* been.

"How the hell did you get them to pull back?" Odin demanded.

Ramsey turned to stare at him. "Obviously, they realized they had the wrong man. I'm not a criminal. I'm an upstanding, respectable member of society." He turned and strode for the bar.

Then he stopped. "Ali..."

She tensed.

"If I find anything, I will let you know."

Relief hit her with the force of a punch. Ramsey didn't say anything else. Just headed into his place.

Ali's cheeks puffed up before she blew out a long breath. "That was certainly...a lot." She rolled back her shoulders. "Why did they let him go? Why did they let us all go?"

Odin's stare was thoughtful. "Because someone with a lot of power told them to back the hell off."

"Yes," Ali whispered. "That's what I was afraid of."

CHAPTER THIRTEEN

"Where in the hell have you been?" Jinx bounded down the beach house's steps and rushed toward Ali.

She lifted her eyebrows and slammed the door of Odin's Jeep behind her. "Well, hello, to you, too, sunshine."

He hurried forward and curled his hands around her arms. She could feel the angry tension snaking through him. Jinx glared at Odin. "You were supposed to keep watch on her."

"He did," Ali assured Jinx before Odin could respond. "He was with me every single moment." Okay, fine, nearly every single moment. He'd stayed outside while she had her private chat with Ramsey. "Want to tell me why you're so growly?"

"Because you're being hunted by some psycho bastard. *And* you just headed out for some kind of merry-ass jaunt."

"Hardly merry," she grumbled. "If you must know—and, FYI, try asking nicely next time, it works so well—I was at Ramsey's bar. Odin and I were there for a friendly chat when a swarm of FBI agents rolled up. I'll give you two guesses as to who was leading that swarm."

A muscle jerked along his jawline.

"No guesses?" That was very un-Jinx-like. Maybe he was worried about his brother. "It was Imari, but don't worry, she had to let Ramsey go. Somebody with a whole lot of power must have called her and told her to back the hell off."

"You were with Ramsey?" Each word rumbled.

A nod. "Got cuffed and nearly pushed into one of the FBI's delightful SUVs."

"They *cuffed* you?"

Not like it was the first time. But she bit that back. She hadn't walked fully down that path with Jinx, not yet. The painful past reveal would have to come soon. Yet...

She hated to do it. Because she rather liked the way Jinx looked at her. Like he wanted to rip her clothes off and have wild, passionate sex with her. Like he...just *wanted* her.

He was having to clean up his brother's mess due to Ramsey's criminal activities. She didn't...Ali never wanted Jinx to think of her as another problem he had to handle.

But doesn't he have to handle your mess right now? Didn't you bring your troubles to his door?

"Odin..." Jinx flickered a glance his way. "I've got her."

Uh, so, that was—

"Bye," from Odin. Simple. Short. His Jeep cranked, and she heard him drive away.

Ali stood there, staring up at Jinx. The waves were pounding. The scent of the ocean teased her nose. The beach appeared empty around them. The other house on the beach still appeared completely shutdown.

We're alone.

Jinx's fingers tightened on her arms. "Why did you go see Ramsey?"

"Because you and I both know that he's using every connection he has in order to find out who sabotaged your ride."

Jinx's brow furrowed. "I don't think that."

"Sure you do." She backed up, pulling out of his hold. "It's what you would do. If someone came after your brother, you wouldn't rest until you stopped the guy." She tilted her head as she studied him. "Ramsey is family. No one comes before family."

Jinx glanced toward the thundering surf. "Come walk with me."

A walk along a gorgeous beach? Sure, count her in. She kicked away her shoes.

His hand reached for hers.

"Is this part of our setup routine?" Ali asked as she leaned toward him. "You think someone is watching us take a romantic walk along the beach?"

"It's not romantic."

They walked toward the wave line. She watched the waves slide up on the beach, then retreat in a beautiful dance.

"If it was romantic, I'd stop to kiss you," he added, voice roughening.

She let the waves roll over her toes. Her body brushed against his. He still hadn't told her if this bit was part of the setup, and Ali found that she didn't care. She just liked being with him. "Why don't you kiss me?"

His gaze fell to her mouth.

"Better idea," Ali decided. Her feet pushed against the wet sand as she rose to her toes. "I'll kiss you." Her mouth brushed over his. He might not think this walk was particularly romantic, but she did. She thought walking with him along the shore, holding Jinx's hand, and kissing Jinx as the waves tickled her feet...it was the most romantic walk of her life.

She kept the kiss brief. Sensual but short. And as she started to pull back—

"No."

Her lashes lifted.

"Don't stop, sweets," he rasped, eyes gleaming. "And believe me, I don't give a fuck who is watching. I want your mouth." Then he took it.

His lips pressed to hers. Her mouth was open and eager, and his tongue thrust inside. He let go of her hand, and his fingers moved to curl around her hips. He hauled her closer so that she was flush against his body. The hard length of his arousal pressed against her, and a moan slipped from her throat.

He kissed her with a stark hunger, a dark need, and she wanted to rip the clothes from his body. They were on the beach. The waves were pounding, and she wondered what would happen if they just slid into the water...went out deep enough that they were covered by the waves...

And they fucked right there. The Gulf would conceal them. He could make love to her. They could drive each other insane...

Right there.

Her hands rose to press to his shoulders. Her nails bit into his skin. She was going to tell him to come into the water with her. They were just going to forget—

His mouth lifted from hers. "Who the hell is Cyrus?"

Cyrus.

The heat that had burned in her body chilled instantly. Dazed, she could only blink up at him.

"And do you still love the bastard?"

Ali tore free of his embrace. She stumbled and nearly fell in the sand.

Cyrus. The name pounded at her. It was a name she hadn't heard in years. "Who told you about him?"

"Does it matter?"

"Yes. It matters very, very much." She wrapped her arms around her stomach. "Who told you?"

His gaze jumped away from her.

"That's where you were today, wasn't it?" The certainty gnawed at her. "When you left and had me stay behind, you were getting briefed on me. On him." She wasn't an idiot. She could put these pieces together—

"Only you didn't stay behind, did you?" He turned to face the water. Drove his hands into the pockets of his jeans. "You ran to Ramsey and nearly got your sexy ass hauled to jail with him."

Shock pulsed through her. "You knew about the FBI raid before I told you." Her head was spinning. "How?"

"I learned about it the same way I learned about Cyrus."

Her toes dug into the sand. "Landon came to you."

A hard jerk of his head that she took to be agreement.

"He ordered you not to bring me to the meeting because he wanted to tell you all the dirty parts of my past without doing it in front of my face." Sneaky Landon.

"Is it so dirty?" Jinx's voice was low.

What did he know? How much? "Dirty enough." She wasn't the same person any longer. That girl—that confused kid who'd thought she had the world at her feet—she was dead. "I paid for my mistakes. I moved on."

"You made a deal to stay out of jail."

The waves were crashing. Pounding so hard. She stared at them and wanted nothing more than to just go out there and get lost in the water. To lose herself for just a little while.

"But the deal wasn't just for you, was it?" Jinx's voice was too flat. Too unlike him. "You wanted to protect your boyfriend, too. You got pulled into his mess. Whatever damn laws he was breaking, whatever crimes he was committing— that Cyrus bastard pulled you in until you were desperate. Then you had to take a deal and you *still* wanted to protect him—"

She moved closer to the water. "You have it wrong." The beach was still deserted. Just her. Just him. No one else for miles.

"I don't think so. I think you fell in love with some twisted SOB when you were a kid, and he used you. And maybe—just maybe—he's the one who is after you now."

"Is that what Landon thinks? That Cy is the one doing all of this to me?" She shook her head. "I don't believe it."

Jinx spun toward her and locked his hands around her shoulders. His grip was fierce, but it didn't hurt. Jinx had never hurt her. "Why?" Not so flat. Ragged. "Because some part of you still loves the bastard?"

"Cy isn't a bastard."

His eyes glittered. "You do still love him."

"You have this so wrong—"

"*Do* you love him?"

The waves pounded.

"Are you still hooked on the freaking jerk who turned you into a criminal?"

She shoved aside his hands. Stumbled back. "I told you, Jinx. You have this *wrong*." Tears burned her eyes, but Ali refused to let them fall. "Cy didn't turn me into a criminal. I turned *him* into one. He was my best friend. He always had my back. He was sweet and shy and good, and he was also brilliant. I am the one who pulled him into my mess. He didn't lead me down any dark path. He didn't do anything to hurt me. *I'm* the one who destroyed his life. Me." The same way that she feared she was destroying Jinx's life. She was bringing her madness and danger to him...

And would it wreck him, the same way that Cy's world had been wrecked?

"I was promised that Cy would get a normal life." Her hands slashed at her cheeks. Stupid tears. "Promised that if I did everything they wanted, he'd be okay. They'd let him go." *Liar, liar.* She'd learned that truth too late.

She didn't want Jinx seeing her tears. She didn't want to stand on the beach and have to look into Jinx's eyes and see that his illusion of her had shattered.

The water was beautiful. A bright, brilliant blue that was nearly the same color as Jinx's eyes. Her hands went to the hem of her shirt.

"Uh, Ali?"

"I'm going for a swim." She tossed the shirt to the sand. Shimmied out of her shorts.

"Ali...oh, damn. Wait. You're in your underwear—"

"Good of you to notice. Your observational skills are on point." She was also already knee deep in the water and moving fast. The tears were coming harder, and she wanted to wash them away. She wanted to wash everything away.

Ali leaned forward and dove into the next wave.

CHAPTER FOURTEEN

He'd screwed up. Jinx watched as Ali swam gracefully through the waves like some kind of freaking mermaid, and he knew that he should have handled things differently. Way, way differently.

But he'd been battling a very unfamiliar emotion as he squared off with her on the beach.

Jealousy.

He'd been jealous of the faceless Cyrus. Jealous that a young Ali had loved him so much that she'd been willing to make any deal necessary with the government. Loved him so much that she'd broken the law for the jerk—

And then Ali said she'd been the one to turn Cyrus into a criminal.

Her head broke the surface of the waves. She pushed back her hair and turned toward him. She was about twenty feet from the shore.

"Are you just going to stand there?" Ali called out. "Or do you want to join me?"

He looked around. Saw no one. The main height of the tourist season had passed, and this stretch of beach—no one ever came there even when it *was* the busy time. They should have privacy.

Provided, of course, that they didn't get any unexpected company.

Like Ali's stalker...

Or War. Or Ramsey. Or—

"Didn't expect you to be a prude," Ali taunted. Her hands drifted in the water before her. A wave gently lifted her up. Lowered her back down.

She'd just called him a prude. Him? Oh, hell, no.

"Or maybe you just don't want to swim with me." Her voice was lower. Less taunting. Almost...sad. "Maybe you don't want to do anything with me, now that you know who I really am."

Who she really was? Screw that. Jinx yanked his shirt over his head. "I don't like having conversations where we're twenty feet apart." His hands went to his jeans. Shoved them down even as he kicked off his shoes. Damn. His precious kicks were gonna be covered in sand.

He strode into the water.

Even as he approached, he could see that her eyes had widened. "*Jinx.*"

The waves crashed into his legs. "Sorry, but I didn't bother with underwear today. Hope you don't mind."

The water was warm as it swirled around him. A wave was rolling his way, so Jinx dove expertly through it and swam toward Ali. He broke the surface and immediately reached for her. She was sleek and gorgeous, and her mouth gaped as she told him, "You're naked!"

"Your observational skills..." He lowered his head and pressed a soft kiss to her neck before he finished, "are on point."

He took her deeper into the water. He could still touch with his feet, and they slid over the sandy bottom. The bright blue water was so transparent. He could see right through to her tight, thrusting nipples. Her wet bra did little to hide the tempting sight from him.

"*Jinx.*" Her hands clamped around his arms.

"You asked me to join you." He curled his hands around her hips. Lifted her higher so he could continue kissing a hot path down her neck. "Wasn't this what you had in mind?"

"I-I said *swim!*"

"Are you sure..." He lightly nibbled on her skin. "You didn't say sex?"

She moaned. Then pushed at him. "*Stop.*"

Immediately, he did. She had to feel his thick, heavy cock shoving against her. He locked his jaw and stared down at her.

"You...you still want me?" Ali whispered.

Still want her? "Baby, that will *never* stop." How could she even ask that? "Don't you feel the giant dick that's bobbing in the water?"

Her lips started to curl, but Ali seemed to catch herself. She blinked water from her eyes.

Wait...is that water from the waves...or tears?

It had better not be fucking tears.

"I'm not the woman you thought. *I'm* the criminal, Jinx. You're already paid for someone else's sins, and I don't want you to feel that—"

He kissed her. Took her lips and drove his tongue right into the hot heaven of her mouth. He loved the way she tasted. Loved the way her mouth moved on his. Loved the way she gave a little moan in the back of her throat.

And he damn well loved the way her legs lifted to wrap around his hips.

He savored her. Explored her and got greedy for *more*. Jinx forced his head to rise. "I've always known exactly who you are."

Her lashes lifted.

"You're mine," he said simply. Her past was over. Dead and buried. Yes, he'd get the full story about what had happened when she was seventeen, but he *knew* Ali. She was good. Fierce. Strong. She'd risked her life on missions again and again. She wasn't some cold-blooded criminal.

She was the woman he wanted. The woman who'd taken his heart and didn't even realize it.

He'd been playing his game so carefully. Trying to draw Ali to him. Trying to keep things light and easy because in the past, light and easy had worked for him.

The smile had worked. It had made him seem less threatening. The jokes had disarmed. The casual, easy attitude had made him seem charming.

Screw all of that.

He wasn't playing any longer. Ali *was* his. He'd long since broken one of those rules she'd set out for him.

Good sex doesn't equal love. So no falling in love.

Hell, truth be told, he'd been in love with her even before they'd had sex. So maybe he hadn't *technically* broken the rule. The sex had been fantastic, but he'd been lost in Ali long before the first time he'd taken her body.

His hand snaked between them. Slid under the wet fabric of her panties. He dipped into her sex. Made her moan again. Made her arch eagerly against him. His thumb rubbed over her clit. The waves were hitting them, rocking their bodies over and over again. It would be so easy to shove the crotch of her panties to the side and to drive into her. He could fuck her right there, and it would be fantastic.

He pushed a second finger into her.

"Jinx!" She breathed his name into his ear, then her mouth sensually tugged on his earlobe. Damn. The woman was driving him crazy.

She was tight and hot around his fingers. He wanted to pound deep into her and explode.

His thumb rubbed faster over her clit because he knew what she liked. He knew exactly how to give her the pleasure she craved.

"I want you to make love to me." Her words were husky. Sensual. "I want *you* in me."

"No condom, baby, can't put one on while we are—"

She pulled back—moved her upper body just enough so that she could look into his eyes. "I'm protected. I don't have any STDs or anything like that."

His heart slammed into his chest. "I don't either."

"Then...*make love to me.*"

The sun beat down on them. The waves were warm and soft around them. When he kissed her, she tasted of the sea and sin.

The best kind of sin.

His fingers slipped out of her, but only so he could shove the crotch of her panties to the side. He fit his cock to her opening and sank into her.

It will be a miracle if we both don't drown.

That was the last coherent thought Jinx had because he was in her, she was heaven, and his control shattered. He was in her—freaking *bare*—in her, and there was no slowing down or stopping. There was just an avalanche of need that consumed everything else. He couldn't be careful. Couldn't be gentle. He was taking and taking, and Ali was with him.

He felt her come around his cock. Felt the sensual contractions of her sex around him as her thighs tightened around his hips.

She was beautiful when she came. Gorgeous. He stared at her and saw every single flash of pleasure on her face.

And he followed—followed her right into oblivion as his own climax ripped through him. Jinx emptied into her and held her with a fierce grip. Ali...*His* Ali.

***

He didn't have a clear shot at them. They were too freaking far away and the waves kept shifting their position.

What in the hell were they doing in the water?

Why the fuck had they decided to go for a swim right then?

He'd been taking aim. He'd had them in his scope. Then Ali had stripped off her clothes and dove into the water. *Dammit.* He'd been sure she would come back out in moments.

She hadn't. Instead, he'd been treated to a bare-assed view of Jinx as he followed her into the surf. A fast dive from him, too, and Jinx had slipped from the shooter's sights.

The waves were tossing them about. Ali and Jinx kept drifting under, coming up.

Sweat slipped down his spine.

His phone rang.

He gave a little jerk. Sonofabitch. He should *not* be disturbed right now. Not when he was on a job.

But the ringtone told him it was the boss. The guy paying the big bucks. So he reached for his phone with one hand and kept his eye to the scope.

"Is it done?" the boss demanded.

More sweat. "Not yet."

"Why the hell not?"

"Because they went fucking skinny dipping in the middle of the day, and I don't have a shot, that's why!" Not like it was his fault. "The waves keep moving them. If I fire and miss, they'll know I'm here."

"*Company is coming.* You have five minutes to get this done and get out of there!"

"Yeah, well...don't know that they will be *finished* in five minutes." Because he had a pretty good idea of what else they might be doing in the waves...

Jinx...lucky bastard.

He was even gonna get to leave this world with a bang.

"Take the fucking shot!"

The line went dead.

Someone needed to calm the hell down...

He pulled in a breath. Kept his attention focused through his scope. The couple appeared to be coming closer to shore. Good. As soon as they cleared those deeper waves, he'd have them...

***

He was swimming them toward shore. Jinx had pulled out of Ali, slid her panties back into place, but he'd kept his fierce hold on her waist. Now he was taking her back.

"I don't want to go back." The words slipped from her. One of her arms was around his neck, and her grip tightened, just for a moment.

"Sweets?"

She liked that silly endearment. Did Jinx even realize he used it with her? Probably not. But she'd always liked it. A little more personal than sweetheart, it made her think that...maybe, he used it just for her. Maybe it wasn't the same expression he used with every other woman he'd slept with.

Her arm tightened even more.

"Choking me a little," Jinx growled.

Her bad. *Do not think about those other women.*

"Better." His voice was clearer, and he'd also stopped heading for shore. "Why are you afraid?"

And that was it. He'd just figured out exactly what was happening. Ali was afraid. Afraid to slip out of the water and return to the real world. She'd been running when she first jumped into the waves...

He ran after me. He came after me. Made love to me like the past didn't matter.

Perhaps it wouldn't.

Unfortunately, she feared it would.

"You wanted to be a hero. That's how you wound up on the team." Her legs slid from his hips. She pushed from him and swam a few feet— feet that took her *away* from the shore. Back into the deeper water. Colder water brushed her calves, always a sign that she'd gone deeper. "I just wanted to stay out of jail."

He circled toward her. Closed in like...like a shark.

At the thought, she automatically glanced down. All around.

No sharks. She hadn't even thought about them a few moments before. A shark could have swum right by her when she'd been climaxing with Jinx, and she would never have known.

"What did you do?" Jinx asked her.

Ali bit her lower lip. He was still naked. She was clad in soaking-wet underwear and could swear that she still felt him inside her. When she'd jumped into the water, she hadn't been thinking much beyond that moment. She'd been hurting, crying, and escape had been on her mind.

Now, swimming in the water, her body still aching from him, Ali felt vulnerable. She hated that feeling. She liked to be strong and in control, but for the past few months, her control had been chipped away. Her stalker had seen to that as he made her feel more and more alone. Targeted.

Hunted.

"Ali?" Jinx swam closer. "Tell me what happened back then. If you think I'm going to judge you, you're dead wrong." He stared straight into her eyes. "You are dead—"

Something whizzed right by his face and hit the waves. A splash immediately had water hitting her. Ali blinked and tried to figure out what had just happened. Had a fish jumped out of the water? Had—

Another whiz. A sound like a bee buzzing right past her. Another splash as something hit the water, hard.

"*Gunshot,*" Jinx snarled.

Her gaze flew to his face.

"Coming from back on the beach!"

Her frantic stare darted to the beach. She saw no one. She saw—

A glint in the distance. A glint that was coming from the other massive house much farther down the beach. From the *top* of that house, on the small balcony on the third floor.

"Dive, Ali!" Jinx blasted. "Dive and swim! Head east. Now, baby, *now!*" He pushed her into the waves.

She sank into that water and as she surged east, she saw a bullet go past her head.

***

"Shit."

They'd disappeared under the surface of the water. Had the last shot hit his target? He couldn't tell, not for certain. Dammit. This was so fucked up! He hadn't wanted to take the damn shots, but the boss had given him the order. He was being paid far too richly to ignore a direct order.

He kept his eyes locked on the waves. If he'd hit his target, he should see blood in the water. A body would rise.

If he hadn't hit his target, sooner or later, they'd have to come up for air. And when they came up, he'd be ready. He'd take another shot. He'd finish the job.

He'd get his money and get the hell out of town.

Come on. Come on. Rise up and just take a breath...

CHAPTER FIFTEEN

Ali felt like her lungs were about to burst. She'd swam for as long as she could. She and Jinx had gone a good distance down from their original location. Had they gone far enough? Were they safe?

I can't believe someone was shooting at us!

And, if she'd been right about that gleam she'd caught, it hadn't been just any shooter taking aim. From a perch that high...

Sniper.

A sniper shooting at her made zero sense. None of this nightmare made sense.

She had to take a breath. Ali kicked up—

Jinx grabbed her ankle and hauled her back. Fear twisted inside of her, and she whirled her body so she could face him.

He shook his head.

Bubbles trickled out of her mouth. She couldn't stay down longer. Jinx might have done training with a SEAL team—specifically, with War's SEAL team—but she hadn't. She couldn't hold her breath this long! Her lungs burned, and she could feel dizziness pulsing through her head.

Jinx pointed to himself. Then he pointed up.

What?

He kicked up.

She understood.

He wants to go first. If the shooter is up there, Jinx thinks the guy will shoot at him first.

Jinx was making himself a target.

She grabbed his damn body and hauled him back down. He frowned at her. Hell, at this rate, they'd both drown before the shooter ever had a chance to fire again.

***

They hadn't come to the surface yet. His back wasn't just sweating. His temples were sweating. His chin. He could feel the beads of sweat preparing to drip, drip...

Was it possible that last shot had somehow taken them both out? Sure, he was good, but...not that good. Or was he?

No blood in the water.

He'd thought he saw a dark shadow moving moments before, but it had turned out to be a big ray, not his prey.

"Come on, come on," he muttered.

"What the hell are you doing?" The voice was sharp, angry, and coming from right behind him.

He spun around, instinctively bringing the weapon with him.

He never got the chance to fire.

The bastard standing behind him shot *his* gun. And the bullet slammed into Louis's chest.

***

They broke the surface of the water together. Jinx took in a deep gulp of air, saw Ali do the same, and then he immediately pushed her back under. He wanted to get farther down the beach. He needed to get her to safety, and then he'd be going after the shooter.

Fury pumped through him as they cut through the water. They'd had to go out deep, hoping to get out of range and into the darker water so that they could be better concealed. The water near the shore was too clear. The deeper water provided the best concealment.

They'd gone deep, then focused on heading east.

Ali was a good swimmer. She was fast, too. They cut through the water together, and they put more distance between them and the guy Jinx suspected was a sniper.

The angle of the shots, the position of the shooter...

He was up there. Watching. Waiting.

But because they'd left the beach and gone into the water, the sniper hadn't had a clear shot.

Ali's impromptu trip into the water had saved their asses.

Speaking of asses...

I'm buck-ass naked. When we finally do go to shore, someone will be getting a show.

And when he got to shore...when he got his hands on that shooter...

Someone will be dead.

***

Landon Hatcher stared at the man before him. The guy was still gripping that giant gun of his even as blood soaked the man's shirt. Landon kicked the rifle away and kept his own weapon trained on the sniper.

It didn't take a genius to figure out what had happened. When he'd arrived, he'd heard the shots. He'd seen the gleam that indicated light reflecting off the scope. As fast—and as quietly—as he could, Landon had gotten into the beach house. A beach house that should have been secured and locked up for the season. He'd broken the lock then hauled ass up the stairs to his target.

"Did you kill them?" he asked. Jinx and Ali. There had been no sign of them when he arrived.

Blood dripped from the man's mouth. His eyes were rolling back in his head.

"*Did you kill them?*" he barked.

"W-water..."

What? But then Landon looked up. Looked *over* the wooden railing of the balcony and down at the beach. He saw what looked like discarded clothes. A shirt. Jeans.

Water.

His gaze flew back to the sniper. Only...he wasn't moving. As in, not breathing. More blood covered him—*soaked* him—and he'd gone deathly still.

Shit. Landon hauled out his phone. He wasn't calling nine-one-one. This wasn't some typical civilian case. He needed a cleanup crew out there, and he needed one stat. And right after he made that call, Landon made another.

It was answered on the second ring.

"War, I need you out at Jinx's place. *Now.*"

***

When they strode onto the shore, Jinx made damn sure to keep Ali shielded by his body. She was snarling and muttering as he forced her behind him, but he ignored her protests. Keeping her safe *was* his priority. If she didn't like it, too bad. Keeping her alive was far more important at the moment than keeping her happy.

She could rage at him later.

And now. She can keep raging now, too.

He was pleased to see that they'd gotten far away from his beach house. So far that they were now in front of a high-rise condo—and all of the condo guests who happened to be out on the condo's private beach.

A woman who'd been applying sunscreen to her stomach paused and gaped at him.

"Got an extra towel?" he asked her politely.

"Jesus, son!" An older man called out, "You're naked!"

"Good of you to notice." Jinx inclined his head. Then, spying a towel on the back of the gentleman's chair, he snagged it. "Don't mind if I borrow this, do you?"

The man's companion slowly shook her head. The man just frowned ferociously.

"Great," Jinx said. "Thanks."

Then he turned and wrapped Ali up in the towel.

"Jinx." She clutched the edges of the towel. "You don't have clothes!"

Everyone kept focusing on that. But did Ali realize *her* bra was completely see-through when it was wet? He didn't need all the jerks on the beach staring at her. Speaking of those jerks...he pointed to a nearby guy who was gaping. "Towel," he snapped.

The younger man immediately threw it at Jinx. He secured it around his hips. "Thanks for that." Then, curving his body around Ali's, he started walking, quickly, toward the condo.

"What?" Jinx threw back into the silence that followed them. "Have you never seen a man who lost his trunks in a battle with a shark before?"

"*Jinx.*" Ali sounded torn between horror and laughter.

Considering everything they'd been through in the last half hour, he completely understood her horror.

Some bastard tried to kill her.

He pulled her into the shelter of the condo building. Caged her with his body. "You weren't hit." He'd tried to check her under the water, but he needed to be absolutely certain.

"I wasn't hit," she murmured. Her hair was soaked. Water dripped down her face and body even as she clutched the towel to her chest. "And you weren't? I mean, I looked over every inch of you and I didn't see—"

Oh, he was sure she'd seen every inch of him. Everyone on that private beach had seen him. Some had even taken pictures. Whatever. Good thing he was done with undercover missions...

"Jinx?"

"I'm not hit," he assured her. What he was... "Pissed off." The bastard was using a rifle on them? This piece of shit was a sniper?

"Uh, excuse me, sir." A small, timid voice.

Jinx's head turned. He saw a guy in a pressed, white dress uniform sidling closer.

"Would your name be Jinx?" A fearful question. The name tag on the man's left pocket read Teo.

"Yeah. How the hell did you know?" *Don't attack Teo yet. Don't attack—*

"A man named Landon just called. Told me that you might be walking from the water with, ah, missing clothes." Nervous laughter. "Thought he was crazy and then you...she..." His gaze bobbed between Jinx and Ali. "The man wanted you to get a message."

How the fuck had Landon known they would be there?

"Scene is s-secure," Teo stuttered. "War is coming. Rendezvous at h-home."

"Are you shitting me right now?" Jinx asked.

"No." Teo licked his lips. "Is this like...some sort of role-playing game?" He took another cautious step forward. "If so, can I play? I really love stuff like this. I used to do D&D back in the day, and I would—"

"No, Teo," Jinx told him flatly. "You can't play this game, and trust me, you don't *want* to play."

Teo appeared crestfallen.

"But if you can find some clothes for him to wear," Ali cleared her throat to say. "I mean, clothes for *both* of us to wear, I'll pay you a hundred dollars."

Teo's brows rose. "You have the money on you?"

She barely had a towel on her, and that was clear to see. "Teo..." Jinx sighed out his name. "Keep your eyes on her face, not her body, and we'll make it one fifty."

"One fifty?" Teo's attention swung back to him. "For real?"

"This shit is as real as it gets."

"I think I've got two robes that will fit you perfectly. Would that work?"

Robes were better than nothing.

***

Teo gave them a phone, and Jinx called to confirm with Landon that the scene was, indeed, secure *before* he got his new best buddy to drop him and Ali off back at the beach house. Of course, Teo's ride wasn't free. Jinx promised him another twenty for the drop-off.

And when they arrived, they pulled up at the same time that War was sliding into the graveled drive with his precious Chevy Impala. War jumped out of the car, and when Jinx went to meet him, War's stare swept over him.

"Uh...nice robe?"

Jinx bit back his immediate reply of "fuck off" and instead said, "Give Teo one hundred and seventy bucks, will you? Don't exactly have cash on me."

Teo held out his hand.

War eyed Teo, then Jinx, and, finally, Ali. "Matching robes?"

"It has been a day, all right?" Ali sighed. "*A. Day.*"

War shoved the cash at Teo.

A black SUV rushed up behind their group.

"Better go before you get blocked in," Jinx warned Teo. "You don't want to be a part of what's going down next."

Teo rushed away.

"I need to get changed," Ali said. She'd shoved her hands into the robe's pockets. "Then I want to find Landon and figure out what is going on here."

"Easy enough to explain." Landon's voice boomed out. He marched toward them, heading away from the other house on the stretch of sand. "The sniper is dead. The scene is secure, and I've got a cleanup team..." He motioned toward the black SUV. "Arriving as we speak."

Another SUV appeared.

"Feds?" Ali asked.

A van rolled up, too. Block letters on the side read...*Coroner.*

"Who killed the sniper?" Jinx questioned quietly.

"I did." Landon rolled back his shoulders. "I came to speak with Ali, and when I arrived, I realized what was happening. I saw the glint off his weapon and knew his location." He turned and pointed in the distance, toward the beach house that waited yards away. "I was able to get pretty close to him, but at the last moment, he turned and would have fired his weapon." Landon swallowed. "I fired first."

Jinx studied him. Landon's voice was grim. Almost cold. But his eyes were darting around the group too quickly. There was a fine edge of nervous tension to his body.

Had that been Landon's first kill?

"Get changed," Landon directed. "We all need to talk, but let's not do it while it's looking like you two just got back from a spa day."

"Spa day, my ass," Jinx rumbled right back. "We had to swim for our lives." His head turned toward Ali. "Didn't realize you were so good underwater."

Shadows darkened her eyes as she gave him a weak smile. "I was pretty sure that I was going to drown...at least three times."

His gut clenched. "And then you didn't let me go up without you." He'd wanted to surface first so that he could take any fire and give *her* the chance to suck in some much needed air.

She shook her head. "We're in this together, but you don't get to risk your life for me."

"Um, yes. Of course, I do." As if he'd do anything else. He caught her hand. Pulled her closer. Stared into her eyes and wanted to make absolutely certain she got this point. "I would risk anything for you."

She sucked in a sharp breath. "Jinx?"

Not the time or the place for big declarations. He got that. Especially with a shaky Landing Zone watching him and some stiffs in suits coming to do clean up.

Jinx locked his jaw. "I want an ID on the sniper."

"If he's her stalker, this mess is over," War noted. "We get his ID, and we tie him to Ali. Then she can get her life back."

Jinx wasn't so ready to call the case closed. His gaze remained on Ali. "He didn't kill your previous target with a long-distance shot, did he?"

Once more, Ali shook her head. "All signs indicated the shots were close-up."

"Maybe he's a man of many friggin' deadly talents." War's voice had lowered. "Let's get the ID, then move from there. Try to be more positive, would you, buddy?" He slapped a hand on Jinx's shoulder. "You're alive. Ali's alive. I'll call that a win."

It was a win, hell, yes. But...

But I want Ali alone. He locked his hand with hers and pulled her away from the growing chaos of the scene. He took her inside his house as quickly as he could, but that meant retrieving keys and disarming the security system first. Once they were away from everyone else and the door of his home closed behind them...

He spun around and pinned Ali to the door. His mouth crashed down on hers in a frantic, desperate kiss.

Any one of those bullets could have hit her. Any one of them could have taken her out.

Then there would have been no second chances for him. For them. No chance to show Ali that there was one thing in this world he took very, very seriously...

Her.

He was kissing her too hard. Too desperately. He realized that. But a desperate tension rode him. The feeling that, despite what War hoped, this case wasn't over.

It was just going to get worse.

Jinx had screwed up. He hadn't counted on a sniper. Had never considered that mode of attack. He'd been so sure that the beach's location meant he'd see his target coming...

First that punk showed up last night. Now this.

He'd messed up left and right.

Jinx slammed his hands against the door behind Ali and forced his mouth away from hers. "I'm sorry."

She licked her lips. Lips that were red and swollen from his mouth. Her hair was starting to dry, and it was tousled and thick and gorgeous around her face. "Are you sorry for kissing me?"

His gaze fell to her delectable mouth. "I'll never be sorry for that." He freaking loved her mouth. And he was staring at it too hard. Jinx gave a rough shake of his head. "I didn't protect you well enough." The failure burned in his gut. "I was distracted." *Because I want you so much.* "Because I can't keep my damn hands off you." A stark truth. "I never should have put you in a position where you could be vulnerable. If we hadn't been able to sink into those waves..."

Her hand rose. Pressed to his stubble-covered cheek. "You are not seriously blaming yourself right now."

He was.

"Jinx." She said his name like it was some kind of caress. "There was a crazy man with a gun shooting at us. Not your fault. Not mine. *His.* He's the one who pulled the trigger." She offered him a tentative smile. "And we got lucky—probably because you *are* the luckiest man I know."

No, he wasn't. Most days, his luck was shit. *That* was why he was always tossing salt and making sure he didn't duck under any ladders. He'd already had more than enough bad luck to last him a lifetime, thank you very much.

If others wanted to believe he was lucky, fine. He let them run wild with that idea. But deep inside, he'd always known the truth.

He didn't feel lucky. Jinx felt cursed. Like he was the bad luck that could destroy people who got too close.

"It's a good thing Landon was there." She squeezed her eyes shut after making that announcement. "I can't believe I just said that because the man annoys me most days..."

Ditto. Except, Jinx felt a whole lot more than *annoyance.*

Her eyes opened. "He stopped the shooter. Now we have a real lead. And maybe War is right. Maybe this is where it ends. We just have to figure out this guy's ID. I'm sure Landon will have his prints run, his DNA checked. Every single thing that can be done will be done. And we can go from there. We can figure all of this out and perhaps it will be over."

If it was over, what happened next for them? "You slip away?" He was still caging her. He needed to stop. He couldn't physically hold her to him...

Though the thought was helluva tempting. Jinx wanted to hold Ali close and never, ever let go.

Back off. She's dealing with enough right now.

He shoved away and put space between them. "I want a look at the guy's face." Because if he'd been working for the government, as Ali had suspected, then the sniper might not be in the system at all. He could be a ghost...

"Me, too." Ali was definite.

He stared at her. "About Cyrus..."

"It's not going to be him." She was adamant. "Cy would never stare down the scope of a gun and try to kill me."

She sure had a lot of faith in the bastard. The jealousy was back, stronger than ever. "Maybe he wasn't aiming for you."

Her horrified gaze held his.

"We wanted him to come and get me. Maybe that's what he was trying to do." Or, if she was right and Cy wouldn't stare down the scope himself, perhaps he'd hired someone else for the job.

Jinx had worked plenty of missions in which snipers had been contracted so they could make a hit. Those guys—and ladies—all had a few things in common...

Secretive. Intense. Control freaks.

Ali surged forward. Her index finger jabbed into his chest. "This is over."

His robe had gaped open. Shocker. Her finger hit his skin. He glanced down at it even as dread pooled within him. "You mean us?" *You're saying we are over?*

"I mean *you* risking yourself! That's over! It ends now. I'm tired of you being targeted. I'm tired of you being in danger."

Speaking slowly, Jinx said, "I thought we agreed that I thrive on danger."

She jabbed him again. "You don't thrive on death! And I don't thrive on the idea of something happening to you!" Her expression was stark. Her gaze swirled with emotion.

Jinx tensed. *Well, hello, there…what is that I see?* "Worried about me?" he murmured. "I am touched."

"Jinx!" Her hand yanked away. "Would you be—"

"I am serious. Damn tired of people thinking otherwise." He caught her hand. "I asked you a question, Ali. Are you worried about me?"

Her thick lashes flickered. "Of course, I'm worried."

"Good sign. Very, very good."

"You—you're my friend, Jinx and—"

"No. Try again."

"What?"

"I'm not your *friend*. I'm pretty sure we've covered this before. War is your friend. Odin is your friend. You're not fucking either of them." If she had been, he would have kicked their asses. "Try again," he repeated. "Because this isn't one of those friends-with-benefits situations." Not even close.

"It's not…"

They had to get moving. A dead body waited. So did an investigation. But this was important. She was important.

So I'll say my part and give her time.

Though he'd already given her time…several months. Months while he'd been waiting for her.

Longing for her. Fighting the urge to go out and track her down...

But I'm not a damn stalker. I'm not some freak who wants to control Ali.

He just...wanted her. And he thought she wanted him, too.

Trying to keep his voice level, Jinx told her, "If we were friends with fuck benefits, I wouldn't be jealous of a freaking ghost from your past."

"Cy? You're jealous of—"

A grim nod.

Her eyes widened.

"If we were just friends, I wouldn't be so ready to kill anyone who threatened you." He paused. Considered the matter. "Maybe I would." His hand rose and curled beneath her hair as he tipped back her head. "See, here's the deal. I don't want anyone hurting you. Don't want anyone scaring you. I want to make sure every damn thing in your life is perfect. That you are happy. That you can smile and laugh and jump half-naked into waves, if that's what you want. Sure, I want to fuck you." Like that was in doubt. "Endlessly. But I also—I need to know you're good, Ali. Safe and happy. I'll do anything necessary to make sure that a safe and happy life is what you get." He could not look away from her. "I would not sacrifice you for anyone or anything. Know that."

Shit. Were those tears in her eyes?

"Jinx?" She blinked. "That is probably the nicest thing you've ever said to me."

A tear slid down her cheek. He kissed it away.

"Why?" Ali whispered. "Why are you doing all of this for me?"

His forehead pressed to hers. "Don't you know?" He wanted her mouth. But if he kissed her again, he'd be ripping that robe of hers away in seconds.

He pulled back. *Dead body. Investigation.*

"Jinx, I—"

"*Jinx!*" War thundered from the other side of the main door. "Odin's grandmother is faster than you. Haul ass! Dammit, we *know* this guy! Come on before they take the body away!"

We know this guy...

***

Jinx stared down at the dead man. Blood had covered his chest, soaking his shirt. His eyes were closed. His hand was still outstretched, as if he wanted to grab the rifle that rested near his body.

The dead man was clean shaven. His blond hair had been cut short, a military cut. Made sense. The man *was* former military.

Once upon a time, he'd been a US Army Sniper. He'd been incredible in training. He'd received top ratings for camouflage techniques, target detection, terrain utilization, advanced marksmanship...The list had gone on and on.

It had been expected that he would be just as superior in the field as he was in training.

That expectation had been wrong.

He'd worked one mission with Jinx and War...and Ali. Just one...

And he'd nearly killed two civilians. He *had* shot them both. Ali and War had rushed the civilians to safety while Jinx had run to stop the shooter.

"What the hell were you thinking?" Jinx remembered the exact words he'd shouted to the man...

To Louis Grimshaw, a superstar in training who'd lost his nerve on his first mission. A guy who'd disappeared shortly after that incident and had never been in the field with Ali or Jinx or War again.

"He'll have green eyes," Jinx said as he gazed at the body.

"Louis," War confirmed.

Jinx nodded. His gaze turned to Ali. She'd put on jeans and a loose blouse. Her canvas shoes. He'd dressed, too, as fast as possible, and rushed with War to see the body.

Louis was tied to them all.

"You worked with him?" Landon's surprise was clear.

"Right before you came on board as handler," Jinx confirmed. It had been back in the day when Landon's current supervisor had been in charge. Landon had been doing more of the background work. Jinx kept his voice low, even though Landon had cleared out the men and women on the cleanup crew as soon as Jinx and Ali had appeared. "After that mission, he was sent in for more psych evals. War and I told your boss that the guy didn't have what it took. He couldn't handle the pressure, and he proved to be a risk in the field. From what we know, he was discharged soon after."

"I remember." War's jaw was tight. "When I left service, I also heard word he'd gone freelance. That for the right price, he was taking contract work for Uncle Sam...and other interested parties."

"I'll be checking that," Landon assured them. "In the meantime, my crew found his ride parked down the road. He had left a hotel room key in the glove box." His lips pursed. "Guessing you'll be wanting to see that room?"

"Damn straight, we will," Jinx confirmed.

Louis. He hadn't thought about the man in years.

"If this guy is a rogue sniper, one *we* trained, I want everything kept confidential, you understand what I'm saying?" Landon pushed.

Oh, Landon was clear. He wanted it all swept under the rug.

"Your wife had better not be reporting this story on the evening news," Landon added with a glare at War.

Jinx shook his head. "You don't talk about his wife," he warned.

Too late.

War's shoulders had rolled back. "My wife can report on any fucking thing she wants. You got someone bad, someone dirty who decides to open fire on people? That shit *will* make the news. That shit *is* a problem. That shit—"

"We never spoke." Ali was still staring at the dead man.

Everyone's attention slid to her.

"Not on that one mission. I was doing intel work. My job was to get inside the government funded research facility in Prague and download documents. I saw this man once, and it was just in passing. After everything went to hell, Jinx and War made sure he got out of the field. I never talked to him." She bit her lower lip. "I don't buy that he suddenly became obsessed with me after that. It doesn't make sense."

"Obsessions don't make sense. Emotions don't always make sense." It was War who spoke, and his voice had turned thoughtful. "Sometimes, emotions take control, and even the strong can't stop them."

"Search the hotel," Landon ordered curtly. "I'll handle the scene here. I'm trying to keep the local authorities out of this as much as possible."

Good luck with that.

Jinx turned away from the body.

CHAPTER SIXTEEN

"His hotel is right across the street from my condo unit." Ali stood at the door to room 704. "I'm not thinking that's a coincidence."

Jinx didn't think it was a coincidence, either. In his book, very little was.

He'd donned gloves. So had she. Not like it was their first time to search a room.

"Housekeeping," Jinx called out loudly and tapped his knuckles against the door.

Ali frowned at him.

"Just making sure no one is waiting in the room for us," he murmured. There had been no sound from inside the room in response to his housekeeping call so...

He tapped the keycard against the lock. The light flashed green. Carefully, he eased open the door and stepped inside.

The room was dim. The curtains were drawn, concealing any view, and the silence in the place seemed heavy. They passed the small closet, and through the open door, Jinx saw the duffel bag.

He reached for it.

"Jinx?"

He turned at Ali's call, but didn't drop the bag. He brought it with him. She was standing near the small desk that had been positioned near the bed.

She stared down at the surface of the desk. Or rather, at the pictures on the surface.

Pictures of her. A picture from the first day, when Jinx had met her on the beach. She was wearing the same red bikini, and she lounged back against her chair.

Another shot showed her at Ramsey's—with Jinx. They were standing close together. It looked like they were either about to kiss or scream at each other. Maybe both.

The third shot? Right outside of Jinx's beach house. He was standing beside her. A red circle had been drawn over Jinx's head. "Well, that certainly clears up one thing." He glanced at Ali. "I think it's safe to assume those bullets were meant for me."

He dropped the duffel bag onto the bed. Opened it up...

Fuck me.

"Item two is also cleared up..." He pushed his gloved hand into the bag and lifted a wad of cash. "I don't know that Louis was obsessed with you, but it *does* seem that he was doing some freelance work."

"OhmyGod." Ali grabbed the bag. "How much cash is in there?"

A lot. "Enough to kill for," he said simply. Jinx suspected that was exactly what had happened...

Louis hadn't been on the beach because he was obsessed with Ali. He'd been there because he'd been hired to do a job. That job...

It had been to kill me.

"Who hired him?" Ali's voice notched up. "Dammit. I told you, I think this was from someone *inside* the organization. Someone who knew about Louis and the work he did."

Shoddy work.

"Someone who wanted to use Louis," Ali added. "If only we'd been able to talk to him! To question him!"

Not like they could question the dead. "Keep searching the room. There could be more here for us to find." He also wanted the room scanned by a crime scene team. Maybe Louis had met with his "employer" in that room. Maybe there were prints. Maybe there was—

"Cyrus," Ali said, voice choking.

Jinx's head whipped up. *Not that asshole again.*

She'd gone back to the pictures on the desk. She'd lifted one—the one of her at the beach. She was squinting and staring at the photo. "I-I think that's him."

In a flash, Jinx was at her side.

"The guy in the chair, to the right." Ali's hand was shaking, so the picture trembled. "I don't even remember that man being there..."

Jinx remembered him. "He was looking at your ass."

"What?"

"The dick in the red shirt with the baseball cap...he was looking at your ass on the beach. You stood up, and I saw him do a double-take." It had pissed him off then. It enraged him now. "That sonofabitch was right there!"

"I-I think it's Cy. The jaw is stronger, or at least, the beard makes it look stronger. The nose is the same, though. And he's a lot bigger than he was back then...a *lot* bigger. But..." She pulled the photo closer. Stared at it with narrowed eyes. "It's him." A soft whisper. "I didn't notice him on the beach. He was sitting just a few feet away, and I didn't notice him. Some great agent I am."

"He was angled so that you *wouldn't* see him. So that he could see you. And he probably had on sunglasses for most of the time. Sunglasses, a hat, and the perfect location to watch you." *Cyrus, you are a sonofabitch.*

"You're trying to make me feel better." Her head turned so that she was gazing up at him. "It's just making me feel worse."

"No, sweets, you're feeling worse because you just realized your old friend Cyrus looks guilty as hell. He's right here in the city." He'd been close enough to just get up and *touch* her the first day at the beach. "His photo is in the hired sniper's room. And you don't want it to be true, but it looks like Landon was right, and I fucking *hate* to admit that but..."

"But you think Cy is after me."

Grimly, Jinx nodded.

And I think I'm going to stop him. I think I'm going to make sure that the old friend from your past never has the chance to get touching close to you again.

***

"I want the full story." They'd just entered Armageddon. It was the middle of the day, and the bar was completely empty. Understandable since the place wouldn't open until much later that night.

They were supposed to head upstairs and rendezvous with War and Odin in the Trouble for Hire office. But it looked like Jinx couldn't wait any longer. His voice was hard and rough, and Ali squared her shoulders as she turned to face him.

"Every detail," he ordered. His eyes smoldered with barely banked fury. That heat had been in his gaze ever since they'd discovered the picture of Cyrus in Louis's hotel room. "I get that you thought he was a buddy. That he couldn't possibly be a threat, but you were wrong."

She *had* thought that he was a friend. Once upon a time, he'd been one of the sweetest, shyest guys she'd ever met. She'd been his only friend back in the day. Cy had never talked about his family, but then, he hadn't needed to—she'd been able to see the bruises that darkened his cheeks and jaw every few days.

Cy had wanted to escape. She'd hatched a crazy idea a lifetime ago to help him...

"Ali..." Jinx blocked her path. All big and growly and not flashing his typical smile. "Don't you trust me?"

Surprise had her stepping toward him and putting her hand on his chest. "Of course, I do." She trusted Jinx more than she trusted, well, anyone.

I would trust him with my life in a heartbeat.

"Then tell me everything, sweets. You think I'll judge you for what happened back then? I won't. I wouldn't judge you for a damn thing. But I need to know about this guy."

Because it looked as if Cyrus wanted to kill Jinx. "Yes, you certainly have a right to know." Wearily, she let her hand fall. Ali turned away from him and paced toward the gleaming bar.

"Did you sleep with him?"

There was a mirror behind the bar. She saw her own surprised face staring back at her. Ali laughed, truly shocked by the question. "No, he was more like a brother to me than anything else." She turned toward Jinx and let her back rest against the edge of the bar. "Anything sexual like that—we both would have thought it was gross."

"Gross." His gaze raked her. "Uh, huh. I'm sure that's what he thought."

Jinx wasn't getting it. "He was my best friend. I was his. We didn't fit in with the other kids. They were going to parties and football games, while Cy and I spent our nights..." She swallowed. "It didn't start out with us wanting to break laws, okay? It was a challenge. We just wanted to see what we could do." She bit her lower lip. "Turned out, we could do a lot. Especially when we worked together."

They'd been nearly unstoppable.

"We got past every security block in our way. We started with our school. Then went to the city government files. From there we turned to state data. And then...the Feds." A shrug. "The more we did, the faster we learned how to get better. To be better. We weren't stealing files or anything. We were just testing our skills. No one was getting hurt, or at least, that's what we told ourselves."

He waited. Kept watching.

"Something happened," Ali admitted as her stomach churned with nerves. "Cy needed to get out of town. He needed a fresh start, and he needed cash to do it. This was going to be the first time—the only time—that we used our talents...to steal. We were going to take the money from an account—look, the guy was a criminal," she added quickly. *As if that makes it better.* "We knew what he was because we'd been following the news stories about him. He was this jerk who was tied to a dozen different investigations, and he'd funneled a ton of money to an offshore account. I know it's ridiculous now, but we were kids back then, and we thought if we were going to steal money from someone, it should be taken from a guy like him."

His expression didn't alter. "You said something happened. *Why* did Cyrus need to get out of town?"

She hesitated. This wasn't her story to tell...

"Ali. You told me that you trusted me." He strode forward. Stopped when his body was right in front of hers. "Tell me."

Her breath slowly eased out. "Cy's dad almost killed him."

Jinx blinked.

"I knew he'd hit Cy before. Cy could never please him. See, Cy's dad wanted a big, tough son. A son who scored all the touchdowns on the football field. Prom king. *That* guy. He didn't want a thin, asthmatic son who spent all of his time inside tapping away on a computer. Whenever he'd catch Cy at his computer, he'd lose it." She would never forget the way Cy had looked that last time. Not just one or two bruises. He'd been covered. His left eye had been bulging and bloody. "Cy had to get away. I begged my parents for money, for help first, but they refused. They said...they thought Cy was trouble. Told me to stay away from him." Ali could only shake her head. "Like I was just going to turn my back on him?"

Jinx shook his head. "No. That's not what you would do."

"Stealing wasn't right. I get it. But I needed to help him. Cy was going to vanish. Everything was going to be okay and then..." Her shoulders rose and fell. "I got caught." So much for thinking she'd been invincible. The one and only time she'd thought no one could catch her. "Lots of people with badges and bad suits swarmed my house. I was crying and shaking when they cuffed me and pushed me into the back of an SUV. My parents kept shouting at me and asking what I'd done, and I just kept telling them that I was sorry." The memory burned through her mind. "My dad's face was so red. And my mom—she kept looking to the left and the right, and I heard her telling the neighbors it was all a misunderstanding. Only, it wasn't. Nothing was ever going to be the same again."

"Did your parents get you a lawyer?"

She nodded. "They did, and he was fresh out of law school. He had no idea how to handle the agents telling him that I had violated national security in a dozen different ways. I was told that I'd be locked up, tried as an adult, that I was going to lose everything..." A sad smile twisted her lips. "And just when I thought things were darkest, I was offered a deal."

"Come work for us...and the crimes vanish."

She nodded. It was a deal that she'd learned was made far too often, and most people never even realized it. "I had conditions on my deal. I wanted protection for Cy. I was the one who'd had the idea to take the money, not him. I wanted him to get his freedom. I was told that he got it."

Jinx's eyes narrowed. His lips parted as if he'd say something, but he seemed to catch himself.

But now she was curious. "What is it?"

"You asked for protection, for him?"

She nodded. "I thought I got it. It was only later—much later, when I was working a case—that I realized Cy had never gone free."

His eyes gleamed. "How did you realize it?"

"I was hacking. I mean, that was the main reason they wanted me, right? But I wasn't the only one looking at this particular system. And the thing about hackers—it's like we have fingerprints..." Maybe that wasn't a good enough description. "Or...signatures." That was better. "You can recognize someone else's code. Understand that code belongs to someone in particular."

"And you saw Cyrus's signature."

"At first, I thought he might be—" She stopped. *Tell him everything.* "I thought he might be a threat. I had to report what was happening, but when I informed Landon, I learned that the other hacker—Landon never identified him specifically, just said the 'other hacker'—I learned he was also working for Landon."

"Are you *sure* it was Cyrus?"

"I sent him a message," she confessed. She would not hold back with Jinx. "And he replied. It was the only time we communicated because part of my deal was that I'd end contact with the life I had before."

"Wait..." His fingers circled around her wrist, and Jinx tugged her close. "End contact? Define that."

"I left my hometown. I left my school. I left my family. And I wasn't supposed to look back. The government needed me to become a shadow, and shadows don't have a past." She pressed her lips together, then admitted, voice small and subdued, "There wasn't anything to go back to. Shortly after I was arrested..." *God, this hurt so much.* "My dad had a heart attack. He died. My mom made it clear that I was an embarrassment. She blamed me for what happened to him. Said that I'd caused it. She sent me a note and said she never wanted to see me again. As far as she was concerned, I was dead to her."

"Fucking brutal."

"I rather thought so at the time." It hurt even more to say... "I'd always hoped she might change her mind, but a month after I got the note, she was killed in a hit and run. They were both gone. There was nothing in my old life for me."

"So you just became someone else. You let Landon and the others train you, and you became a dozen different people."

Her hair slid over her shoulder. "I became whoever I needed to be in order to get the job done." A bitter laugh broke from her. "Sometimes, I'm not even sure who I am anymore."

He leaned forward. Pressed a fast, hard kiss to her lips. "I know exactly who you are."

Who am I? She swallowed back the question. "I told you my dirty story. Gave you all the details, and yet you're still staring at me as if..." Her voice trailed away.

"As if—what?"

As if you still care. As if nothing had changed for him. "Tell me about your life."

"You don't want to hear it."

"I want to know everything about you. I always have. Why do you think I looked into your files so much?" She could feel a burn in her cheeks. "I guess some habits are just hard to shake. I still go peeking where I'm not supposed to, and, yes, I tried to learn about you."

"Why? Why would I matter?"

Was he going to play this game? "Oh, Jinx. You've always mattered."

"Always?" One eyebrow rose. "You sure did a good job of hiding that. I thought you barely tolerated me on most missions."

"You were the person who got me through most missions," Ali corrected. "When I was scared or desperate, you'd make some ridiculous statement. You'd toss salt in Odin's eyes or at War...You'd smile at me, and everything would just be...all right." That was it. Her stark truth. Her fear had faded, and her world had been good when Jinx was there. "You helped me get through more dark days than you will probably ever know."

His expression hardened. "You think you didn't do the same for me?"

Her breath caught. "Jinx?"

"I had nothing growing up, Ali. My family was never what you'd call functional. Drugs and alcohol, they were what my parents loved. My dad would do anything for the next fix."

She wanted to throw her arms around him and hold on tight. Her heart ached for him.

"I knew we were heading straight for trouble, but I couldn't stop my old man. The only thing that stopped him was jail. I tried to take care of my brother. When we were sent into foster care, I swear, I tried my hardest..."

"I know." She did hug him. Ali just had to wrap her arms around him and hold on tight.

"When Ram vanished, I didn't have many choices. I stayed with a foster family until I hit legal age, and then the military was an option staring me dead in the face. Once I enlisted, it turned out I had a real aptitude for the life." He was stiff in her embrace. "I soaked up everything I was taught. There was so much to learn, and I wanted to learn *everything*. I couldn't wait for the missions. I wanted to see new places, I wanted to see new things...and like you, I was offered deals. But my deals—"

"They were about your brother."

"I was told he'd gotten into trouble. While I'd been on the other side of the world, he'd been fighting to survive. I know he crossed the line. I know…" If possible, his body became even harder. "He's my brother."

She looked up at him. "You can't turn your back on him." She knew what it was like to have family walk away. *It guts you.*

"Sometimes, you have to turn away," Jinx rasped. "If I could have gotten Ram away from my dad when we were kids, I would have done it. There was nothing good for us there. Your buddy Cyrus isn't the only one with an asshole dad who liked to hit."

"*Jinx.*" Ali wished she could take all of his pain away.

"You get me, Ali." He seemed to be looking straight into her soul. "I kind of always knew that, but it's even more so now. I feel like you understand me. Like you—"

"I would do anything for you," she said clearly. He needed to understand *this*. "I hope you know that." There was no one that she would put before him. Didn't he get how important he was to her? Didn't he see?

No, no, maybe he didn't.

Just…say it! "I love you," Ali blurted.

Silence. The words seem to have fallen hard into the quiet bar.

CHAPTER SEVENTEEN

I love you. Ali's words rang in Jinx's ears. He even shook his head, convinced that he'd imagined them. When you wanted something so badly, sometimes, your mind could start playing tricks on you.

"I haven't confused good sex with love. I remember our rules." Her lush mouth tightened. "We have great sex. Phenomenal. But what I feel for you is completely separate from that."

War had come down the stairs. Jinx had been conscious of his approach. He'd heard the creak of the fourth stair and knew that War was coming to see what the hell was keeping them. War had arranged the meeting, and Jinx had no doubt that his buddy had watched them arrive from one of the windows upstairs. When too much time had passed and they hadn't appeared, War had come looking for them.

Ali's shoulders tensed. She'd obviously heard that little creak, too. "War," she whispered.

Jinx nodded.

"So…" War's steps approached them quickly. "It's not just a problem that Jinx has. You *both* like to overshare about your sex life."

Jinx glared at him. Would it have killed War to have turned around and taken his ass back up the stairs? Could he not tell that he was interrupting a major moment? Because Jinx thought it was more than damn obvious. "Go," he mouthed to his buddy.

War held his ground. "I'm not the only one waiting up there." He looked up. "Landon wants to brief you. He's the one who wanted to come down first, but I volunteered for duty instead. Figured you'd rather have me interrupt than him."

Yes, War had figured correctly. "And Odin?"

"He's running down leads. He'll meet up with us later—"

Even as War said that, the front door to Armageddon swung open. Jinx whirled around, battle-ready tension filling him, but the person in the doorway...it was Rose, War's wife.

She held up her keys. "Thought it was fine if I let myself in." Her sharp gaze took in the scene inside the bar. "Things certainly seem tense in here."

War hurried to her side. "Baby, this isn't a good time for a visit."

No, it was a shit time. Jinx glanced back at Ali. He didn't think she'd met Rose yet.

But Ali's eyes weren't on Rose. They were on him.

Jinx needed her to understand...Voice low, he promised, *"We are going to finish this talk when we're alone."*

She licked her lower lip.

He fought the urge to kiss her. Fought the need to pull her close and demand that she give him those three utterly amazing words one more time.

I love you.

Could it be true? Could something that good have finally happened to him? And to think, all he'd had to do was lie and cheat in order to get her…

"War, I feel terrible!" Rose's voice was strained. "I'm the one who brought Imari into our lives! I'm the one who pushed you to give her a job! I had no idea that she was working undercover to bring down Ramsey Hyde."

At the mention of Ramsey's name, Jinx had to look back at her once more.

Rose's face showed her concern. "I didn't even know that you had dealings with Ramsey," she told War.

Dealings? That was an interesting word.

"I trusted her," she added as she gazed up at her husband. "Because of that trust, I put you and your friends in—"

War kissed her. Leaned down and gently brushed his lips over hers. "It's okay," he said, voice as tender as his kiss had been. "We all knew she was a cop or a Fed the minute she walked through the door."

She pushed against his shoulders. Her narrow-eyed glance darted from him to Jinx to Ali.

"Hi," Ali said, tucking a lock of hair behind her ear. "I'm Ali, and, yes, we all knew."

Rose's gaping mouth closed. Her attention flew back to War. "So I'm feeling guilty for nothing?"

"No, it's something," Jinx assured her.

Ali elbowed him.

Since she'd said she loved him, he chose to ignore the elbow to the ribs.

"Where is your friend?" Jinx asked. Because he'd love to have a chat with Imari.

"I don't know." Rose's heels tapped on the floor as she paced toward him. "She stopped answering my calls. I went by her place, but it's been cleared out. It's like she's just vanished."

Now that was interesting.

"She was certainly far from pleased when she got the call telling her to pull back at Ramsey's place," Ali said thoughtfully. "Maybe her orders weren't just to let him go. Maybe she was supposed to pack up and end the entire investigation."

Right. About Imari and everything that had gone down at Ramsey's bar... "We are really going to need to have a long talk," Jinx began. Jeez, this was gonna be awkward. "Just remember that when we have that talk, you love me. You said the words. Can't go taking them back."

"Jinx!" Her cheeks flushed.

Oh, what? Why the blush? What was embarrassing about her loving him? "You love me," he repeated, voice more definite. Harder. She wasn't gonna take that back. Not after he'd worked so hard.

She cast a glance toward War and Rose. But they were back to whispering to each other. And then Rose was darting out the door.

That had certainly been a fast visit.

"She had a few more leads to follow up on," War rumbled. "A couple of other spots where she wants to search for Imari." He pointed upstairs. "And we have Landon waiting. If it's all the same to you, how about we get up there fast? Because I don't like the idea of Landon being unattended in my office."

That comment made Ali's brow furrow. "Don't you trust him?"

War made his way past them and toward the stairwell. "I trust Rose—I'd trust her with my life. I trust Odin. I trust Jinx. And I trust you." He looked back at her. "No one else is in that special circle just yet, though Odin's lady is working her way real close..." He faced forward again, and a moment later, his steps thudded up the stairs. This time, he was being plenty loud.

Ali moved to follow him.

Jinx reached for her hand. "Who is in your circle of trust, sweets?"

"Isn't it obvious? Though I don't know if it's a circle, so much as a very short line. You're the only one I've ever told all my secrets. You're first."

His heart wasn't going to be able to handle many more of her confessions.

"You, Odin, and War. Cy used to be on that list but..." Her words trailed away. She straightened her shoulders. "Like I said, my list is pretty short and sweet."

"Aw, Ali, you think I'm sweet?" He grinned at her. Despite all the madness happening, he felt happier than he'd felt in...

Hell if I know how long.

"Your smile always makes me want to jump you," she confessed. "But this is not the time."

Unfortunately, it wasn't. Not with Landing Zone waiting impatiently upstairs. There was one thing he was going to say, though. One thing he *had* to say before anything else happened. Any other interruptions or shootings or stalkings... "I love you."

"You—"

"I love you. I broke our rules, too." Another smile. "Come on, you saw that coming, didn't you? You know I hate rules." He leaned down. Brought his mouth near her right ear. "Here's a secret. I broke that rule on day one."

Her head whipped back so she could gape up at him.

"Had to admit that because I couldn't have you thinking that I didn't worship the ground that you fucking walk on," Jinx told her. "Because I do. Have that clear in your mind. I love you. Would have said that as soon as you made your big reveal, but then War had to appear." He considered the situation. "Actually, I'd hoped to be the one to say 'I love you' first." He'd had such grand plans. "But you beat me."

Her own lips started to curl. "Jinx..."

He wanted to haul her against him. To kiss her and savor her and never let go.

And I will never let go. Ali is mine. I will do whatever it takes to keep her with me.

But he backed away. He still had his fingers circled around her wrist, and he lifted her hand to his mouth. Pressed a careful kiss to her knuckles. "Let's go see what Landon has learned." And... "We have to tell him that Cyrus is here." She had to see the threat that her former friend had become.

There was no more denying it. He'd been a victim once, a long time ago, but the evidence had mounted that Cyrus was much, much more now.

He's trying to hurt you, Ali. At least, that was what the signs would indicate.

Jinx knew he had to play this part carefully. A plan was brewing in his head, based on what Ali had already told him.

Jinx picked up the duffel bag he'd brought along. They headed silently up the stairs and made their way into War's office. Landon was pacing when they entered, and his fast glance took them both in. Then narrowed on the bag. "What in the hell is that?"

"I estimate it's about fifty grand in mostly small bills." He tossed the bag over so that it fell near Landon's feet. "We found it in Louis's hotel room. I know you had a crew coming to the hotel, but I just didn't feel right leaving that much cash out, especially considering what else we found."

"Fifty grand?" War whistled.

Landon raked a hand over his face. "What else was there?"

Ali stepped forward. "A picture of Cyrus Hendrix. He's here, in town. And he's been watching me."

Landon's expression didn't alter. "You're sure of that?"

"As sure as I can be after all of this time. Louis was doing surveillance on me, and he took a picture of me at the beach, a picture that had Cyrus in the background." She crossed her arms over her chest. "He printed the photos with a small printer we found in the hotel room. Don't know why he printed them, though. Maybe he was supposed to deliver the photos to Cyrus as evidence that he was doing the job?"

"Plenty of clients still want hard-core proof," War said. He pointed to the small printer on a nearby cabinet. "Guessing his client wanted evidence of—"

"Of me and Jinx together. Because Jinx was in the pictures, too." She rocked forward. "I think Cyrus being in the beach picture was just an accident. Like I said, he was in the background. The focus of the picture was me and Jinx."

"Sonofabitch," Landon swore. "I knew that guy was gonna be a problem."

Oh, he was a problem all right. But one that Jinx now knew how to handle.

"I shot the man who could have helped us to nail Cyrus." Landon's hands clenched into fists. "I didn't have a choice, though. He turned on me with that weapon—"

"I have an idea," Jinx offered. He waved his own hand in the air, all casual-like. "I think it will work nicely."

Everyone turned to stare at him.

He offered them his innocent smile. Then he focused on Ali. "You can send Cyrus a message."

"Uh, Jinx..." She slanted a glance toward Landon.

"Old habits die hard. Both for you and, I'm guessing, for Cyrus." Ali still dipped into government files—not that he was about to tell Landon that fact—but Jinx was betting that if she did it, then Cyrus did, too. She'd found his signature before, and Jinx knew that once she went looking for him—now that she *knew* to look—she'd find him again. If not in the back doors that contained the government's secrets, then on the Dark Web. Ali *could* find him.

She'd wanted to know who was stalking her. Based on the evidence in the hotel, they had a good idea of *who* it was. Now Ali would be able to reach him.

"If he wants you," Jinx continued carefully, "then you lure him out. You exchanged messages with him before, and you can do it again."

"Exchanged messages?" Landon's body jerked as if he'd been hit by electricity. "When? How?"

Ali ignored him. She inclined her head toward Jinx. "Now that I know Cy is here...now that I know it might be him..."

"Might be?" Landon exploded. "Everything certainly is pointing to—"

"I can set up a meeting. I want to question him," she added quickly before Landon could snarl again. Jinx thought Landing Zone sure looked as if he was ready to snarl. "I want to know why. I want to know how Cy went so off the rails that he would do this to me."

"You can't explain obsession," Landon gritted. "The man is dangerous. You don't get to have some catch-up session with him. You arrange the meeting, and we will be there every second to watch. My team will take control when he appears."

Jinx could tell by the fierce gleam in Ali's eyes that she didn't like that plan.

"You take him into custody," Ali said, "and then *I* get to question him."

Landon spared a glance for Jinx.

Jinx inclined his head.

"Fine," Landon agreed. "We have a deal." But he didn't sound happy about that deal. "Now how do you contact him?"

"Not like I just pick up the phone and reach out to him. He's rather unlisted." Her hands fell to her sides. "Don't worry about the how. I'll just let you know when the meeting is planned. And...it may take some time for me to find him, okay? So go do your work. Finish your investigation. I'll be sure and let you know as soon as we have anything."

Landon appeared less than thrilled, but Jinx knew the man didn't have other options. After a grim nod, Landon marched for the door. Except...

He paused by Jinx. "A word. Outside."

"Since you asked so nicely..."

Ali was frowning worriedly at him. Jinx gave her a reassuring wink.

Then he went out with Landon. Only they didn't just stop outside that door. They headed down the stairs. Moved back into the bar. When Landon seemed satisfied that they were alone...

"Our deal stands?" Landon asked.

Jinx had figured that was the point of this little one-on-one session. "You seem to be making deals with everyone lately. Me, Ali..."

"I could have pushed up there. It's obvious *you* know how she's going to contact Cyrus, and I'm guessing it's some way that's not going to make me feel all freaking warm and tingly."

"I don't particularly want to know what makes you feel warm and tingly, but thanks." Jinx lifted his eyebrows. "And as far as how, I think that's above your tech pay grade."

Landon surged closer. "You *tell* me when the meeting is set up. Cyrus isn't going to come in solo."

No, he hadn't thought that the man would. "Ali won't be there solo, either. I'll have her back."

"Cyrus wants to take *you* out. You're standing in his way."

"It's one of my favorite places to stand." Between Ali and any threat.

"Jinx, I stuck my neck out for you! I covered your brother and kept him out of jail, and I want to help Ali, too. Dammit, I *shot* that bastard who was waiting to kill you! I am not the bad guy here! You need to work with me."

"Thought I was working with you," he murmured.

Landon searched his gaze before swinging away. He took a few, fast steps for the door.

"Was that the first time you've had to kill someone?"

Landon's hands flexed at his sides. "Yes."

"It will stay with you."

Landon threw a haunted glance over his shoulder. "Tell me something I haven't already figured out." He wrenched open the door.

And nearly ran right into the pretty blonde who stood uncertainly in the doorway.

"Oh, sorry." She offered him a weak smile. "I, uh, Maisey Bright told me that Trouble for Hire was located in this building? I know this is the bar, but, I—"

Landon side-stepped around her. "I think she's here for you," he threw back to Jinx. "Excuse me, ma'am." He walked away with a fast, determined stride.

Jinx took a hard look at the woman in the doorway. This visit was the last thing he needed right now.

"There are exterior stairs that lead up to Trouble for Hire," he told her as he tried to buy some time. "You don't have to come through the bar."

"I tried those stairs. The door at the top was locked. The door to Armageddon was locked, too. I was just standing outside, trying to figure out what to do and...then it swung open." She took a nervous step inside.

Whitney Augustine. Yes, he knew who she was.

The woman who'd been thought dead. The woman with no memory of the six months before her attack. The woman who owned Ramsey's heart.

And she doesn't have any clue.

But if she was coming to Trouble for Hire... "Is everything all right?" Jinx asked her.

Her left hand clutched the strap of her purse in a death grip.

"Are you in danger?" Because if she was being threatened...*Ram will lose his mind.*

"No, no, it's not that. I'm safe. Perfectly safe." Her hand twisted around the strap. "I just—I need to hire a PI. Maisey said Odin was wonderful." She looked around, as if expecting Odin to appear.

Not like there was any place in the bar for that giant to hide. "I'm afraid Odin isn't here right now." *And I'm afraid the world is on fire so if you could possibly come back...* Instead of saying that, he gave her his friendly-client grin. War would have been proud. "Want me to get him to follow up with you when he returns?"

More twisting of the strap. "Uh, maybe..." Her lips pressed together. "No, no, forget it. I-I can't do this."

She whirled and rushed back through the doorway.

Well, that had been damn odd. Jinx made a mental note to pass along this odd visit to Ramsey. Though, of course, his brother would deny any interest in Whitney.

But if something is rattling her so much that she came to Trouble for Hire, he needs to know...

Ram might act like he was done with Whitney, but Jinx knew the truth. The woman who'd just walked out of Armageddon was his brother's biggest weakness in the world.

And the woman upstairs is mine.

CHAPTER EIGHTEEN

Don't trust Jinx.

It had taken Ali approximately seven hours to make contact with Cyrus. Every moment during that time, she'd kept hoping that more evidence would emerge. Something that would come along and prove that Cy couldn't be the one stalking her. He couldn't be the one behind the attacks on Jinx.

She stared at the computer screen before her. War and Jinx had made sure she had the best possible tech to do her work. She'd been hunched over the keyboard for hours, and now that she'd finally tracked down Cy and gotten him to communicate with her...the message she received was the last one that she'd ever expected.

She stared at the screen, her eyes feeling dry and glassy.

Don't trust Jinx.

She fired out a quick response. One word. *Why?*

Ali didn't even breathe as she waited for the reply.

He's lying to you.

The hinges of the door squeaked. "Baby..."

Her head whipped up. Jinx stood in the doorway. No shirt. Abs for days and days. Jeans loose around his hips.

"It's too late, and you've been at that too long." His worried stare swept over her. "Come to bed."

"I just made contact."

He surged forward.

She almost covered the screen. Almost. Such a weird instinct, to hide the words that accused Jinx—

"Sonofabitch." Jinx leaned over her. His hand slammed into the desk. "He's trying to turn you against me."

"It's not going to happen." She had faith in Jinx. Her head turned. "I know you wouldn't betray me."

His gaze cut from hers and flew back to the screen. "He's sending another message."

In danger. Meet me now.

Ali licked her dry lips and typed, *Where?*

He gave her coordinates, and when she plugged them in the map app on her phone, she realized that he wanted her to meet him at an old fort, a historic site in the area.

"That fort is filled with tunnels and passageways. There will be a million places for Cyrus to hide." Jinx's voice boiled with frustration. "It's on the beach, so it can be accessed by land or sea. That gives him two escape options. Dammit, I don't like this. Type in an alternate location. Tell him to meet *you—*"

But when she typed, there was no response, and she realized— "He's gone."

"No, he's there. He saw what you wrote. He's just playing some game."

"No." Ali was adamant. "He wouldn't want to stay on too long because he'd be afraid someone else might be able to reach him. I wasn't trying to back tunnel to get his location—I just wanted to talk to him. But Cyrus knows that the longer he's on, the longer he talks to me, someone else *could* be trying to find him." She'd deliberately avoided that tactic because she'd feared he'd have too many red herring safeguards in place.

Ali exhaled heavily. "We need to get to that fort."

"Ali, it's a freaking trap."

"Yes, and we're the one setting it." She rose from the chair. Started to push past him. But Jinx caught her and pulled her back. He lifted her onto the edge of the desk.

His mouth crashed onto hers.

Ali couldn't help herself. She leaned into him. Gave herself up to that hot, wild, frantic kiss. Fear and adrenaline pumped in her. She knew this was bad. She knew going to that fort would put her in danger.

And Jinx. Jinx will be in danger.

Her hands rose. Her fingers bit into his shoulders. Her mouth tore from his. "Don't come with me."

"Yeah, not happening." His expression was hard with intent. Almost brutal. "I would walk through hell with you in a heartbeat. There is no way—*no way*—that I let you go off into the night alone and face this guy."

"He's tried to kill you already."

"I won't be alone. We'll make sure War and Odin have our backs." A muscle flexed along his jaw. "And Landon. I have to call Landon."

That was a ton of reinforcement. War and Odin were the best trained men she knew, after Jinx. But they were her friends...*I hate risking them all.*

"We've gone out on missions way riskier," Jinx reminded her.

She knew that. Of course, she knew that. But this was different. It was different because it was because of her. The risk they faced wasn't because they were trying to protect their country. It was because they were trying to protect *her*.

Jinx stood between her legs. His hands were locked around her hips. "If I was in danger, sweets, what would you do?"

"Fight for you." Her immediate reply. She'd fight dirty and hard and do whatever it took to protect him.

"Then you understand why I will do the same for you." Another kiss. Deeper. Longer. "I love you."

His words rolled through her. Warmed her in all the cold places that fear had created.

"I will stand with you, I will fight for you, and I will not let *anything* happen to you." His forehead pressed to hers. "You see, I want a future with you. A life where I get to wake up and see you first thing in the morning and make love to you last thing every night."

That sounded pretty good to her. It was a dream she wanted. It was one they *would* have.

"Trust me," Jinx said.

She nodded. She did. She absolutely did...

Don't trust Jinx.

Ali pushed the warning from her mind. Cy didn't know Jinx. She did. The person she *didn't* know, not any longer...

Cyrus.

***

The fort was spooky. No other word for it. There were no lights inside, and the myriad of tunnels that cut through the historic site seemed dark and menacing. The wind blew off the Gulf and swept through those tunnels, and the sound of the wind blowing sounded like moans. Ghostly echoes.

The moon and stars shone down from overhead. The bastions of the fort rose like angry beasts in the night, and the scent of salt air surrounded her.

Ali slowly strode forward. She had a flashlight in her left hand and a gun in her right. She didn't have the light on yet. The minute she turned it on, she'd be a beacon to anyone hunting for—

"*Ali.*"

She whirled to the left. Toward the gaping tunnel. Her name echoed through that tunnel.

She knew Jinx was watching her. Jinx. War. Odin. Landon. They were all there, hiding in the shadows. Ready to swarm at a moment's notice.

She took a step toward the tunnel. "You're a fool if you think I'm just blindly walking in there." She made sure her voice was clear and that it carried easily. "I came to the fort. I followed your directions, now you follow mine." A pause. "If you want to talk to me, Cy, then come out." If she went into that tunnel, Jinx wouldn't be able to see her. She'd promised him that she'd stay in the open.

Ali had no intention of breaking a promise to Jinx. She kept her gun aimed at the entrance to that old tunnel. The waves were pounding against the nearby shore. The fort was on a small barrier island, and the surf was rough and hard as the wind blew with the promise of an oncoming storm.

Over the pounding, she heard the light pad of steps.

A dark shadow emerged from the tunnel. Came toward her. Closer and closer...

She turned on her light. It illuminated the man in the dark hoodie who stood at the entrance to that gaping tunnel. A tall man with wide shoulders and a muscled chest. A beard covered his hard jaw, and beneath the top of the hood, she could see thick, dark hair.

He had changed a lot from the too thin, hesitant teen that she'd known.

But she knew that she was staring straight at Cyrus. "Why?" Ali asked him softly, sadly. "Why did you do all this?"

***

"Contact," Jinx barely breathed the word into his comm link. They'd all linked up before Ali went inside. "I can see him."

"Take him out." An order that came from Landon.

Jinx saw Ali's shoulders jerk. He knew she'd heard that order, too. She was on the link, a small bit of tech that most wouldn't be able to see. In the dark, they'd been counting on Cyrus not noticing her comm as it hid in her left ear.

"Take him out," Landon blasted. "He is a security threat. My orders are to remove him from the equation. If Ali isn't going to do it...Jinx, you know what you have to do."

Remove him from the equation? Who said shit like that?

"Jinx!" Landon was snarling in his ear. "He's reaching for a weapon! Don't you see him, don't you see—"

Cyrus *was* reaching into the pocket of his hoodie.

Jinx sprang from the darkness.

***

"Drop it!" Ali ordered.

Cyrus lifted up what appeared to be a small box—barely any bigger than a matchbox. "It's a signal jammer. I just made sure that whoever you're talking to on your comm link—those people won't be whispering in your ear any longer. You won't hear them, and they won't hear us."

"What makes you think I have a comm link?" She could now hear *nothing* from the link. Landon had been snarling about Cyrus reaching for his gun, and then everything had gone quiet.

"Oh, Ali." Cyrus sighed and dropped the little box to the ground. He raised his hands toward her. "It's predictable. It's exactly what the people in the agency would want. Control. You do know that you've been under their control for years? They've lied to you. Manipulated you. Used you."

"But they haven't tried to kill me. That would be something *you* did. You came after me. After Jinx. After—"

Jinx burst out of the darkness.

Cyrus tensed. "I warned you about him, Ali."

Jinx was trying to move between her and Cyrus.

"Dammit, Ali! I told you he was lying to you!" Cyrus shouted. "I told you that you couldn't trust him, I told you—"

A gunshot blasted. Cyrus stumbled back, then slammed into the ground.

Ali hadn't fired. Neither had Jinx.

"War? Odin?" Ali called.

There was no response on her comm.

Cyrus was on the ground, rolling to his side and swearing as he grabbed his shoulder. "Ali, help me!"

Jinx had his gun aimed at Cyrus, but he was also glancing around the fort, no doubt searching for the shooter's position.

"Ali!" Cyrus sat up, but he'd dragged himself partially into the mouth of that tunnel once again. *It gives him cover. The shooter might not be able to hit him from that angle.* "Ali, you need to get away from him!" Cyrus urged her, seemingly desperate.

Ali had her weapon trained on him. "Are you armed, Cy?"

"I'm *shot!* That's what I am! Because your new boyfriend over there set us both up! And if you don't listen to me—you and I will be dead soon!"

What?

"I'm here to protect Ali," Jinx snapped. "Not hurt her. You're the freak who has been stalking her. You hired Louis Grimshaw to take me out because I was in your way."

"Who the hell is Louis Grimshaw?" Cyrus wanted to know.

He sounded genuinely confused. But the confusion was probably a lie.

A bullet sank into the stone near Cyrus's head.

"Dammit, Ali! Get your ass in this tunnel! You're in his range!" Cyrus scuttled back, still holding his shoulder. "I told you that I was in danger! You should have believed me!"

Wait...*he* was in danger?

She remembered the message he'd sent...

In danger. Meet me now.

She'd thought that Cy meant *she* was in danger. But he'd been talking about himself?

"He's been hunting me for over a year!" Cy was inside the tunnel. "You led him right to me! I came down here to help you, I thought I could count on you—*but you led him to me!*"

She inched forward, then scooped up the jamming device he'd dropped. She hit the button and immediately demanded, "War, Odin? Who is shooting?"

"Not me," War's grim response came over the comm.

"Fucking take cover!" From Odin.

"Landon?" Ali whispered.

Nothing.

And—

Gunfire.

But it missed her because Jinx had grabbed her and hurtled them both into the mouth of the tunnel.

CHAPTER NINETEEN

"Get away from her, asshole!"

Jinx raised his head. His body shielded Ali's, and he had his gun aimed toward the snarling voice.

Cyrus.

"I don't think so," Jinx replied, quiet clearly. "But, Ali, how about you reach into my back pocket and pull out the cuffs there so we can make sure this prick is no threat to either of us—"

"I would *never* be a threat to Ali!"

"The comm has gone out again," Ali said, voice tight. "I don't hear War and Odin any longer."

He'd noticed the same thing.

"Of course, the links have gone out!" Cyrus exclaimed. "Landon took them offline as soon as he realized that he was about to be screwed! His second shot missed me, I'm still living, and I can tell you about all the crap he's done!"

They were too close to the tunnel's entrance, and Jinx didn't know where the damn thing exited. He didn't have a light on, and Ali's light had fallen to the ground.

"Ali, get away from that guy!" Cyrus's voice notched even higher. "I told you, he's using you! He's working with Landon!"

Jinx rose to his feet. He pulled Ali to his side. She'd grabbed the cuffs, but she didn't move toward Cyrus.

"What is he talking about?" she asked Jinx.

Jinx swallowed. "Nothing, sweets. We just need to get the cuffs on him and—"

"*Jinx is working with Landon!* They had this whole deal in place—Jinx was going to get close to you. Going to do anything he had to do in order to get close—and then he was supposed to use you to draw me out." The ragged sound of Cyrus's breathing seemed to fill the air. "You drew me out, all right. Now Jinx gets his prize—his brother gets to stay a free man."

How the hell did Cyrus know all this? Jinx didn't dare risk a glance at Ali. He was afraid Cyrus would pull a weapon and attack at any moment.

"Why do you think the raid at Ramsey's place was called off?" Cyrus pushed.

"How do you know about that?" Ali edged a little closer to him.

"Because I was there! I was trying to get to you! You are trusting the wrong people, and I wanted to help you!"

"Bullshit," Jinx called. He pulled the cuffs from Ali's hand. "Keep your gun on him." He didn't want Ali getting closer to this jerk. He rushed toward Cyrus. Spun him around so the guy had to face the wall.

Jinx put his gun to the back of Cyrus's head.

"Ali!" Cyrus screamed her name, and the sound echoed in the tunnel. "I'm telling you the truth! Jinx is using you so he can help his brother! Don't let him kill me—*I'm not the villain!* You know me, Ali, you know—"

Jinx lowered his weapon and shoved it into the holster under his arm. He needed both hands free while he cuffed this dumbass. "She knows me, too," he snapped. He grabbed Cyrus's hand, and the guy bellowed in agony as Jinx wrenched it—and his shoulder—back.

Oh, yeah, you're shot, right, buddy? Tough shit.

Jinx clamped the cuffs around Cyrus and patted him down quickly to look for weapons but...

There were no weapons on him. Not a single one.

"You came unarmed?" Jinx asked.

"I came for Ali! I would never hurt her—*I'm not you!*"

"Yeah, asshole, look, you've got it all wrong." Not that he was going to explain himself to this jerk. *But I have to explain to Ali. I can't have her buying this load of bull.* The explanations would come after they were out of that tunnel and safe. *After* they made sure the shooter was handled. "Ali—" He looked back.

He could see her because his eyes had adjusted to the darkness. She was standing just a few feet away. She still had her weapon up.

"Is he lying?" Ali asked, voice cracking.

Shit. "Ali, we have a lot going on right now."

"Are you using me, Jinx?"

"Fuck, Ali, I—"

"Of course, he is," Landon's voice boomed out. "What did you expect?"

Jinx whirled toward the depths of the tunnel, but it was too late. Gunfire exploded and he took the hit in the chest. It slammed hard into him, and Jinx flew back into the air before he crashed down on the rough, stone floor of the fort.

"Jinx!" Ali shouted.

Landon fired again.

"Ali!" Jinx's roar. Jinx shoved upward and ignored the burning in his chest. The bullet hadn't hit him—he'd taken the liberty of donning a bulletproof vest beneath the tactical jacket that he wore. A vest that Landon hadn't realized he was wearing.

Or you would have aimed for my head, wouldn't you, you sonofabitch?

Ali hadn't been hit. Cy had been shot again. He'd heaved his body in front of her. Jinx could just make out their forms. Cy was facing Ali, half on *top* of Ali and blocking her as she tried to raise her arm and shoot at Landon. Cy's weight seemed to be dragging her down.

"Always planned to take you both out," Landon snarled. "What better time than—"

Jinx still had his weapon. He fired it at the bastard. A fast, hard hit to Landon's stomach. The blast echoed around them, just as the others had done.

Landon staggered. His knees buckled beneath him, but he still tried to lift his weapon and take aim at Jinx once more.

Jinx kicked the gun out of his hand. "I don't think so." He had his gun aimed dead center between Landon's eyes. "I'm not in the mood to get shot again."

"H-how...?"

"How am I not bleeding all over the place, the way *you* are? Easy. I put on a vest. So did Ali. So did Odin and War. Because I'm not an overly trusting bastard and because things in Louis's room were a little too perfectly placed." He'd been suspicious as hell. It had been the photo that tipped it over the line for him. A photo that just *happened* to include Cyrus?

Footsteps raced from the depths of the tunnel.

He needed a damn light! Those could be reinforcements for Landon—

"*Jinx.*" War's voice.

Relief surged through him. "Get me a light! Cyrus is hit and so is Landon!"

Even as he said those words, Landon crashed against the floor.

A bright light fell on him. War swore when he saw the damage. "Who the hell did that?"

"I did," Jinx replied grimly. "He was going to kill Ali, so I made the shot. *I did it.*" And he'd do it again. Over and over. He would protect her, no matter what.

"He sent us to the east side," Odin rumbled. "Told us he saw the shooter there, then the comm link died again."

Landon had deliberately led them away. He'd probably wanted time to kill Ali and Cyrus...*and me, too.*

Landon was bleeding out in front of them. War wrenched out a phone and called for an ambulance even as Odin crouched and began to apply pressure to Landon's wound. That was Odin for you—even trying to save the enemy.

A man who'd betrayed them all.

"Help me!" Ali's frantic cry.

Jinx whirled and fear poured through his veins. Had Ali been hit, after all? Was she—

"It's too much blood!" Ali was half-sprawled across Cyrus's body. "He's shaking and the bleeding is too heavy! We can't let him die! *Help me!* Help *me!*"

***

Jinx watched through the hospital window as Ali stood by the bed of her old buddy, Cyrus. The man had been in surgery for three hours, then he'd spent some touch-and-go time in the ICU, but the doc had just assured them that Cyrus was now on the road to recovery.

Ali had been allowed in to visit with him as soon as Cyrus had been moved to a private room.

"Are you gonna glare all day or you gonna tell me what's happening?"

Jinx spared a glance for War. "Glaring feels good. I'll stay with that."

"We caught the bad guy. He's currently cuffed to a bed down the hallway, and you and I just got special permission to pay him a private visit." War's smile looked like a shark's. "Tell me you don't want to pass up this opportunity."

Hell, no, he didn't want to pass up this opportunity. But his gaze slid back to Ali.

She was smiling at Cyrus.

He saved her life. Jumped between her and a bullet. Cyrus hadn't known that Ali had on a bulletproof vest. He'd just wanted to protect her. "I want to hate him," Jinx admitted.

"Yeah, I can see that."

"But I have to be grateful to him because Ali is still breathing." His hand fisted. "And she's fucking smiling at him."

Just then, Ali looked up. She stared through the glass. Her gaze met Jinx's. And the smile that had been on her face vanished.

Her whole expression closed down.

I can explain. Just give me a chance…

"Guessing she found out about the deal with Landon?" War asked quietly.

"It was a bullshit deal. You know I just told him that I'd use her to get Cyrus." *I never intended to betray her.* "I wanted my brother safe, and I wanted Ali safe. I wasn't pretending with her. I meant every damn thing that I said and did with her." But…

I'm a liar.

I'm a user.

And he'd screwed up with Ali.

"What if it had come down to a choice between them?" Again, War's voice was quiet.

Ali had turned away.

"What in the hell kind of question is that?" Jinx demanded, annoyed.

"One that she might ask. If it had come down to protecting your brother or helping Ali, what would you have done?"

"Ali isn't gonna ask that question." Was she? Jinx rubbed his hand over his aching chest. *Look at me again, sweets. Look at me and smile. I want to see your eyes warm up like they used to do when you looked at me.*

"And why not?" War seemed honestly confused. "If I were in her place, I sure might ask."

"Ali knows how I feel about her. I *told* her."

But...

War's hand curled around his shoulder.

"Ali knows," Jinx mumbled.

Then...

God, I hope she knows.

***

"He's...a dick." Cy's voice was weak. *He* was weak. That happened when you were shot twice. Especially when one of the bullets hit far too close to your spine and you were nearly paralyzed...

"He's a dick who helped to save your life." When she'd asked for help in that tunnel, Jinx had lunged to her. He'd stayed with her. Even ridden in the ambulance. He'd helped Cy every single moment until the other man had been wheeled away to surgery.

"He...lied to you."

She wouldn't look back toward that little window. An observation window that should have been used by nurses and doctors, but, somehow, Jinx had gotten access. He'd probably flashed a smile at a nurse and gotten her to let him sneak over there.

"Did you...hear...me?"

Ali nodded. "How do you know Jinx lied?"

"Imari."

The name caught her by surprise.

"Been...working with her." Cy was far too pale. He'd lost a dangerous amount of blood. "Landon told her. When he called...c-called and got her to b-back off the raid..."

"The raid at Ramsey's place?"

A nod. "Jinx agreed to...d-deal...he would g-get close to you, g-get your trust...and then help deliver m-me..."

Tears stung her eyes. She wasn't going to let them fall. She also wasn't going to look back toward that window. She would *not*. "Jinx said he loved me."

"*Lie...*"

Had it been? Or had he lied to Landon? Because Jinx hadn't told Landon about the bulletproof vests. He'd just insisted that she slide one on, when Landon *hadn't* been around. Had Jinx already suspected Landon? It sure seemed that way. But if so, why hadn't he told her? Why keep that info from her?

"Jinx...chose his...b-brother..."

She looked up at the ceiling. It was a technique Ali used when she didn't want to cry. If you looked up, it seemed harder for the tears to fall down. "Jinx loves his brother. He wants to help him. I know what it's like to have family turn their back on you, and Jinx isn't going to do that to—"

"L-lie..."

Her stare flew to him. "It's not a lie. Jinx does want to help his brother."

"No, I-I meant...your family, your mom...she didn't turn her back on you." The machines around him beeped faster. "That's one of th-the things I learned..."

Ali crept closer to the bed. "What are you talking about?"

"She...didn't send that note..."

***

Imari stood beside an armed guard in front of Landon's hospital room. "Well, well..." Her gaze drifted between War and Jinx. "If it's not my old bosses..."

"And if it's not the woman who had more secrets than I could count," War returned. But there was no humor in his voice or in his expression. "You said we could question him."

Imari nodded. "You're getting permission to go in only because when the people over his head realized what he'd done, they went ballistic. I tried to warn them, but they didn't listen. Now, they have no choice but to hear me." Her chin lifted. "He's on lots of pain meds, so he may not be conscious for long. Get what you can from him."

"Oh, I'll get plenty," Jinx assured her.

He'd already learned that Imari wasn't actually an FBI agent. From what War had learned—and passed on to Jinx—Imari was a fairly new recruit for the same government group that had once employed their team. But Imari and

Cyrus had some sort of friendship, a connection that hadn't been fully revealed yet, and she'd suspected her boss was dirty. She'd been working covertly with Cyrus to bring down Landon.

Imari led the way into the room. Sure enough, Landon was cuffed to the railing of the bed. He was awake, his eyes slits, and when he saw Jinx...

"*You.*"

Jinx inclined his head. "Me."

"Sonofabitch! Get out!"

No, he'd rather get closer. Jinx stalked toward the bed. He looked down at Landon's stomach. "Gut shots are bitches," he said flatly. "They've got you all stitched up, and word on the street is that you're riding high on lots of pain pills..." He lifted his hand. "But I bet if I just press down real hard, you can still feel plenty of pain." He let his hand begin to lower.

"*Don't!*" A sharp cry from Landon.

Because the guy was a freaking wimp. He'd never had to handle pain. Never had to do anything but appear at the landing zone. "Why the hell did you go after my Ali?"

"I-I had to get Cyrus!" Heaving breaths. Beeping machines. "He...he found out what I was doing."

"And what were you doing?" War wanted to know.

Landon's squinty gaze jerked around the room. Landed on Imari. "You sold me...out."

"You sold yourself out. Literally—to the highest bidder. That guy who died in Paris—*you* made the hit on him. Cyrus told me he learned it was you who fired the shots. That you'd been paid two hundred grand to do the job. You had the man's location. The whole mission was a ruse. I bet when we start digging, we'll find plenty of other missions like that one."

War's face twisted with disgust. "Why the stalking job on Ali?"

But Jinx had already figured that out. "Because if she was threatened, Landon thought she'd turn to Cyrus. She'd get him out of the shadows, then Landon could kill him." Because Cyrus had been the one with the initial suspicions against Landon.

"She...didn't go to h-him." Landon's voice was slurring. "Had to threaten her more...she turned to *you.*"

It had taken her too long to come to Jinx. *She wanted to protect me.*

"Had to...try and take you out of the p-picture...without y-you..." But the slurring words stopped.

"Without me, you thought that maybe she'd contact Cyrus for help. Only your attempts on me failed, so you got creative." Jinx knew where this part was going. "That's why you left all that fake-ass evidence in Louis's hotel. You thought we'd see the picture of Cyrus and the case against him would be sealed. I'd be in a killing fury—hell, maybe I'd even kill Cyrus for you. Either way, he'd be gone soon enough. A big problem eliminated for you."

"He came down here...for her." Ragged breaths. "Got...l-lucky...that picture...Louis took it...he *told* me...Cyrus..."

"Cyrus figured out Ali was in danger, and he came to help her because she was his best friend. He didn't hate her. He never hated her." Jinx didn't let emotion enter his voice. "That setup in the hotel—the money, the pictures—that was where you screwed up. I mean, you *gave* me the damn hotel room key. You gave it to me because you were the one who set up the evidence in there. I suspected it when I was searching the room. I didn't have proof to back up my suspicions, but I also didn't have proof that Cyrus was a killer. If anything, just the opposite..."

Imari's stare jumped to him. "What do you mean?"

"I mean, I did what Landon wanted. I learned Ali's secrets. I learned about Cyrus. Everything she told me made me doubt what Landon had said. In the end, I had two choices...I could believe the story Ali had told me—a story about a best friend who'd been desperate for help—or I could believe Landon." His gaze raked the cuffed man. "I went with Ali. It was an easy choice, especially considering that I never really fucking liked you."

Landon tried to lunge out of the hospital bed.

Jinx drove his fist into Landon's jaw. Knocked Landon right out.

"Dammit, Jinx!" Imari hit the call button for the nurse. "We can't question him when he's out cold!"

True...but hitting him had sure felt damn good.

CHAPTER TWENTY

Jinx stormed out of Landon's hospital room and nearly rammed right into Ali. A *crying* Ali. Tears were on her cheeks.

He staggered to a stop right in front of her, and Jinx could have sworn that his heart had just been cut out. Her tears just kept falling as she stared at him. Her eyes were gleaming pools. Her lips were trembling. And he'd never, ever felt worse in his entire life.

All he wanted to do was haul her into his arms. Hold her tight. *Stop* her pain. But he was the asshole who'd caused her pain. "I'm so sorry." His voice was ragged. "Hurting you was the last thing that I ever intended to do, I swear it."

More tears.

He was pretty sure his heart was on the floor. "Baby...sweets...I only told Landon I was going along with the deal. I didn't mean it. I am a fucking lying bastard, you know that—but I am a bastard who is loyal to you. If it means you are protected, I will lie, steal, cheat, or kill in an instant." He'd do it, over and over again. "I was buying time. Time for Ramsey to get his damn ass out of trouble and time for me to find out what intel Landon might have. You know I've never trusted that jerk. Couldn't wait to stop working with him."

More tears. She wasn't speaking. She was destroying him, one tear at a time.

So he kept talking, desperately. "I suspected him. When we were at Louis's hotel room, everything seemed too pat. Like Louis just *happened* to leave all the cash there. I mean, he didn't even put it in the hotel safe. He was going to leave it there for the cleaning staff to find? And the photos? He might as well have circled Cyrus's face with a big, red pen." That was exactly what had been done to Jinx's image. "It was too obvious."

Her arms curled around her body, as if she was hugging herself.

"I couldn't say anything in the room because I was afraid it might be bugged. I was also worried I'd be wrong. I didn't want to get your hopes up about Cyrus being innocent just to have to dash them and shoot the guy in the chest in front of—" Jinx stopped. Wrong thing to say. Way too graphic. But if it had come to it, if Cyrus had been a threat to Ali, Jinx would have shot him.

She didn't speak.

He kept going. "I wanted you wearing the bulletproof vest because honestly—I trust you. I trust War. I trust Odin. Most days, I trust Ramsey, when he isn't being insane." Jinx sucked in a heaving breath. "I didn't trust Landon. I was waiting for him to hang himself, and he did. He's going down, your friend has been exonerated, and the nightmare for you is over. You are safe and clear, and I'm so fucking sorry that I hurt you. I will be sorry for a thousand years because your tears are wrecking me and I know I destroyed your faith in me, and all I fucking wanted to do was love you and…"

She shook her head.

Jinx had to swallow because a damn lump was in his throat, choking him. *Ali doesn't love me*. She was too hurt. Too angry. He'd feared he'd screw this up with her. From the beginning. From the moment he'd met her, he'd just wanted…

I wanted her to be mine. I wanted to love her.

And he did.

But by keeping the deal with Landon from her, he'd destroyed everything. He'd wanted to protect her. Wanted to make Landon think he was safe, but…

Jinx's head fell forward. He stared down at his shoes. There were some things in the world that couldn't be fixed. He knew that.

Hadn't he tried and tried to fix his family? Tried so desperately to get his dad to stop the drugs and the drinking? It hadn't worked.

Then hadn't he fought to keep Ramsey with him, only to have his brother run away?

And when he'd fallen for Ali, hadn't he known that he wouldn't be good for her? That his cursed life would wind up hurting her and Ali would leave him? He'd tried to be so careful, but in the end, he'd screwed up.

"It would have been you," he rasped.

He lifted his hands. Realized he'd clenched them into fists. *All I do is hurt and destroy.* Jinx cleared his throat. "Just so you know…it would have been you. If I had to choose between you and my brother, I would choose you, every time. Because I love my brother, but you are my life." There. Done.

His head lifted.

She stared at him in shock. Her eyes were wide, and the tear tracks glistened on her cheeks.

"Ali…?"

Her lips parted. She tried to speak. Stopped. Shook her head.

Right. He was making this hard on her. Ugly. She didn't want some dramatic breakup scene, but he'd had to try and explain. And he'd *needed* her to know how he felt.

Jinx turned away, then realized he was just facing Landon's room again. War and Imari were still in there.

Ali grabbed him. Wrenched him back around. "I—" She heaved out a breath. "I was coming to tell you that my mother didn't give up on me."

What?

"Cyrus found out that my mom's note to me was fake. Landon did that. He wanted to make sure that I'd cut all ties with the life I had before. He *and* his boss worked together on that. They did the same shit to Cyrus, only he got suspicious because he said his family *never* cared a shit about him. Didn't make sense for them to send him some cut-you-out-of-my-life note. Cyrus talked to my mom before she passed. She loved me. She *always* loved me."

"That's wonderful, sweets. But I'm not surprised. You're easy to love." Jinx gave her a small smile. "Excuse me." He pulled away from her, narrowed his eyes, and spun for Landon's door.

"Wait! What are you doing?" She tugged on him, but he didn't stop.

"Going to cause someone a whole hell of a lot of well-deserved pain."

Ali jumped into his path. "Do you know why I came to tell you about my mom?"

She needed to scoot so he could go and rip open Landon's stitches.

"It's because you are the person who matters most to me. I had this news that changed the way I looked at my life—my past and my present and my future, and I couldn't wait to find you and tell you about it."

But...she'd been crying.

Because the news had been good and bad and it had hurt her. "I...thought you were angry with me."

Her head tilted. "Jinx..."

Ali...

Her lips lifted into a small smile. "You really think that I didn't know you lied to Landon?"

"I—"

She slid closer to him. "You really think that I didn't know you would tell him anything necessary to protect your brother? Family matters to you, it always has."

"Ali..."

"Ramsey is family to you, I get that. But I also get that I'm family. War is. Odin is. You would protect us all, and if you had to lie to do it, I get that you wouldn't think twice." She leaned up on her toes. "Spoiler alert, I'd do the same thing for you."

His heart was racing far too fast. Just moments before, he'd been sure his heart had been ripped out and tossed on the floor, but now, it was shaking in his chest.

"Do you know why I went to see Ramsey the day that Imari had her raid at his place?" Ali asked him softly.

Uh, actually... "Why?"

"Because I didn't want your brother doing something stupid—"

"Oh, he does stupid shit all the time. Can't help himself."

Her eyes seemed to gleam. "I didn't want him doing something stupid—like chasing down the bad guy without you and me as backup—and getting himself killed. I didn't want him getting hurt because I know how much you do love him. I was ready to threaten Ramsey, to make deals with him, to do anything I needed to do because I wanted to protect *you*." She paused a beat. "Sound familiar?"

He could not look away from her. "You forgive me for that BS deal with Landon?"

She grabbed his shirtfront. Fisted her hands in the fabric. "I love you. I trust you. Love and trust go hand in hand with me. Because I love you, I trust that you won't sell me out. That's just how it works."

He wanted to scoop her up and get her the hell out of that hospital and far away from everyone else and just keep her locked in his bedroom for at least a week. But... "What about Cyrus?"

"Oh, he doesn't like you at all."

Jinx frowned. Then realized he didn't give a damn.

"But he'll come around," Ali promised. She pulled him toward her. "Because he wants me to be happy and the best way for me to be happy? It's for me to be living my life with you for the next fifty years. For you to love me, for me to love you, and for us to make and break rules left and right."

"Sweets…" If he started kissing her, he would not stop. Screw being in a hospital and having a cop or agent or whoever he was just a few feet away. The guy had been uncomfortably witnessing the whole scene between them.

"But just one thing first." She was on her tiptoes. So very, very close to his mouth. "A point that we need to cover."

Anything. Everything. He just wanted to carry her out of there.

"We," Ali said very definitely, "are not a mistake."

He blinked. Then remembered…the first time they'd hooked up, she'd said what they were doing was a mistake. At the time, he'd agreed.

Of course, he'd been lying…

"We are great," Ali told him. "When we are together, the world makes a lot more sense to me."

That was fucking sweet. His head bent toward her.

"Jeez, man," War's disgruntled voice boomed. "Get a room. How many times do I have to tell you? Keep your personal shit *personal*."

When Jinx glanced over Ali's shoulder, he saw that his buddy was smiling. Jinx scooped Ali into his arms, and her laugh truly was music to his ears. "Get a room. Right. On it." He hesitated. "Do you happen to know which nearby hospital room is empty right now?"

Horror flashed on War's face. "*Jinx.*"

"Kidding," Jinx assured him.

Well, mostly, he had been.

***

"What do you mean...this house is *yours*?"

Ali seemed stunned as she held the sheet over her world-class breasts.

Jinx pouted as he glanced at the sheet. Why was she blocking his view?

"*Jinx.* Focus here."

He had been focusing.

"When you just said... 'by the way, the house is mine' what exactly did you mean?"

"I said the wrong thing." He yanked his eyes up. "I meant the house is ours. If you want it to be. If you hate it, we can get something else."

"This place is a freaking mansion, Jinx."

"Um..." He let his index finger slide down her shoulder and edge carefully toward the top of the sheet.

"How did you get the house?"

"Did some favors for a guy. He offered to pay cash, but I mean, that would have been a lot of cash. Then I saw this house, and I had this vision of you on the beach. Of us watching the sunset. I thought, Ali would love it here. So I took the house instead of the cash."

Her mouth hung open.

"That a yes?" Jinx asked. "Or no?"

Her mouth snapped closed. Her eyes immediately narrowed. "What is the question, again?"

He should do this properly. Jinx stopped tugging on the sheet. He slid from the bed. He had boxers on, so at least he wasn't doing this routine totally nude. He pulled a small box from the nightstand. Opened the box and took a knee near the bed.

"*Where did you get that?*" Ali seemed to be choking.

"A jewelry store."

"*When* did you get that?"

If he told her the truth, would it terrify her?

"Jinx!"

"I got it right after I got the house. If you came back into my life, I wanted to make sure I was ready for you. No screwing up this time."

She started to speak, but a little squeak emerged.

He stayed on his knee. "Will you marry me?"

Her gaze lifted from the ring to meet his stare.

"Will you marry me," this was the most important moment of his life, "and make me the luckiest guy in the world?"

"Yes."

Shit, had she just said—"Yes?"

"Yes!"

He shot to his feet and jumped back into the bed with her. He took her mouth and kissed her with all of the desire, need, and love that churned through him.

She said yes.

She said yes!

He couldn't ever remember being so happy.

And he would never, *ever* let anyone take away his happiness. Whatever he had to do...

He would protect Ali.

Protect her and love her...for the rest of his life.

***

"You could have gotten your fool-ass killed."

Jinx didn't jump or dramatically whirl around when that low voice came out of the darkness. It was the middle of the night. He'd slipped from bed because he wanted something to drink, but he was hardly surprised to find an unexpected visitor in his kitchen.

He was just surprised that Ramsey hadn't shown up sooner.

Jinx hit the lights and turned to see Ramsey sitting on a barstool. "I think I need to change my alarm codes."

Ramsey merely lifted one eyebrow. "*That's* your response?"

"That and...you are invited to the wedding."

Ramsey almost fell off the stool. "What wedding?"

"Mine and Ali's." Yeah, he had to lead with this news. "She said yes, and I'm thinking she'll probably want a beach wedding. Maybe something at sunset. It will be awesome. You *will* be there."

"We don't want people to know about my connection to you. We don't want—"

"Screw other people." On this, he was dead serious. "You're my brother, and you will be at my wedding." Jinx stalked toward him. "I don't care if this town is terrified of you or what kind of big, bad reputation you have—you are my brother. I want you there."

Ramsey looked away. "I'm a criminal. The Feds want to take me down—"

"There is no case against you."

Ramsey glanced back at him.

"You know it, and I know it. So do War and Odin, by the way. The scene with the agents storming your place? That was just for show. Imari told me that there is no actual evidence against you. Guess you've just been too careful over the years." Ramsey made no response to that statement, so Jinx added, "No one is going to come along and haul you off to jail."

"It's not the cops and Feds I worry about. I have plenty of other enemies out there who—"

"You're not alone," Jinx cut in. "Stop acting like you are. You've got threats out there? Then let me help you. Let Odin, War, and Ali—let *all* of us. Because if there is one thing I've learned, the world is fucking frigid place when you are alone."

Ramsey shoved from the stool. "Just wanted to check on you. I'll see myself out." He marched away.

"It wasn't just Landon." Ramsey knew exactly who Landon was. Jinx revealed, "Turns out, his old boss was pretty crooked, too. He's been taken into custody as well. Ali is safe. Her case is closed." He waited just a moment and added, "That means that Trouble for Hire will be looking for new clients…"

"Good luck finding them." Ramsey threw up his hand and didn't look back.

"Actually…" Jinx just could not resist saying this part. *Could not.* "I think we already have one lined up. She wanted to see Odin recently, but we were busy tying up things for Ali. No worries, though. I heard she booked a new appointment. Whitney Augustine will be in for her meeting tomorrow."

Ramsey jerked to a stop. Then he spun around. "Why the hell would Whitney be coming to Trouble for Hire?"

"Seriously?" Jinx squinted at him. "We're amazing. Why wouldn't she come see us?"

Ramsey growled.

"And, of course, there's the fact that the poor woman lost a ton of her memory. Can you imagine what it must be like for her? How scared and uncertain she must be? She survived two crazy killers trying to murder her, but in the process of that truly epic survival experience, she lost the memory of six months of her life. She doesn't know what happened during that time. If she made friends, lost friends, if she had a lover…if she got her heart broken…"

"*Stop.*"

"I'm just saying…she had a lot going on. Maybe she's coming to Trouble for Hire because she wants answers to the questions that plague her." *Questions you won't answer*. But he didn't say that part. Jinx figured it was understood.

Ramsey's nostrils flared. "She...she came to my bar."

This was news. "And...?"

"And I escorted her out! She doesn't belong there! She doesn't belong—" He broke off.

But Jinx knew where he'd been going. "With you?"

A grim nod.

"Keep telling yourself that," Jinx advised. "Maybe one day, you'll actually believe it." He heard a creak to the right. Ali was coming down the hallway. "Or maybe..." His voice deepened. "You'll wake the hell up. You'll realize that there are some people in this world worth fighting for. People who will love you and trust you and say *yes* when you ask them the most important question ever..."

Ali slipped from the hallway. "Hi, Ramsey." No shock. No surprise. "Came to make sure Jinx was all right?"

An inclination of his head. "Jinx...and you."

"That's sweet. Thank you." A beaming smile. She hurried toward Jinx. Wrapped her arms around him. "We're great. Did you hear the news? We're getting married!"

Over her head, Jinx met Ramsey's stare. "You *will* be at the wedding."

"Of course, he will be." Ali turned in his arms and stared at Ramsey. "He's family."

Yes, he was.

Ramsey inclined his head, then hurried out.

"That was a yes, wasn't it?" Ali asked.

"I think it was more of a 'Hell, yes, I'm thrilled and will be there' reply."

She laughed.

He loved her laugh.

Once more, she eased back around to face him. "I missed you," Ali confessed. "The bed was empty and cold."

"Oh, no," Jinx said dramatically. He scooped her into his arms. "We cannot have that. We must both jump in the bed right away and make it very..." A kiss. "*Very.*" Another kiss. "Hot."

And they did just that.

***

"Jinx."

"Five more minutes."

"Jinx, I need to tell you something."

His eye cracked open.

Damn but she was beautiful in the morning. Even when she was frowning.

"You don't have to make me laugh."

She was beautiful and...confusing?

"You don't have to tell me jokes or give me smiles that you don't mean."

It was still dark outside. Definitely not morning yet. He'd been wrong about the time.

And Ali seemed nervous.

"You don't have to do any of that," she rushed to say. "When you're mad, be mad. When you're sad, be sad. I will take you any way that you are. I need you to know that."

Dammit. She was back to being freaking adorable. He smiled at her.

She'd turned on the nearby lamp, so he knew she could see his smile.

"I just told you that you don't have to do that," Ali whispered. "I want you to know that I love you no matter what."

"And that's why I'm smiling. Because *you* make me happy." Because with Ali, the jokes and the laughter and everything else—they were all real. She made him feel good. Complete. He didn't have to pretend with her. With Ali...

He was home.

"Oh." Now she smiled. "You make me happy, too."

He pulled her down on top of him. "I love you."

"I love you, too."

And those were words that he would never *ever* grow tired of hearing.

EPILOGUE

Odin stared at the blonde woman who sat with her back perfectly straight in the chair before him. Whitney Augustine had arrived at his office just after nine. Her tension was apparent, and her fingers trembled every few moments—or, they *had* trembled, before she'd clenched them in her lap.

He'd been waiting for her to explain why she'd come to Trouble for Hire. So far, he'd gotten nothing.

Carefully, he cleared his throat. "Is there anything in particular I can do for you?"

"Yes."

He waited. There was no more.

Well, well. Usually, he was the one with the one-word responses. Being on the receiving end was new. His fingers drummed on the desktop.

"Maisey said you were the best."

Maisey was the love of his life, so she was hardly unbiased. She was also Whitney's closest friend. "Did you tell Maisey that you were coming to see me today?" Odin asked, trying to feel his way through this conversation.

Whitney shook her head.

"Why not?"

"It's...private."

"Well, we *are* a private investigation firm."

His joke fell flat. Her lips did not lift at all. Dammit. Jinx would have done a way better job.

More silence. More tension. More...

Screw it. "I can't help you if I don't know the problem."

One of her clenched hands went to her stomach. Opened. Pressed...protectively?

Uh, oh. His eyes widened. "Whitney?"

"I'm pregnant."

Before he could speak, she jumped to her feet and whirled for the door.

"Stop!"

She froze.

"Whitney, let me help you."

She turned back to him. Tears were in her eyes. "It's a miracle. After what happened to me...the baby was safe all that time. The doctor said that's what the body does. It protects the baby. A perfect design." She licked her lips. Took a step toward him. "Then I came back here, and I thought—surely the father will make an appearance. He *has* to be someone in my life. Someone I-I knew, but the attack made me forget him."

It was a good thing he was sitting down.

"But no one showed up. No man came to tell me that we were involved or that—that we..." She crept closer. "It could have been a one-night stand."

"I don't think so," Odin said automatically because he *knew*—

"Um, why do you say that?"

Because I know who fathered your baby. Or, rather, he had a very, very strong suspicion.

But she shook her head. "Look, that's why I'm here, okay? Because I'm pregnant and I can't remember who is the father of this child. This child that is so tiny and precious inside of me and... I just—can you help me?" Her eyes begged him. "Can you help me to figure out what was happening to me during that period of my life that I forgot? Help me to find the man I forgot?"

"I can do better than that." He didn't normally make promises to clients but in this case—*special circumstances*. "I'm taking the case. Pro Bono."

"But, no, I will pay—"

The hell she would.

"I'm taking the case." Grim. "And I think I may know the father."

"Already?" Her eyes seemed to double. "How?"

This wasn't going to be an easy talk. Then again, nothing about Ramsey Hyde was ever easy. "You might want to take a seat..."

***

When Whitney left thirty minutes later, Odin pulled out his phone and dialed Jinx. His buddy answered on the second ring.

"Personal day, man!" Jinx called out. "I am taking a personal day and living my best life with my lady—"

"Whitney Augustine was just here." He wasn't violating confidentiality because Jinx *was* part of

Trouble for Hire, and technically, he was going to be working this case, too.

"Yeah, yeah, I know that you had a visit with her planned. Even told Ramsey about it when he—"

"She's pregnant."

"*What?*"

"Is the baby your brother's? Because she wants us to find the father. The woman has no memory of that time or who she was involved with and she just hired *us* to solve the mystery for her."

"Oh, damn." Jinx sounded shaken. "Ramsey will lose his mind."

Yes, Odin rather suspected he might...

THE END

A NOTE FROM THE AUTHOR

Thank you for reading Jinx's story! From the moment that Jinx first snuck onto the page of DON'T PLAY WITH ODIN, I knew that I would have to write a story for him. Jinx is such a fun character, but beneath his easy grin, he was just as dangerous as the other PIs at Trouble for Hire. And, of course, now I have to write a book for his brother, Ramsey...

If you'd like to stay updated on my releases and sales, please join my newsletter list.

https://cynthiaeden.com/newsletter/

Again, thank you for reading JINX, YOU'RE IT.

Best,
Cynthia Eden
cynthiaeden.com

ABOUT THE AUTHOR

Cynthia Eden is a *New York Times*, *USA Today*, *Digital Book World*, and *IndieReader* best-seller.

Cynthia writes sexy tales of contemporary romance, romantic suspense, and paranormal romance. Since she began writing full-time in 2005, Cynthia has written over one hundred novels and novellas.

Cynthia lives along the Alabama Gulf Coast. She loves romance novels, horror movies, and chocolate.

For More Information

- *cynthiaeden.com*
- *facebook.com/cynthiaedenfanpage*

HER OTHER WORKS

Trouble For Hire

- No Escape From War (Book 1)
- Don't Play With Odin (Book 2)
- Jinx You're It (Book 3)
- Remember Ramsey (Book 4)

Death and Moonlight Mystery

- Step Into My Web (Book 1)
- Save Me From The Dark (Book 2)

Wilde Ways

- Protecting Piper (Book 1)
- Guarding Gwen (Book 2)
- Before Ben (Book 3)
- The Heart You Break (Book 4)
- Fighting For Her (Book 5)
- Ghost Of A Chance (Book 6)
- Crossing The Line (Book 7)
- Counting On Cole (Book 8)
- Chase After Me (Book 9)
- Say I Do (Book 10)
- Roman Will Fall (Book 11)
- The One Who Got Away (Book 12)

Dark Sins

- Don't Trust A Killer (Book 1)
- Don't Love A Liar (Book 2)

Lazarus Rising

- Never Let Go (Book One)
- Keep Me Close (Book Two)
- Stay With Me (Book Three)
- Run To Me (Book Four)
- Lie Close To Me (Book Five)
- Hold On Tight (Book Six)
- Lazarus Rising Volume One (Books 1 to 3)
- Lazarus Rising Volume Two (Books 4 to 6)

Dark Obsession Series

- Watch Me (Book 1)
- Want Me (Book 2)
- Need Me (Book 3)
- Beware Of Me (Book 4)
- Only For Me (Books 1 to 4)

Mine Series

- Mine To Take (Book 1)
- Mine To Keep (Book 2)
- Mine To Hold (Book 3)
- Mine To Crave (Book 4)
- Mine To Have (Book 5)
- Mine To Protect (Book 6)
- Mine Box Set Volume 1 (Books 1-3)
- Mine Box Set Volume 2 (Books 4-6)

Bad Things

- The Devil In Disguise (Book 1)
- On The Prowl (Book 2)
- Undead Or Alive (Book 3)
- Broken Angel (Book 4)
- Heart Of Stone (Book 5)
- Tempted By Fate (Book 6)
- Wicked And Wild (Book 7)
- Saint Or Sinner (Book 8)
- Bad Things Volume One (Books 1 to 3)
- Bad Things Volume Two (Books 4 to 6)
- Bad Things Deluxe Box Set (Books 1 to 6)

Bite Series

- Forbidden Bite (Bite Book 1)
- Mating Bite (Bite Book 2)

Blood and Moonlight Series

- Bite The Dust (Book 1)
- Better Off Undead (Book 2)
- Bitter Blood (Book 3)
- Blood and Moonlight (The Complete Series)

Purgatory Series

- The Wolf Within (Book 1)
- Marked By The Vampire (Book 2)
- Charming The Beast (Book 3)
- Deal with the Devil (Book 4)
- The Beasts Inside (Books 1 to 4)

Bound Series

- Bound By Blood (Book 1)

- Bound In Darkness (Book 2)
- Bound In Sin (Book 3)
- Bound By The Night (Book 4)
- Bound in Death (Book 5)
- Forever Bound (Books 1 to 4)

Stand-Alone Romantic Suspense

- Never Gonna Happen
- One Hot Holiday
- Secret Admirer
- First Taste of Darkness
- Sinful Secrets
- Until Death
- Christmas With A Spy

Stand-Alone Paranormal Romance

- Immortal Danger
- Come Back To Me
- Put A Spell On Me
- Slay All Day
- Midnight Bite
- A Vampire's Christmas Carol